THE SHOOTING PARTY

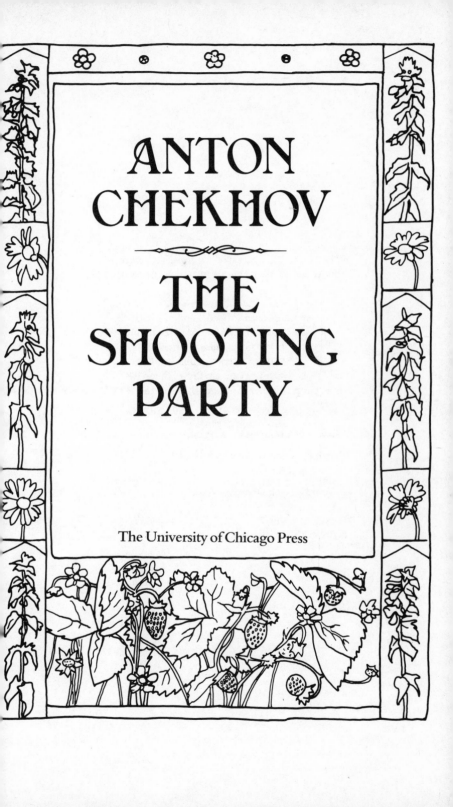

ANTON CHEKHOV

THE SHOOTING PARTY

The University of Chicago Press

A. E. Chamot's translation of *The Shooting Party*, revised for
this edition by Julian Symons, was first published in 1926.

The University of Chicago Press, Chicago 60637
André Deutsch Limited, London WC1B 3LJ
Revised Translation © André Deutsch Limited 1986
Introduction © Julian Symons 1986
All Rights reserved. Published 1986
University of Chicago Press Edition 1987
Printed in Great Britain by Ebenezer Baylis and Son Ltd, Worcester

96   95   94   93   92   91   90   89   88   87   54321

Library of Congress Cataloging-in-Publication Data

Chekhov, Anton Pavlovich, 1860-1904.
The Shooting party.

Translation of: Drama na okhote.
I. Title.
PG3456.D7   1987   891.73'3   86-14605
ISBN 0-226-10241-6 (pbk.)

INTRODUCTION

The general view of Anton Chekhov's work held in the West is a misleading one. We think of him as the author of four great plays who also wrote some interesting but comparatively minor short stories – 'The Lady with the Little Dog' is sure to be mentioned, and also perhaps 'The Duel', 'The Kiss' and 'The Party' (the titles vary with the translator). The view is misleading because it gives no sense of the way in which Chekhov's art developed. Chekhov became famous as a short story writer, and when in 1888 he was awarded the Pushkin Prize it was for a collection of stories, *In the Twilight*. The first of the great plays, *The Seagull*, was not written until 1895, and was a disastrous failure when performed at St Petersburg in the following year. Success did not come until the play's production in 1898 by the Moscow Arts Theatre under the guidance of Stanislavsky and the playwright's old friend Nemirovich-Danchenko. The triumphs of the later plays, all produced at the Moscow Arts Theatre, were compressed into the last six years of his life.

Chekhov was not then a playwright who produced short stories on the side, but a professional writer who found that he could make a living most easily from writing short narratives, many of them fictional. In part he earned his living as a doctor, but his tendency to treat patients for nothing if they were poor meant that from the beginning he relied on writing as a major source of income. He once said that medicine was his lawful wife and literature his mistress, and that when bored with one he spent the night with the other, but as the years passed most nights in the week were spent with the mistress. And that mistress was the short story. The inclination that Chekhov undoubtedly felt towards the theatre was checked by his inability to get his youthful melodrama *Platonov* performed, and by the irritation he felt with actors and actresses even after the critical praise given to *Ivanov* on its performance in 1889 at St Petersburg. Varying the wife and mistress metaphor, he called prose narrative his wife, drama the mistress.

Again it should be emphasized that in the English-speaking world we have read almost nothing Chekhov wrote in his first five years as an author, because so little of it has been translated. By way of explaining this, the often-told story of his early years needs brief repetition. Anton Chekhov was born in 1860 and brought up in Taganrog, a small port six hundred miles south of Moscow. His grandfather was a serf known simply as Chekh, who managed to buy the family's freedom. This was not well used by his son Pavel, who combined a severe upbringing of his six children with grandiose ambitions to have not one but two grocer's shops, and to build his own house. Deep in debt and trouble Pavel Chekhov fled to Moscow and there, after finishing his education at Taganrog, Anton joined the rest of the family. He enrolled at the Medical Faculty of the University for the five years of study necessary before he could become a doctor, and set out to help maintain the rest of the family by his pen. Some of the other children worked too, but Anton soon became their principal financial support. From the age of twenty until he qualified as a doctor in 1884, Chekhov was a punctilious medical student who in his spare time wrote dozens – indeed, hundreds – of sketches and stories, mostly for St Petersburg comic papers.

From the description given by Chekhov's English biographer Ronald Hingley, it would seem that *Oskolki*, the magazine to which Chekhov most frequently contributed, was a kind of Russian equivalent of the contemporary *Punch*. Its staple sources of comedy included mothers-in-law, drunks, foreigners and Russian citizens unable to speak good Russian, bureaucratic officials, young men and women awkwardly courting before marriage, husbands and wives quarrelling after marriage. . . . Yes, very reminiscent of *Punch*, and resembling the English magazine also in a relentless insistence on brevity. A thousand words was the limit imposed by the editor, and within this length Chekhov had to be amusing, light-hearted, whimsical, never for a moment serious. He wrote notes and sketches, provided captions to pictures or comic mock-advertisements, and produced similar trivia. It is no wonder that all this was done under assumed names, most often that of A. or Antosha Chekhonte. Not until 1886, in a contribution to the St Petersburg daily *Novoye vremya*, did Chekhov use his own name.

The ability to do such hackwork speedily and successfully indicates his extreme flexibility as a writer. He often referred to what he was doing as excrement, he often railed against Leykin, the editor of *Oskolki*, but still he conformed without much trouble to what was needed. He was in practice the reverse of the long-fingered aesthete we might expect to have written the plays, a man distinctly robust in expression, and at times coarse in his treatment of sexual matters. The man and what he produced were not identical. In 'The Kiss' the shy bespectacled lieutenant Ryabovich is overwhelmed by the kiss mistakenly given him in the dark and feels on his left cheek a faint delicious tingling sensation as from peppermint drops, but this was not the view of his creator who called actresses cows, and said of ballerinas that they all smelt like horses after their performances. If one asks what kind of man Chekhov was, and what beliefs he held, the questions are difficult to answer. He certainly had opinions, powerfully expressed, but they were often contradictory. He might say in letters that Leykin was a cheat and a villain, but when Chekhov moved in 1892 from Moscow to Melikhovo in Moscow province, the editor of *Oskolki* was a welcome visitor. He insisted that he must leave Moscow because as a doctor he needed patients (in a year he treated without payment hundreds of peasants), and as a writer found it essential to have a permanent home away from city life, but when he got to Melikhovo he filled the house with friends so that he had to build a small cottage away from the house as a place to work.

It is a mistake, then, to take any expression of opinion by Chekhov as final, especially in relation to serious subjects. He was much more nearly a mirror of his times than a moralist pronouncing on them, hence his uneasy relationship with the ideas of Tolstoy, which Chekhov at first tried to absorb in some not very

successful stories and then rejected almost completely. He admired
the novelist but criticized the philosopher, often in sharp practical
detail. And it is a particular mistake, common in the last half-
century, to claim Chekhov as a political progressive, consciously
and deliberately charting the decay of Imperial Russia in his plays.
No doubt it is true that Lopakhin is the most significant character
in *The Cherry Orchard*, and certainly Chekhov conceived the play
as very funny and quarrelled with Stanislavsky because the pro-
ducer insisted on treating it as heavy drama, but when Chekhov
called the play a comedy (a term he never defined) he did not have
in mind the kind of crude social criticism that would see in the
chopping down of the orchard a prophecy of the fall of the Tsarist
régime. Edmund Wilson, watching the play performed in Moscow during the thirties, noted with apparent surprise that it seemed
just as usual, without any special socialist interpretation. Chekhov
was never dogmatic, and his political views were not partisan. In
1900, along with Tolstoy, he was elected an honorary member of
the newly-created section of Belles Lettres in the Academy of
Sciences, but a couple of years later he resigned because Gorky had
been expelled from the Academy by personal order of the Tsar. An
ardent liberal, then? Yet probably Chekhov's closest literary friend
was the renegade liberal and anti-Semite Alexey Suvorin, owner
and editor of *Novoye vremya*, although their relations cooled over
the Dreyfus affair, Suvorin of course being an ardent anti-
Dreyfusard.

But although Chekhov often changed his tune about what he
believed and what he wished to do, he never had any doubt that
most of what he had written was rubbish, up to that time in 1886
when he signed his name to an article for the first time. He said this
often and variously, perhaps most memorably to the novelist
Dmitry Grigorovich, remembered now principally because of his
early perceptiveness in seeing Dostoievsky's genius and his much
later appreciation of Chekhov, but then an established and greatly
respected novelist. Grigorovich, almost forty years Chekhov's
senior, wrote in 1886 what might be called a fan letter to the young
man, but one which urged him to take his own talent seriously,
deprecated the use of a pseudonym, and said that Chekhov must
not sin against his own genius by flippancy, or by the use of erotic

material. Chekhov's reply was fulsome. He was, after all, a young man in his middle twenties being praised by a respected elder, and it is not surprising that he should say Grigorovich's letter had struck him like a thunderbolt and had left a deep mark on his soul. He continued:

> If I have a gift that should be respected, I confess before the purity of your heart that hitherto I have not respected it. . . .
> Up till now my attitude towards my literary work has been extremely frivolous, casual, thoughtless. . . . I cannot think of a *single* story at which I worked for more than a day, and 'The Huntsman', which you liked, I wrote in a bathing cabin. I wrote my stories the way reporters write notices of fires: mechanically, half-consciously, without caring a pin either about the reader or myself.

He ends by promising to do better, and asks for a photograph of Grigorovich. The fulsomeness of this letter receives a typically Chekhovian corrective, in a note about it sent to the assistant editor of *Oskolki* saying that the old boy had rather laid it on with a trowel.

In 1899 Chekhov sold the rights to his collected works for 75,000 roubles, and a ten-volume edition was published between that year and 1901. He made the selection himself, and used a ruthless hand in dealing with the work written by A. Chekhonte, although retaining the majority of his contributions to *Novoye vremya*. Among the work omitted was *The Shooting Party*.

The Shooting Party appeared in 1884 as a serial in the daily paper *Novosti dnya* ('News of the Day'), published in thirty-two more or less weekly instalments (although with one considerable gap) between August 1884 and April of the following year. It has been generally ignored or dismissed as juvenilia by writers about Chekhov. One of the few to have considered it in any detail, Ronald Hingley, changed his mind about the story between his book about Chekhov published in 1950 and his full-scale biography of 1976. In the first book he remarked on the ingenuity of the plot and commended the tale as 'excellent light reading', although 'not a completely homogeneous work', but later he called it a juvenile thriller, a semi-absurdity. Chekhov himself never referred to the story in his correspondence.

The only translation into English was that made by A. E. Chamot in 1926. The novel was, however, the basis of the film *Summer Storm*, made in Hollywood in 1944, directed by Douglas Sirk, with George Sanders in the principal part and Linda Darnell and Edward Everett Horton in the cast. Horton, known for his comedy roles, was cast against type as the Count, apparently very successfully. I have not seen the film, but since it was set in 1912 it can only have provided an approximation to Chekhov's picture of nineteenth-century rural Russia. The plot, a prefiguring of Agatha Christie's *The Murder of Roger Ackroyd* in which the narrator is finally revealed as the murderer, is one that cannot satisfactorily be reproduced on screen or stage, something shown when the Christie story was made into the play *Alibi*. Sirk tried to solve the problem by setting the main story as a flashback within a framework of post-revolutionary Russia, with dialogue referring to the revolutionary period and the moral drawn that, as Sirk said in an interview, 'with guys like him [the magistrate] and the Count going round there had to be a revolution'. This ingenious device, however, must have changed the balance and effect of the story.

It is surprising that *The Shooting Party* should have been so briskly dismissed or simply ignored. It has several points of interest: as the longest piece of fiction Chekhov ever wrote, a work far removed in tone and style from the flippant stuff he was turning out for the comic papers; as a novel of considerable atmospheric power; and as a rare example of the nineteenth-century detective puzzle, not a thriller but a precursor of the tale that sets out deliberately to deceive.

The first half of the book renders the sights and sounds of rural Russia with a sort of desolate romanticism Chekhov rarely evoked so directly. The walk beside the lake in the opening chapter, the Count's gardens with their pavilions, grottoes, foreign fruit trees and avenue of limes, the vivid picture of the forester's cottage, all this is descriptive writing of a high order. And the relationship between the principal characters is both curious and convincing. The examining magistrate, handsome, conceited and egotistical, both envies and despises the drunken lecherous Count who has drowned in alcohol any notion of decent behaviour. The Count on his side shows the fawning affection for the magistrate often felt by the weak for the strong. Although the Count is the magistrate's social superior he cannot bring himself to use this as a way of bringing the magistrate to heel, so that when Kamyshev insults the Count's mysterious Polish friend out of sheer ill-will, the Count does not show the outrage one might expect, but merely pleads that Kamyshev should restrain himself, and changes the subject by talking about the rational management of his estate.

Within this subtle picture of a dominant personality and a weak one, both bent on self-destruction, are set scenes of drunkenness and debauchery which are presumably the kind of thing deprecated by Grigorovich. And certainly there are distinctly outspoken passages, like the Count's casual mention of his two planned seductions, and Kamyshev's reluctant acknowledgement that one ought not to touch married women. There is, however, a change of gear at the end of Chapter XII when we are told that 'the introduction is finished and the drama begins'. From this point onwards we are less concerned with rural Russia and social relationships, more with a murder story.

There is no doubt that the second half of the book does not fit easily with the first. Ronald Hingley suggests that Chekhov's editor insisted on excisions and changes designed to speed up the story, and to emphasize melodrama at the expense of style and tone. There is no direct evidence of this, although some of the comments in the 'Postscript' about material omitted suggest it, and one can imagine an editor who had commissioned a melodramatic mystery becoming impatient with the leisureliness of the early chapters. Whatever the reason the emphasis changes, and we are confronted with an ingenious murder mystery.

That Chekhov had an interest in crime and crime stories is shown by the early short story 'The Swedish Match', in which a trail of false clues leads to the conclusion that a man has been murdered, when he turns out to have been kidnapped by his mistress. In the novel Chekhov offers, as has been mentioned, the kind of deception used by Agatha Christie in what is probably her most famous story. In the context of time and place this was a stroke of extraordinary ingenuity, and there is nothing else at all like it in crime stories of the period. The actual use of the device, however, is comparatively unsophisticated. The footnotes appended by Chekhov in the role of editor make clear his scepticism about the magistrate's story, and this is true particularly of the footnote about Kamyshev's insistence to the dying Olga that she must name her murderer, who will be sent to penal servitude. Such a use of footnotes to make editorial comment on what is supposed to be authentic narrative is, again, a strikingly original device, and would be so even today, but for twentieth-century readers Chekhov gives too much away. Did he mean to show us the identity of the murderer? It is hard to think anything else, but those who bought *Novosti dnya* were undoubtedly more innocent about the devious ways of crime writers, so perhaps they were deceived. A suggestion that the story is in part a parody, rather on the lines of 'The Swedish Match', does not seem to me to have any firm basis.

One should not make extravagant claims for *The Shooting Party*. It is a landmark in the history of the crime story, not in the work of Chekhov. Yet it is a continuously interesting although uneven novel, far from mere juvenilia, a diamond among the trivia and rubbish of the early work. In its melodramatic manner, its outspokenness and deliberate gloom, it represents a kind of writing recognizably Russian, although very unlike what we think of as Chekhovian. Dostoievsky was a writer Chekhov found uncongenial in the fervency of his beliefs and the extravagance of his temperament, but there is something Dostoievskian about the early part of *The Shooting Party*. Perhaps Chekhov rejected the story less for any lack of literary merit than because he knew the path of melodrama and violence taken by such a tale was one that did not suit him, the expression of an attitude alien to his natural genius.

I must give thanks to Arnold Hinchliffe, who first drew my attention to *The Shooting Party* (and has produced a version of it for radio) and to Francis Wyndham who told me of the film *Summer Storm*. The translation used is that made by A. E. Chamot, to which I have made many minor textual changes under the guidance of Julian Graffy, of the London School of Slavonic Studies. Howard Davies has also made many helpful suggestions. I have sometimes interpreted their suggestions rather freely, and any errors resulting from such freedom are mine, not theirs. All of the footnotes are those in the original, except for two on pages 20 and 104, which are mine.

JULIAN SYMONS

THE SHOOTING PARTY

PRELUDE

On an April day of the year 1880 the doorkeeper Andrey came into my private room and told me in a mysterious whisper that a gentleman had come to the editorial office and demanded insistently to see the editor.

'He appears to be a chinovnik,'★ Andrey added. 'He has a cockade. . . .'

'Ask him to come another time,' I said, 'I am busy today. Tell him the editor only receives on Saturdays.'

'He was here the day before yesterday and asked for you. He says his business is urgent. He begs, almost with tears in his eyes, to see you. He says he is not free on Saturday. . . . Will you receive him?'

I sighed, laid down my pen, and settled myself in my chair to receive the gentleman with the cockade. Young authors, and in general everybody who is not initiated into the secrets of the profession, are generally so overcome by holy awe at the words 'editorial office' that they make you wait a considerable time for them. After the editor's 'Show him in,' they cough and blow their noses for a long time, open the door very slowly, come into the room still more slowly, and thus rob you of no little time. The gentleman with the cockade did not make me wait. The door had scarcely had time to close after Andrey before I saw in my office a tall, broad-shouldered man holding a paper parcel in one hand and a cap with a cockade in the other.

This man, who had succeeded in obtaining an interview with

★ A government official.

me, plays a very prominent part in my story. It is necessary to describe his appearance.

He was, as I have already said, tall and broad-shouldered and as vigorous as a fine cart horse. His whole body seemed to exhale health and strength. His face was rosy, his hands large, his chest broad and muscular and his hair as thick as a healthy boy's. He was around forty. He was dressed with taste, according to the latest fashion, in a new tweed suit, evidently just come from the tailor's. A thick gold watch-chain with little ornaments on it hung across his chest, and on his little finger a diamond ring sparkled with brilliant tiny stars. But, what is most important, and so essential to the hero of a novel or story with the slightest pretension to respectability, is that he was extremely handsome. I am neither a woman nor an artist. I have but little understanding of manly beauty, but the appearance of the gentleman with the cockade made an impression on me. His large muscular face remained for ever impressed on my memory. On that face you could see a real Greek nose with a slight hook, thin lips and nice blue eyes from which shone goodness and something else, for which it is difficult to find an appropriate name. That 'something' can be seen in the eyes of little animals when they are sad or ill. Something imploring, childish, resignedly suffering. . . . Cunning or very clever people never have such eyes.

His whole face seemed to breathe candour, a broad, simple nature, and truth. . . If it be not a falsehood that the face is the mirror of the soul, I could have sworn from the very first day of my acquaintance with the gentleman with the cockade that he was unable to lie. I might even have betted that he could not lie. Whether I should have lost my bet or not, the reader will see further on.

His chestnut hair and beard were thick and soft as silk. It is often said that soft hair is the sign of a sweet, sensitive, 'silken' soul. Criminals and wicked obstinate characters have, in most cases, coarse hair. If this be true or not the reader will also see further on. Neither the expression of his face, nor the softness of his beard was as soft and delicate in this gentleman with the cockade as the movements of his bulky form. These movements seemed to denote education, lightness, grace, and if you will forgive the expression, something womanly. It would cause my hero but a slight effort to bend a horseshoe or to flatten out a sardine tin with his fist, yet at the same time not one of his movements showed his physical strength. He took hold of the door handle or of his hat, as if they were butterflies – delicately, carefully, hardly touching them with his fingers. He walked noiselessly, he pressed my hand lightly. When looking at him you forgot that he was as strong as Goliath, and that he could lift with one hand weights that five men like our office servant Andrey could not have moved. Looking at his light movements, it was impossible to believe that he was strong and heavy. Spencer might have called him a model of grace.

When he entered my office he became confused. His delicate, sensitive nature was probably shocked by my frowning, dissatisfied face.

'For God's sake forgive me!' he began in a soft, mellow baritone voice. 'I have broken in upon you not at the appointed time, and I have forced you to make an exception for me. You are very busy! But, Mr Editor, you see, this is how the case stands. Tomorrow I must start for Odessa on very important business. . . . If I had been able to put off this journey till Saturday, I can assure you I would not have asked you to make this exception for me. I submit to rules because I love order. . . .'

'How much he talks!' I thought as I stretched out my hand towards the pen, showing by this movement I was pressed for time. (I was heartily sick of visitors just then.)

'I will only take up a moment of your time,' my hero continued in an apologetic tone. 'But first allow me to introduce myself. . . . Ivan Petrovich Kamyshev, Bachelor of Law and former examining magistrate. I have not the honour of belonging to the fellowship of authors, nevertheless I appear before you from motives that are purely those of a writer. Notwithstanding his forty years, you have before you a man who wishes to be a beginner. . . . Better late than never!'

'Very pleased. . . . What can I do for you?'

The man wishing to be a beginner sat down and continued, looking at the floor with his imploring eyes:

'I have brought you a novel which I would like to see published in your journal. Mr Editor, I will tell you quite candidly I have not written this story to attain an author's celebrity, nor for the sake of sweet-sounding words. I am too old to enjoy such things. I venture on the writer's path from purely commercial motives. . . . I want to earn something. . . . At the present moment I have absolutely no occupation. I was a magistrate in the S— district for more than five years, but I did not make a fortune, nor did I keep my innocence either. . . .'

Kamyshev glanced at me with his kind eyes and laughed gently.

'Service is tiresome. . . . I served and served till I was quite fed up, and chucked it. I have no occupation now, sometimes I have nothing to eat. . . . If, despite its unworthiness, you will publish my story, you will do me more than a great favour. . . . You will help me. . . . A journal is not an alms-house, nor an old-age asylum . . . I know that, but . . . if you'd be so kind . . .'

'He is lying,' I thought.

The ornaments on his watch-chain and the diamond ring on his little finger belied his having written simply for money. Besides, a slight cloud passed over Kamyshev's face such as only an experienced eye can trace on the faces of people who seldom lie.

'What is the subject of your story?' I asked.

'The subject? What can I tell you? The subject is not new. . . . Love and murder. . . . But read it, you will see. . . . "From the Notes of an Examining Magistrate" . . .'

I probably frowned, for Kamyshev looked confused, his eyes began to blink, he started and continued speaking rapidly:

'My story is written in the conventional style of former examining magistrates, but . . . you will find in it facts, the truth. . . . All that is written, from beginning to end, happened before my eyes. . . . Indeed, I was not only a witness but one of the actors.'

'The truth does not matter. . . . It is not absolutely necessary to see a thing to describe it. That is unimportant. The fact is our poor readers have long been fed up with Gaboriau and Shklyarevsky.★ They are tired of all those mysterious murders, those artful devices

---

★ A. A. Shklyarevsky was a well-known Russian author who wrote a number of novels and tales on criminal and detective subjects in the years 1860–80. – A. Ch. [Shklyarevsky was known as 'the Russian Gaboriau'. Among his most celebrated works were *Tales of an Examining Magistrate* (1872), *Murder Without Trace* (1878) and *The Undiscovered Crime* (1878). – J. S.]

of the detectives, and the extraordinary resourcefulness of the examining magistrate. The reading public, of course, varies, but I am talking of the public that reads our newspaper. What is the title of your story?'

'The Shooting Party.'

'Hm! . . . That's rather sensational, you know. . . . And, to be quite frank with you, I have such an amount of copy on hand that it is quite impossible to accept new things, even if they are of undoubted merit.'

'Pray look at my work. . . . You say it is sensational, but . . . it is difficult to tell what something is like until you have seen it. . . . Besides, it seems to me you refuse to admit that an examining magistrate can write serious works.'

All this Kamyshev said stammeringly, twisting a pencil about between his fingers and looking at his feet. He finished by blinking his eyes and becoming exceedingly confused. I was sorry for him.

'All right, leave it,' I said. 'But I can't promise that your story will be read very soon. You will have to wait . . .'

'How long?'

'I don't know. Look in . . . in about two to three months. . . .'

'That's a pretty long time. . . . But I dare not insist. . . . Let it be as you say. . . .'

Kamyshev rose and took up his cap.

'Thank you for the audience,' he said. 'I will now go home and dwell in hope. Three months of hope! However, I am boring you. I have the honour to bid you good-bye!'

'One word more, please,' I said as I turned over the pages of his thick copy-book, which were written in a very small handwriting. 'You write here in the first person. . . . . You therefore mean the examining magistrate to be yourself?'

'Yes, but under another name. The part I play in this story is somewhat scandalous . . . . It would have been awkward to give my own name. . . . In three months, then?'

'Yes, not earlier, please. . . . Good-bye!'

The former examining magistrate bowed gallantly, turned the door handle gingerly, and disappeared, leaving his work on my writing table. I took up the copy-book and put it away in the table drawer.

Handsome Kamyshev's story reposed in my table drawer for two months. One day, when leaving my office to go to the country, I remembered it and took it with me.

When I was seated in the railway coach I opened the copy-book and began to read from the middle. The middle interested me. That same evening, notwithstanding my want of leisure, I read the whole story from the beginning to the words 'The End', which were written with a great flourish. That night I read the whole story through again, and at sunrise I was walking about the terrace from corner to corner, rubbing my temples as if I wanted to rub out of my head some new and painful thoughts that had suddenly entered my mind. . . . The thoughts were really painful, unbearably sharp. It appeared to me that I, neither an examining magistrate nor even a psychological juryman, had discovered the terrible secret of a man, a secret that did not concern me in the slightest degree. I paced the terrace and tried to persuade myself not to believe in my discovery. . . .

Kamyshev's story did not appear in my newspaper for reasons that I will explain at the end of my talk with the reader. I shall meet the reader once again. Now, when I am leaving him for a long time, I offer Kamyshev's story for his perusal.

It is not an unusual story. There are *longueurs* in it, there are things crudely expressed. . . . The author is too fond of effects and melodramatic phrases. . . . It is evident that he is writing for the first time, his hand is unaccustomed, uneducated. Nevertheless his narrative reads easily. There is a plot, a meaning, too, and what is most important, it is original, very characteristic and what may be called *sui generis*. It also possesses certain literary qualities. It is worth reading. Here it is.

THE SHOOTING PARTY

FROM THE NOTEBOOK OF AN EXAMINING MAGISTRATE

I

'The husband killed his wife! Oh, how stupid you are! Give me some sugar!'

These cries awoke me. I stretched myself, feeling indisposition and heaviness in every limb. One can lie upon one's legs or arms until they are numb, but now it seemed to me that my whole body, from the crown of my head to the soles of my feet, was benumbed. An afternoon snooze in a sultry, dry atmosphere amid the buzzing and humming of flies and mosquitoes does not act in an invigorating manner but has an enervating effect. Broken and bathed in perspiration, I rose and went to the window. The sun was still high and baked with the same ardour it had done three hours before. Many hours still remained until sunset and the coolness of evening.

'The husband killed his wife!'

'Stop lying, Ivan Dem'yanych!' I said as I gave a slight tap to Ivan Dem'yanych's nose. 'Husbands kill their wives only in novels and in the tropics, where African passions boil over, my dear. For us such horrors as thefts and burglaries or people living on false passports are quite enough.'

'Thefts and burglaries!' Ivan Dem'yanych murmured through his hooked nose. 'Oh, how stupid you are!'

'What's to be done, my dear? In what way are we mortals to blame for our brain having its limits? Besides, Ivan Dem'yanych, it is no sin to be a fool in such a temperature. You're my clever darling, but doubtless your brain, too, gets addled and stupid in such heat.'

My parrot is not called Polly or by any other of the names given to birds, but he is called Ivan Dem'yanych. He got this name quite by chance. One day, when my man Polycarp was cleaning the cage, he suddenly made a discovery without which my noble bird would still have been called Polly. My lazy servant was suddenly blessed with the idea that my parrot's beak was very like the nose of our village shopkeeper, Ivan Dem'yanych, and from that time the name and patronymic of our long-nosed shopkeeper stuck to my parrot. From that day Polycarp and the whole village christened my extraordinary bird 'Ivan Dem'yanych'. Thanks to Polycarp the bird became a personage, and the shopkeeper lost his own name, and to the end of his days he will be known among the villagers by the nickname of the 'magistrate's parrot'.

I had bought Ivan Dem'yanych from the mother of my predecessor, the examining magistrate, Pospelov, who had died shortly before my appointment. I bought him together with some old oak furniture, various rubbishy kitchen utensils, and in general the whole of the household goods that remained after Pospelov's death. My walls are still decorated with photographs of his relatives, and the portrait of the former occupant is still hanging above my bed. The departed, a lean, muscular man with a red moustache and a thick under-lip, sits looking at me with staring eyes from his faded nutwood frame all the time I am lying on his bed. . . . I had not taken down a single photograph, I had left the house just as I found it. I am too lazy to think of my own comfort, and I don't prevent either corpses or living men from hanging on my walls if the latter wish to do so.*

Ivan Dem'yanych found it as sultry as I did. He fluffed out his feathers, spread his wings, and shrieked out the phrases he had been taught by my predecessor, Pospelov, and by Polycarp. To occupy in some way my after-dinner leisure, I sat down in front of the cage and began to watch the movements of my parrot, who was industriously trying, but without success, to escape from the torments he suffered from the suffocating heat and the insects that dwelt among his feathers. . . . The poor thing seemed very unhappy. . . .

---

* I beg the reader to excuse such expressions. Kamyshev's story is full of them, and if I do not omit them it is only because I thought it necessary in the interest of the characterization of the author to print his story *in toto*. – A. Ch.

'At what time does he awake?' was borne to me in a bass voice from the lobby.

'That depends!' Polycarp's voice answered. 'Sometimes he wakes at five o'clock, and sometimes he sleeps like a log till morning. . . . Everybody knows he has nothing to do.'

'You're his valet, I suppose?'

'His servant. Now don't bother me; hold your tongue. Don't you see I'm reading?'

I peeped into the lobby. My Polycarp was there, lolling on the large red trunk, and, as usual, reading a book. With his sleepy, unblinking eyes fixed attentively on his book, he was moving his lips and frowning. He was evidently irritated by the presence of the stranger, a tall, bearded muzhik, who was standing near the trunk persistently trying to inveigle him into conversation. At my appearance the muzhik took a step away from the trunk and drew himself up to attention. Polycarp looked dissatisfied, and without removing his eyes from the book he rose slightly.

'What do you want?' I asked the muzhik.

'I have come from the Count, your honour. The Count sends you his greetings, and begs you to come to him at once. . . .'

'Has the Count arrived?' I asked, much astonished.

'Just so, your honour. . . . He arrived last night. . . . Here's a letter, sir. . . .'

'What the devil has brought him back!' my Polycarp grumbled. 'Two summers we've lived peacefully without him and this year he'll again make a pigsty of the district. It reflects on us, it's shameful.'

'Hold your tongue, your opinion is not asked!'

'I need not be asked. . . . You'll come home drunk again, and go in the lake just as you are, in all your clothes. . . . It's I who have the job of cleaning them afterwards! And it takes three days and more!'

'What's the Count doing now?' I asked the muzhik.

'He was just sitting down to dinner when he sent me to you. . . . Before dinner he was fishing from the bathing cabin, sir. . . . What answer can I take?'

I opened the letter and read the following:

My Dear Lecoq,

If you are still alive, well, and have not forgotten your ever-drunken friend, do not delay a moment. Get dressed immediately and come to me. I only arrived last night and am already dying from ennui. The impatience I feel to see you knows no bounds. I wanted to drive over to see you and carry you off to my den, but the heat has utterly exhausted me. I simply sit about, fanning myself. Well, how are you? How is your clever Ivan Dem'yanych? Are you still at war with your scolding Polycarp? Come quickly and tell me everything.

Your A. K.

It was not necessary to look at the signature to recognize the drunken, sprawling, ugly handwriting of my friend, Count Alexey Karnéev. The shortness of the letter, its pretension to a certain playfulness and vivacity proved that my friend, with his limited capacities, must have torn up much notepaper before he was able to compose this epistle.

The pronoun 'which' was absent from this letter, and adverbs were carefully avoided – both being grammatical forms that were seldom achieved by the Count at a single sitting.

'What answer can I take, sir?' the muzhik repeated.

At first I did not reply to this question, and every decent, honest man in my place would have hesitated too. The Count was fond of me, and quite sincerely obtruded his friendship on me. I, on my part, felt nothing like friendship for the Count; I even disliked him. It would therefore have been more honest to reject his friendship once for all than to go to him and dissimulate. Besides, to go to the Count's meant to plunge once more into the life my Polycarp had characterized as a 'pigsty', which two years before during the Count's residence on his estate and until he left for Petersburg had injured my health and dried up my brain. That loose, unaccustomed life so full of show and drunken madness, had not yet shattered my constitution, but it had made me known throughout the province. . . . Yet I was popular . . . .

My reason told me the whole truth, a blush of shame for the not distant past suffused my face, my heart sank with fear that I would not possess sufficient manliness to refuse to go to the Count's, but I did not hesitate long. The struggle lasted not more than a minute.

'Give my compliments to the Count,' I said to his messenger, 'and thank him for thinking of me. . . . Tell him I am busy, and that . . . Tell him that I . . .'

And at the very moment my tongue was about to pronounce a decisive 'No', I was suddenly overpowered by a feeling of dullness. . . . Here I was, a young man, full of life, strength and desires, who by the decrees of fate had been cast into this forest village, seized by a sensation of ennui, of loneliness. . . .

I remembered the Count's gardens with the exuberant vegetation of their cool conservatories, and the semi-darkness of the narrow, neglected avenues. . . . Those avenues protected from the sun by arches of the entwined branches of old limes know me well; they also know the women who sought my love in semi-darkness. . . . I remembered the luxurious drawing-room with the sweet indolence of its velvet sofas, heavy curtains and thick carpets, soft as down, with the laziness so common to young healthy animals. . . . I recalled my drunken audacity, limitless in its scope, its satanic pride and its contempt for life. My large body wearied by sleep again longed for movement. . . .

'Tell him I'll come!'

The muzhik bowed and retired.

'If I'd known, I wouldn't have let that devil in!' Polycarp grumbled, quickly turning over the pages of his book in a purposeless manner.

'Put that book away and go and saddle Zorka,' I said. 'Look sharp!'

'Look sharp! Oh, of course, certainly. . . . I'm just going to rush off. . . . It would be all right if he were going on business, but he's just off on some spree!'

This was said in an undertone, but loud enough for me to hear it. Having whispered this impertinence, my servant drew himself up before me and waited for me to flare up in reply, but I pretended not to have heard his words. My silence was the best and sharpest weapon I could use in my contests with Polycarp. This contemptuous custom of allowing his venomous words to pass unheeded disarmed him and cut the ground away from under his feet. As a punishment it acted better than a box on the ear or a

flood of vituperation. . . . When Polycarp had gone into the yard
to saddle Zorka, I peeped into the book which he had been
prevented from reading. It was *The Count of Monte Cristo*, Dumas'
dreadful romance. . . . My civilized fool read everything, beginning with the signboards of the public houses and finishing with
Auguste Comte, which was lying in my trunk together with other
neglected books that I did not read; but of the whole mass of
written and printed matter he only approved of exciting, sensational novels with 'celebrated personages', poison and subterra-
nean passages; all the rest he dubbed 'nonsense'. I shall have again
to refer to his reading, now I had to ride off. A quarter of an hour
later the hoofs of my Zorka were raising the dust on the road from
the village to the Count's estate. The sun was near setting, but the
heat and the sultriness were still felt. The hot air was dry and
motionless, although my road led along the banks of an enormous
lake. . . . On my right I saw the great expanse of water, on the left
my sight was caressed by the young vernal foliage of an oak forest;
nevertheless, my cheeks suffered the dryness of Sahara. 'If there
could only be a storm!' I thought, dreaming of a good cool
downpour.

The lake slept peacefully. It did not greet with a single sound the
flight of my Zorka, and it was only the piping of a young snipe
that broke the grave-like silence of the sleeping lake. The sun
looked at itself in it as in a huge mirror, and shed a blinding light
on the whole of its breadth that extended from my road to the
distant banks opposite. And it seemed to my blinded eyes that
nature received light from the lake and not from the sun.

The sultriness impelled to slumber the whole of that life in
which the lake and its green banks so richly abounded. The birds
had hidden themselves, the fish did not splash in the water, the
field crickets and the grasshoppers waited in silence for coolness to
set in. All around was a waste. From time to time my Zorka bore
me into a thick cloud of mosquitoes along the bank of the lake, and
far away on the water, scarcely moving, I could see the three black
boats belonging to old Mikhey, our fisherman, who leased the
fishing rights of the whole lake.

II

I did not ride in a straight line as I had to make a circuit along the road that skirted the circular lake. It was only possible to go in a straight line by boat, while those who went by the road had to make a large detour, the distance being almost eight versts farther. All the way, looking across the lake, I could see beyond it the muddy banks opposite, on which the bright strip of a blossoming cherry orchard gleamed white, while farther still I could see the roofs of the Count's barns dotted all over with many coloured pigeons, and rising still higher the small white belfry of the Count's chapel. At the foot of the muddy banks was the bathing cabin with sailcloth nailed on the sides and sheets hanging to dry on its railings. I saw all this, and it appeared to me as if only a verst separated me from my friend the Count, yet in order to reach his estate I had to ride about sixteen versts.

On the way, I thought of my strange relationship with the Count. I was interested in examining and trying to define it, but the task proved beyond me. However much I thought, I could come to no satisfactory decision, and at last I arrived at the conclusion that I was a bad judge of myself and of men in general. The people who knew both the Count and me had an explanation for our mutual connection. The narrower-minded, who see nothing beyond the tip of their nose, were fond of asserting that the illustrious Count found in the 'poor and undistinguished' magistrate a congenial hanger-on and boon companion. In their view I, the writer of these lines, fawned and cringed before the Count for the sake of the crumbs and scraps that fell from his table. In their opinion the illustrious millionaire, who was both the bugbear and the envy of the whole of the S— district, was very clever and liberal; otherwise his gracious condescension that went as far as friendship for an indigent magistrate and the genuine liberalism that made the Count tolerate my familiarity in addressing him as 'thou', would be quite incomprehensible. Cleverer people explained our intimacy by our common 'spiritual interests'. The Count and I were of the same age. We had finished our law studies in the same university, and we both knew very little: I still had a smattering of legal lore, but the Count had forgotten and drowned in alcohol the little he had ever known. We were both proud, and by virtue of some reason which was only known to ourselves, we shunned the world like misanthropes. We were both indifferent to the opinion of the world – that is of the S— district – we were both immoral, and would certainly both end badly. These were the 'spiritual interests' that united us. This was all that the people who knew us could say about our relations.

They would, of course, have spoken differently had they known how weak, soft and yielding was the nature of my friend, the Count, and how strong and hard was mine. They would have had much to say had they known how fond this infirm man was of me, and how I disliked him! He was the first to offer his friendship and I was the first to say 'thou' to him, but with what a difference in the tone! In a fit of kindly feeling he embraced me, and asked me timidly to be his friend. I, on the other hand, once seized by a feeling of a contempt and aversion, said to him:

'Canst thou not cease jabbering nonsense?'

And he accepted this 'thou' as an expression of friendship and submitted to it from that time, repaying me with an honest, brotherly 'thou'.

Yes, it would have been better and more honest had I turned my Zorka's head homewards and ridden back to Polycarp and my Ivan Dem'yanych.

Afterwards I often thought: 'How much misfortune I would have avoided bearing on my shoulders, how much good I would have brought to my neighbours, if on that night I had had the resolution to turn back, if only my Zorka had gone mad and carried me far away from the immensities of the lake! What numbers of tormenting recollections which now cause my hand to quit the pen and seize my head would not have pressed so heavily on my mind!' But I must not anticipate, all the more as farther on I shall often have to dwell on misfortunes. Now for gaiety. . . .

My Zorka bore me into the gates of the Count's yard. At the very gates she stumbled, and I, losing the stirrup, almost fell to the ground.

'An ill omen, sir!' a muzhik, who was standing at one of the doors of the Count's long line of stables, called to me.

I believe that a man falling from a horse may break his neck, but I do not believe in prognostications. Having given the bridle to the muzhik, I beat the dust off my top-boots with my riding-whip and ran into the house. Nobody met me. All the doors and windows of the rooms were wide open, nevertheless within the house the air was heavy, and had a strange smell. It was a mixture of the odour of ancient, deserted apartments with the tart narcotic scent of hothouse plants that have but recently been brought from the conservatories into the rooms. . . . In the drawing-room, two tumbled cushions were lying on one of the sofas that was covered with a light blue silk material, and on a round table before the sofa I saw a glass containing a few drops of a liquid that exhaled an odour of strong Riga balsam. All this denoted that the house was inhabited, but I did not meet a living soul in any of the eleven rooms that I traversed. The same desertion that was round the lake reigned in the house. . . .

A glass door led into the garden from the so-called 'mosaic' drawing-room. I opened it noisily and went down the marble stairs into the garden. I had gone only a few steps along the avenue when I met Nastasia, an old woman of ninety, who had formerly been the Count's nurse. This little wrinkled old creature, forgotten by death, had a bald head and piercing eyes. When you looked at her face you involuntarily remembered the nickname 'Scops-Owl' that had been given her in the village. . . . When she saw me she trembled and almost dropped a glass of milk she was carrying in both hands.

'How do you do, Scops?' I said to her.

She gave me a sidelong glance and silently went on her way. . . . I seized her by the shoulder.

'Don't be afraid, fool. . . . Where's the Count?'

The old woman pointed to her ear.

'Are you deaf? How long have you been deaf?'

Despite her great age, the old woman heard and saw very well, but she found it useful to pretend otherwise. I shook my finger at her and let her go.

Having gone on a few steps farther, I heard voices, and soon after saw people. At the spot where the avenue widened out and formed an open space surrounded by iron benches and shaded by tall white acacias, stood a table on which a samovar shone brightly. People were seated at the table, talking. I went quietly across the grass towards the gathering and, hiding behind a lilac bush, began to peer about for the Count.

My friend, Count Karnéev, was seated at the table on a cane-bottomed folding chair, drinking tea. He was dressed in the same many-coloured dressing-gown in which I had seen him two years before, and he wore a straw hat. His face had a troubled, concentrated expression, and it was very wrinkled, so that a man not acquainted with him might have imagined he was troubled at that moment by some serious thought or anxiety. . . . The Count had not changed at all in appearance during the two years since last we met. He had the same small thin body, as frail and wizened as the body of a corncrake. He had the same narrow, consumptive shoulders, surmounted by a small red-haired head. His small nose was as red as formerly, and his cheeks were flabby and hanging like rags, as they had been two years before. On his face there was nothing of boldness, strength or manliness. . . . All was weak, apathetic and languid. The only imposing thing about him was his long, drooping moustache. Somebody had told my friend that a long moustache was very becoming to him. He believed it, and every morning since then he had measured how much longer the growth on his pale lips had become. With this moustache he reminded you of a moustached but very young and puny kitten.

Sitting next to the Count at the table was a stout man with a large closely-cropped head and very dark eyebrows, who was unknown to me. His face was fat and shone like a ripe melon. His moustache was longer than the Count's, his forehead was low, his lips were compressed, and his eyes gazed lazily into the sky. . . . The features of his face were bloated, but nevertheless they were as hard as dried-up skin. He did not look like a Russian. . . . The stout man was without his coat or waistcoat, and on his shirt there were dark spots caused by perspiration. He was not drinking tea but Seltzer water.

At a respectful distance from the table a short, thick-set man with a stout red neck and protruding ears was standing. This man was Urbenin, the Count's bailiff. In honour of the Count's arrival he was dressed in a new black suit and was now suffering torments. The perspiration was pouring in streams from his red, sunburnt face. Next to the bailiff stood the muzhik, who had come to me with the letter. It was only here I noticed that this muzhik had only one eye. Standing at attention, not allowing himself the slightest movement, he was like a statue, and waited to be questioned.

'Kuz'ma, you deserve to be thrashed black and blue with your own whip,' the bailiff said to him in his reproachful soft bass voice, pausing between each word. 'Is it possible to execute the master's orders in such a careless way. You ought to have requested him to come here at once and to have found out when he could be expected.'

'Yes, yes, yes . . .' the Count exclaimed nervously. 'You ought to have found out everything! He said: "I'll come!" But that's not enough! I want him at once! Pos–i–tively at once! You asked him to come, but he did not understand!'

'What do you want with him?' the fat man asked the Count.

'I want to see him!'

'Only that? To my mind, Alexey, that magistrate would do far better if he remained at home today. I have no wish for guests.'

I opened my eyes. What was the meaning of that masterful, authoritative 'I'?

'But he's not a guest!' my friend said in an imploring tone. 'He won't prevent you from resting after the journey. I beg you not to stand on ceremonies with him. . . . You'll like him at once, my dear boy, and you'll soon be friends with him!'

I came out of my hiding place behind the lilac bushes and went up to the tables. The Count saw and recognized me, and his face brightened with a pleased smile.

'Here he is! Here he is!' he exclaimed, getting red with pleasure, and he jumped up from the table. 'How good of you to come!'

He ran towards me, seized me in his arms, embraced me and scratched my cheeks several times with his bristly moustache. These kisses were followed by lengthy shaking of my hand and long looks into my eyes.

'You, Sergey, have not changed at all! You're still the same! The same handsome strong fellow! Thank you for accepting my invitation and coming at once!'

When released from the Count's embrace, I greeted the bailiff, who was an old friend of mine, and sat down at the table.

'Oh, golubchek!'* the Count continued in an excitedly anxious tone. 'If you only knew how delighted I am to see your serious countenance again. You are not acquainted? Allow me to introduce you – my good friend, Kaetan Kazimirovich Pshekhotsky. And this,' he continued, introducing me to the fat man, 'is my good old friend, Sergey Petrovich Zinov'ev! Our magistrate.'

The stout, dark-browed man rose slightly from his seat and offered me his fat, and extremely sweaty hand.

'Very pleased,' he mumbled, examining me from head to foot. 'Very glad!'

Having given vent to his feelings and become calm again, the Count filled a glass with cold, dark brown tea for me and moved a box of biscuits towards my hand.

'Eat. . . . When passing through Moscow I bought them at Einem's. I'm very angry with you, Serezha, so angry that I wanted to quarrel with you! . . . Not only have you not written me a line during the whole of the past two years, but you did not even think a single one of my letters worth answering! That's not friendly!'

'I don't know how to write letters,' I said. 'Besides, I have no time for letter writing. Can you tell me what could I have written to you about?'

'There must have been many things!'

'Indeed, there was nothing. I admit of only three sorts of letters: love, congratulatory, and business letters. The first I did not write to you because you are not a woman, and I am not in love with you; the second you don't require; and from the third category we are relieved as from our birth we have never had any business connection together.'

'That's perfectly true,' the Count said, agreeing readily and quickly with everything; 'but all the same, you might have written, if only a line. . . . And what's more, as Pëtr Egorych tells

---

* Little dove; a much used term of endearment.

me, all these two years you've not set foot here, as though you were living a thousand versts away or disdained my property. You could have made your home here, shot over my grounds. Many things might have happened here while I was away.'

The Count spoke much and long. When once he began talking about anything, his tongue chattered on without ceasing and without end, quite regardless of the triviality or insignificance of his subject.

In the utterance of sounds he was as untiring as my Ivan Dem'yanych. I could hardly stand him for that facility. This time he was stopped by his butler, Il'ya, a tall, thin man in a well-worn, much-stained livery, who brought the Count a wineglass of vodka and half a tumbler of water on a silver tray. The Count swallowed the vodka, washed it down with some water, making a grimace with a shake of the head.

'So it seems you have not yet stopped tippling vodka!' I said.

'No, Serezha, I have not.'

'Well, you might at least drop that drunken habit of making faces and shaking your head! It's disgusting!'

'My dear boy, I'm going to drop everything. . . . The doctors have forbidden me to drink. I drink now only because it's unhealthy to drop habits all at once. . . . It must be done gradual-ly. . . .'

I looked at the Count's unhealthy, worn face, at the wineglass, at the butler in yellow shoes. I looked at the dark-browed Pole, who from the very first moment for some reason had appeared to me to be a scoundrel and a blackguard. I looked at the one-eyed muzhik, who stood there at attention, and a feeling of dread and of oppression came over me. . . . I suddenly wanted to leave this dirty atmosphere, having first opened the Count's eyes to the unlimited antipathy I felt for him. . . . There was a moment when I was ready to rise and depart. . . . But I did not go away. . . . I was prevented (I'm ashamed to confess it!) by physical lazi-ness. . . .

'Give me a glass of vodka, too!' I said to Il'ya.

Long shadows began to be cast on the avenue and on the open space where we were sitting. . . .

The distant croaking of frogs, the cawing of crows and the

singing of orioles greeted the setting of the sun. A gay evening was just beginning. . . .

'Tell Urbenin to sit down,' I whispered to the Count. 'He's standing before you like a boy.'

'Oh, I never thought of that! Pëtr Egorych,' the Count addressed his bailiff, 'sit down, please! Why are you standing there?'

Urbenin sat down, casting a grateful glance at me. He who was always healthy and gay appeared to me now to be ill and dull. His face seemed wrinkled and sleepy, his eyes looked at us lazily and as if unwillingly.

'Well, Pëtr Egorych, what's new here? Any pretty girls, eh?' Karnéev asked him. 'Isn't there something special . . . something out of the common?'

'It's always the same, your Excellency. . . .'

'Are there no new . . . nice little girls, Pëtr Egorych?'

The virtuous Pëtr Egorych blushed.

'I don't know, your Excellency. . . . I don't occupy myself with that. . . .'

'There are, your Excellency,' broke in the deep bass voice of one-eyed Kuz'ma, who had been silent all the time. 'And quite worth notice, too.'

'Are they pretty?'

'There are all sorts, your Excellency, for all tastes. . . . There are dark ones and fair ones – all sorts. . . .'

'O, ho! . . . Stop a minute. . . . I remember you now. . . . My former Leporello, a sort of secretary. . . . Your name's Kuz'ma, I think?'

'Yes, your Excellency. . . .'

'I remember, I remember. . . . Well, and what have you now in view? Something new, all peasant girls?'

'Mostly peasants, of course, but there are finer ones, too. . . .'

'Where have you found finer ones. . . .' Il'ya asked, winking at Kuz'ma.

'At Easter the postman's sister-in-law came to stay with him . . . Nastasia Ivanovna. . . . A girl all on springs. She's good enough to eat, but money is wanted. . . . Cheeks like peaches, and all the rest as good. . . . There's something finer than that, too. It's only waiting for you, your Excellency. Young, plump, jolly . . . a

beauty! Such a beauty, your Excellency, as you've scarcely found
in Petersburg. . . .'

'Who is it?'

'Olenka, the forester Skvortsov's daughter.'

Urbenin's chair cracked under him. Supporting himself with his
hands on the table, purple in the face, the bailiff rose slowly and
turned towards the one-eyed Kuz'ma. The expression on his face
of dullness and fatigue had given place to one of great anger.

'Hold your tongue, serf!' he grumbled. 'One-eyed vermin! Say
what you please, but don't talk about respectable people!'

'I'm not speaking of you, Pëtr Egorych,' Kuz'ma said imperturbably.

'I'm not talking about myself, blockhead! Besides . . . Forgive
me, your Excellency,' the bailiff turned to the Count, 'forgive me
for making a scene, but I would beg your Excellency to forbid
your Leporello, as you were pleased to call him, to extend his zeal
to persons who are worthy of all respect!'

'I don't understand . . .' the Count lisped naively. 'He has said
nothing very offensive.'

Insulted and excited to a degree, Urbenin went away from the
table and stood with his side towards us. With his arms crossed on
his breast and his eyes blinking, hiding his purple face from us
behind the branches of the bushes, he stood plunged in thought.

Had not this man a presentiment that in the near future his moral
feelings would have to suffer offences a thousand times more
bitter?

'I don't understand what has offended him!' the Count whispered in my ear. 'What a caution! There was nothing offensive in
what was said.'

After two years of sober living, the glass of vodka acted on me
in a slightly intoxicating manner. A feeling of lightness, of
pleasure, was diffused in my brain and through my whole body.
Added to this, I began to feel the coolness of evening, which little
by little was supplanting the sultriness of the day. I proposed to
take a stroll. The Count and his new Polish friend had their coats
brought from the house, and we set off. Urbenin followed us.

III

The Count's gardens in which we were walking demand special description for their lushness and splendour. From a botanical or an economical point of view, and in many other ways, they are richer and grander than any other gardens I have ever seen. Besides the avenue already mentioned with its green vaults, you found in them everything that capricious indulgence can demand from pleasure gardens. You found here every variety of indigenous and foreign fruit tree, beginning with the wild cherry and plum and finishing with apricots that were the size of a goose's egg. You came across mulberry trees, barberry bushes, and even olive trees at every step. . . . Here there were half-ruined, moss-grown grottoes, fountains, little ponds destined for goldfish and tame carp, hillocks, pavilions and costly conservatories. . . . And all this rare luxury which had been collected by the hands of grandfathers and fathers, all this wealth of large, full roses, poetical grottoes and endless avenues had been barbarously abandoned, given over to thieves who attacked the trees with their axes, and to the rooks who unceremoniously built their ugly nests on the branches of rare trees! The lawful possessor of all this wealth walked beside me, and the muscles of his lean, satiated face were no more moved by the sight of this neglect, this crying human slovenliness, than if he had not been the owner of these gardens. Once only, by way of making some remark, he said to his bailiff that it would not be a bad thing if the paths were sanded. He noticed the absence of the sand that troubled nobody else, but not the bare trees that had been frozen in the hard winters, or the cows that were walking about in the garden. In reply to his remark, Urbenin said it would require ten men to keep the garden in order, and as his Excellency was not pleased to reside on his estate, the outlay on the garden would be a useless and unproductive luxury. The Count, of course, agreed with this argument.

'Besides, I must confess I have no time for it!' Urbenin said with a wave of the hand. 'All the summer in the fields, and in winter selling the corn in town. . . . There's no time for gardens here!'

The charm of the principal, the so-called 'main avenue', consisted in its old broad-spreading limes, and in the masses of tulips that stretched out in two variegated borders at each side of its length and finished at the end in a yellow stone pavilion, which at one time had contained a refreshment room, billiards, skittles and other games. We wandered, somewhat aimlessly, towards this pavilion. At its door we were confronted by a reptile whose appearance somewhat unsettled the nerves of my companion, who was never very courageous.

'A snake!' the Count shrieked, seizing me by the hand and turning pale. 'Look!'

The Pole stepped back, and then stood stock still with his arms outstretched as if he wanted to bar the way for the apparition. On the upper step of the crumbling stone stair there lay a young snake of our ordinary Russian species. When it saw us it raised its head and moved. The Count shrieked again and hid behind me.

'Don't be afraid, your Excellency. . . .' Urbenin said lazily as he placed his foot on the first step.

'But if it bites?'

'It won't bite. Besides, the danger from the bite of these snakes is much exaggerated. I was once bitten by an old snake, and, as you see, I didn't die. A man's sting is worse than a snake's!' Urbenin said with a sigh, wishing to point a moral.

Indeed, the bailiff had not had time to mount two or three steps before the snake stretched out to its full length, and with the speed of lightning vanished into a crevice between two stones. When we entered the pavilion we were confronted by another creature. Lying on the torn and faded cloth of the old billiard table was an elderly man of middle height in a blue jacket, striped trousers, and a jockey cap. He was sleeping sweetly and quietly. Around his toothless gaping mouth and on his pointed nose flies were making themselves at home. Thin as a skeleton, with an open mouth, lying there immovable, he looked like a corpse that had only just been brought in from the mortuary to be dissected.

'Franz!' said Urbenin, poking him. 'Franz!'

After being poked five or six times, Franz shut his mouth, sat up, looked round at us, and lay down again. A minute later his mouth was again open and the flies that were walking about his nose were again disturbed by the slight vibration of his snores.

'He's asleep, the dirty pig!' Urbenin sighed.

'Isn't that our gardener, Tricher?' the Count asked.

'The very same. . . . That's how he is every day . . . He sleeps like a dead man all day and plays cards all night. I was told he gambled last night till six in the morning.'

'What do they play?'

'Games of hazard. . . . Chiefly stukolka.'

'Well, such gentlemen work badly. They draw their wages for nothing!'

'It was not to complain, your Excellency,' Urbenin hastened to say, 'that I told you this, or to express my dissatisfaction; it was only . . . I am only sorry that so capable a man is a slave to his passions. He really is a hard-working man, capable too. . . . He does not receive wages for nothing.'

We glanced again at the gambler Franz and left the pavilion. We then turned towards the garden gate and went into the fields.

There are few novels in which the garden gate does not play an important part. If you have not noticed this, you have only to inquire of my man Polycarp, who in his lifetime has swallowed multitudes of dreadful and not so dreadful novels, and he will doubtless confirm this insignificant but characteristic fact.

My novel has also not escaped the inevitable garden gate. But my gate is different from others in this, that my pen will have to lead through it many unfortunate and scarcely any happy people; and even this in a direction contrary to the one found in other novels. And what is worse, I had once to describe this gate not as a novel-writer but as an examining magistrate. In my novel more criminals than lovers will pass through it.

A quarter of an hour later, supporting ourselves on our walking sticks, we wound our way up the hill to what is known as the 'Stone Grave'. In the surrounding villages there is a legend that under this heap of stones there reposes the body of a Tartar Khan, who, fearing that after his death the enemy would desecrate his ashes, had ordered that a mound of stones was to be made above his body. This legend, however, is scarcely correct. The layers of stone, their size and relative position, exclude the possibility of man's hand having had a part in the formation of this mound. It stands solitary in the midst of fields and has the aspect of an overturned dome.

From the top of this mound we could see the whole of the lake's magnificent extent, and grasp its indescribable beauty. The sun, no longer reflected in it, had set, leaving behind a broad purple stripe that illuminated the surroundings with a pleasing rosy-yellow tint. The Count's manor and homestead with their houses, church and gardens, lay at our feet, and on the other side of the lake the little village where it was my fate to live looked grey in the distance. As before, the surface of the lake was without a ripple. Old Mikhey's little boats, separated from one another, were hurrying towards the shore.

To the left of my little village the buildings of the railway station stood out dark beneath the smoke from the engines, and behind us at the foot of the Stone Grave the road was bordered on either side by towering old poplars. This road leads to the Count's forest that extends to the very horizon.

The Count and I stood on the top of the hill. Urbenin and the Pole being heavy men preferred to wait for us on the road below.

'Who's that cove?' I asked the Count, nodding towards the Pole. 'Where did you pick him up?'

'He's a very nice fellow, Serezha; very nice!' the Count said in an agitated voice. 'You'll soon be the best of friends.'

'Oh, that's not likely! Why does he never speak?'

'He is silent by nature! But he's very clever!'

'But what sort of a man is he?'

'I became acquainted with him in Moscow. He is very nice. You'll hear all about it afterwards, Serezha; don't ask now. Let's go down.'

We descended the hill and went along the road towards the forest. It began to be perceptibly darker. The cry of the cuckoo, and the tired vocal warbles of a possibly youthful nightingale were heard in the forest.

'Hollo! Hollo! Catch me!' we heard the high-pitched voice of a child shout as we approached the forest.

A little girl of about five with hair as white as flax, dressed in a sky-blue frock, ran out of the wood. When she saw us she laughed aloud, and with a skip and a jump put her arms round Urbenin's knee. Urbenin lifted her up and kissed her cheek.

'My daughter Sasha!' he said. 'Let me introduce her!'

Sasha was pursued out of the wood by a schoolboy of about fifteen, Urbenin's son. When he saw us he pulled off his cap hesitatingly, put it on, and pulled it off again. He was followed quietly by what looked like a patch of red, which attracted our attention. 'What a beautiful vision!' the Count exclaimed, catching hold of my hand. 'Look! How charming! Who is this girl? I did not know that my forests were inhabited by such naiads!'

I looked round at Urbenin in order to ask him who this girl was, and, strange to say, it was only at that moment I noticed that he was terribly drunk. He was as red as a crawfish, he tottered and, seizing my elbow, he whispered into my ear, exhaling the fumes of spirit on me:

'Sergey Petrovich, I implore you prevent the Count from making any further remarks about this girl! He may from habit say too much; she is a most worthy person!'

This 'most worthy person' was represented by a girl of about nineteen, with beautiful fair hair, blue eyes and long curls. She was dressed in a bright red frock, made in a fashion that was neither that of a child nor of a young girl. Her legs, straight as needles, in red stockings, were shod with tiny shoes that were small as a child's. All the time I was admiring her she moved about her well-rounded shoulders coquettishly, as if they were cold or as if my gaze disturbed her.

'Such a young face, and what a figure!' whispered the Count, who from his earliest youth had lost the capacity of respecting women, and never looked at them otherwise than from the point of view of a spoilt animal.

I remember that I felt a surge of warmth in my heart. I was still a poet, and in the company of the woods, of a May night, and the first twinkling of the evening stars, I could only look at a woman as a poet does. . . . I looked at 'the girl in red' with the same veneration I was accustomed to look upon the forests, the hills and the blue sky. I still had a certain amount of the sentimentality I had inherited from my German mother.

'Who is she?' the Count asked.

'She is the daughter of our forester Skvortsov, your Excellency!' Urbenin replied.

'Is this the Olenka the one-eyed muzhik spoke of?'

'Yes, he mentioned her name,' the bailiff answered, looking at me with large, imploring eyes.

The girl in red let us go past her, turning away without taking any notice of us. Her eyes were looking at something at the side, but I, a man who knows women, felt her gaze resting on my face.

'Which of them is the Count?' I heard her whisper behind us.

'That one with the long moustache,' the schoolboy answered.

And we heard silvery laughter behind us. It was the laughter of disenchantment. She had thought that the Count, the owner of these immense forests and the broad lake, was I, and not that pigmy with the worn face and long moustache.

I heard a deep sigh issue from Urbenin's powerful breast. That man of iron could scarcely move.

'Dismiss the bailiff,' I whispered to the Count. 'He is ill or – drunk.'

'Pëtr Egorych, you seem to be unwell,' the Count said, turning to Urbenin. 'I do not require you just now, so I will not detain you any longer.'

'Your Excellency need not trouble about me. Thank you for your attention, but I am not ill.'

I looked back. The girl in red had not moved, but was looking after us.

Poor, fair little head! Did I think on that quiet, peaceful May evening that she would afterwards become the heroine of my troubled romance?

Now, while I write these lines, the autumn rain beats fiercely against my warm windows, and the wind howls above me. I gaze at the dark window and on the dark background of night beyond, trying by the strength of my imagination to conjure up again the charming image of my heroine. . . . I see her with her innocent, childish, naive, kind little face and loving eyes, and I wish to throw down my pen and tear up and burn all that I have already written.

But here, next to my inkstand, is her photograph. Here, the fair little head is represented in all the vain majesty of a beautiful but deeply-fallen woman. Her weary eyes, proudly lecherous, are still. Here she is the serpent, the harm of whose bite Urbenin would scarcely have called exaggerated.

She gave a kiss to the storm, and the storm broke the flower at the very roots. Much was taken, but too dearly was it paid for. The reader will forgive her her sins!

IV

We walked through the wood.
The pines were dull in their silent monotony. They all grow in the same way, one like the others, and at every season of the year they retain the same appearance, knowing neither death nor the renewal of spring. Still, they are attractive in their moroseness: immovable, soundless, they seem to think mournful thoughts.

'Hadn't we better turn back?' the Count suggested.

This question received no reply. It was all the same to the Pole where he was. Urbenin did not consider his voice decisive, and I was too much delighted with the coolness of the forest and its resinous air to wish to turn back. Besides, it was necessary to kill time till night, even by a simple walk. The thoughts of the approaching wild night were accompanied by a sweet sinking of the heart. I am sorry to confess that I looked forward to it, and had already mentally a foretaste of its enjoyments. Judging by the impatience with which the Count constantly looked at his watch, it was evident that he, too, was tormented by expectations. We felt that we understood each other.

Near the forester's house, which nestled between pines on a small square open space, we were met by the loud-sounding bark of two small fiery-yellow dogs, of a breed that was unknown to me; they were as glossy and supple as eels. Recognizing Urbenin, they joyfully wagged their tails and ran towards him, from which one could deduce that the bailiff often visited the forester's house. Here, too, near the house, we were met by a lad without boots or cap, with large freckles on his astonished face. For a moment he looked at us in silence with staring eyes, then, evidently recognizing the Count, he gave an exclamation and rushed headlong into the house.

'I know what he's gone for,' the Count said, laughing. 'I remember him. . . . It's Mit'ka.'

The Count was not mistaken. In less than a minute Mit'ka came out of the house carrying a tray with a glass of vodka and a tumbler half full of water.

'For your good health, your Excellency!' he said, a broad grin suffusing the whole of his stupid, astonished face.

The Count drank off the vodka, washed it down with water in lieu of a snack, but this time he made no wry face. A hundred paces from the house there was an iron seat, as old as the pines above it. We sat down on it and contemplated the May evening in all its tranquil beauty. . . . The frightened crows flew cawing above our heads, the song of nightingales was borne towards us from all sides; these were the only sounds that broke the pervading stillness.

The Count does not know how to be silent, even on such a calm spring evening, when the voice of man is the least agreeable sound.

'I don't know if you will be satisfied?' he said to me. 'I have ordered a fish-soup and game for supper. With the vodka we shall have cold sturgeon and sucking-pig with horse-radish.'

As if angered at this prosaic observation, the poetical pines suddenly shook their tops and a gentle rustle passed through the wood. A fresh breeze swept over the glade and played with the grass.

'Down, down!' Urbenin cried to the flame-coloured dogs, who were preventing him from lighting his cigarette with their caresses. 'I think we shall have rain before night. I feel it in the air. It was so terribly hot today that it does not require a learned professor to prophesy rain. It will be a good thing for the corn.'

'What's the use of corn to you,' I thought, 'if the Count will spend it all on drink? No need to worry about the rain.'

Once more a light breeze passed over the forest, but this time it was stronger. The pines and the grass rustled louder.

'Let us go home.'

We rose and strolled lazily back towards the little house.

'It is better to be this fair-haired Olenka,' I said, addressing myself to Urbenin, 'and to live here with the beasts than to be a magistrate and live among men. . . . It's more peaceful. Is it not so, Pëtr Egorych?'

'It's all the same what one is, Sergey Petrovich, if only the soul is at peace.'

'Is pretty Olenka's soul at peace?'

'God alone knows the secrets of other people's souls, but I think she has nothing to trouble her. She has not much to worry her, and no more sins than an infant. . . . She's a very good girl! Ah, now the sky is at last beginning to threaten rain. . . .'

A rumble was heard, somewhat like the sound of a distant vehicle or the rattle of a game of skittles. Somewhere, far beyond the forest, there was a peal of thunder. Mit'ka, who had been watching us the whole time, shuddered and crossed himself.

'A thunderstorm!' the Count exclaimed with a start. 'What a surprise! The rain will overtake us on our way home. . . . How dark it is! I said we ought to have turned back! And you wouldn't, and went on and on.'

'We might wait in the cottage till the storm is over,' I suggested.

'Why in the cottage?' Urbenin said hastily, and his eyes blinked in a strange manner. 'It will rain all night, so you'll have to remain all night in the cottage! Please, don't trouble. . . . Go quietly on, and Mit'ka shall run on and order your carriage to come to meet you.'

'Never mind, perhaps it won't rain all night. . . . Storm clouds usually pass by quickly. . . . Besides, I don't know the new forester as yet, and I'd also like to have a chat with this Olenka. . . . and find out what sort of girl she is. . . .'

'I've no objections!' the Count agreed.

'How can you go there, if – if the place is not – not in order?' Urbenin mumbled anxiously. 'Why should your Excellency sit there in a stuffy room when you could be at home? I don't understand what pleasure that can be!. . . How can you get to know the forester if he is ill?'

It was very evident that the bailiff strongly objected to our going into the forester's house. He even spread his arms as if he wanted to bar the way. . . . I understood by his face that he had reasons for preventing us from going in. I respect other people's reasons and secrets, but on this occasion my curiosity was greatly excited. I persisted, and we entered the house.

'Come into the drawing-room, please,' bare-footed Mit'ka spluttered almost choking with delight.

Try to imagine the very smallest drawing-room in the world,

with unpainted deal walls. These walls are hung all over with oleographs from the *Niva*, photographs in frames made of shells, and testimonials. One testimonial is from a certain baron, expressing his gratitude for many years of service; all the others are for horses. Here and there ivy climbs up the wall. . . . In a corner a small lamp, whose tiny blue flame is faintly reflected on the silver mounting, burns peacefully before a little icon. Chairs that have evidently been only recently bought are pressed close together round the walls. Too many had been purchased, and they had been squeezed together, as there was nowhere else to put them. . . . Here, also, there are armchairs and a sofa in snow-white covers with flounces and laces, crowded up with a polished round table. A tame hare dozes on the sofa. . . . The room is cosy, clean and warm. . . . The presence of a woman can be noticed everywhere. Even the whatnot with books has a look of innocence and womanliness; it appears to be anxious to say that there is nothing on its shelves but wishy-washy novels and mawkish verse. . . . The charm of such warm, cosy rooms is not so much felt in spring as in autumn, when you look for a refuge from the cold and damp.

After much loud snivelling, blowing, and noisy striking of matches, Mit'ka lit two candles and placed them on the table as carefully as if they had been milk. We sat down in the armchairs, looked at each other, and laughed.

'Nikolai Efimych is ill in bed,' Urbenin said, to explain the absence of the master, 'and Olga Nikolaevna has probably gone to accompany my children. . . .'

'Mit'ka, are the doors shut?' we heard a weak tenor voice asking from the next room.

'They're all shut, Nikolai Efimych!' Mit'ka shouted hoarsely, and he rushed headlong into the next room.

'That's right! See that they are all shut,' the same weak voice said again. 'And locked – firmly locked. . . . If thieves break in, you must tell me. . . . I'll shoot the villains with my gun . . . the scoundrels!'

'Certainly, Nikolai Efimych!'

We laughed and looked inquiringly at Urbenin. He grew very red, and in order to hide his confusion he began to arrange the curtains of the windows. . . . What does this dream mean? We again looked at each other.

We had no time for perplexity. Hasty steps were heard outside, then a noise in the porch and the slamming of doors. And the girl in red rushed into the room.

'I love the thunder in early May,' she sang in a loud, shrill soprano voice, and she cut short her song with a burst of laughter, but when she saw us she suddenly stood still and was silent – she became embarrassed, and went as quietly as a lamb into the room in which the voice of Nikolai Efimych, her father, had been heard.

'She did not expect to see you,' Urbenin said, laughing.

A few minutes later she again came quietly into the room, sat down on the chair nearest the door and began to examine us. She stared at us boldly, not as if we were new people for her, but as if we were animals in the Zoological Gardens. For a minute we too looked at her in silence without moving. . . . I would have agreed to sit still and look at her for a whole hour in this way – she was so lovely that evening. As fresh as the air, rosy, breathing rapidly, her bosom rising and falling, her curls scattered wildly on her forehead, on her shoulders, and on her right hand that was raised to arrange her collar; with large, sparkling eyes. . . . And all this was found on one little body that a single glance could envelop. If you glanced for a moment at this small object you saw more than you would if you looked for a whole century at the endless horizon. . . . She looked at me seriously, from my feet upwards, inquiringly; when her eyes left me and passed to the Count or to the Pole I began to read in them the contrary: a glance that passed from the head to the feet, and laughter. . . .

I was the first to speak.

'Allow me to introduce myself,' I said, rising and going up to her. 'Zinov'ev. . . . And let me introduce my friend, Count Karnéev. . . . We beg you to pardon us for breaking into your nice little house without an invitation. . . . We would, of course, never have done so if the storm had not driven us in. . . .'

'But that won't cause our little house to tumble down!' she said, laughing and giving me her hand.

She displayed her splendid white teeth. I sat down on a chair next to her, and told her how quite unexpectedly the storm had overtaken us on our walk. Our conversation began with the weather – the beginning of all beginnings. While we were talking, Mit'ka had had time to offer the Count two glasses of vodka with the inseparable tumbler of water. Thinking that I was not looking at him, the Count made a sweet grimace and shook his head after each glass.

'Perhaps you would like some refreshments?' Olenka asked me, and, not waiting for an answer, she left the room.

The first drops of rain rattled against the panes. . . . I went up to the windows. . . . It was now quite dark, and through the glass I could see nothing but the raindrops creeping down and the reflection of my own nose. There was a flash of lightning, which illuminated some of the nearest pines.

'Are the doors shut?' I heard the same tenor voice ask again. 'Mit'ka, come here, you vile-spirited scoundrel! Shut the doors! Oh, Lord, what torments!'

A peasant woman with an enormous, tightly laced stomach and a stupid, troubled face came into the room, and, having bowed low to the Count, she spread a white table-cloth on the table. Mit'ka followed her carefully carrying a tray with various *hors d'œuvres*. A minute later, we had vodka, rum, cheese, and a dish of some sort of roasted bird on the table before us. The Count drank a glass of vodka, but he would not eat anything. The Pole smelt the bird mistrustfully, and then began to carve it.

'The rain has begun! Look!' I said to Olenka, who had re-entered the room.

Olenka came up to the window where I was standing, and at that very moment we were illuminated by a white flash of light. . . . There was a fearful crash above us, and it appeared to me that something large and heavy had been torn from the sky and had fallen to earth with a terrible racket. . . . The window panes and the wineglasses that were standing before the Count jingled and emitted their tinkling sound. . . . The thunderclap was a loud one.

'Are you afraid of thunder-storms?' I asked Olenka.

She only pressed her cheek to her round shoulders and looked at me with childish confidence.

'I'm afraid,' she whispered after a moment's reflection. 'My mother was killed by a storm. . . . The newspapers even wrote about it. . . . My mother was going through the fields, crying. . . . She had a very bitter life in this world. God had compassion on her and killed her with His heavenly electricity.'

'How do you know that there is electricity there?'

'I have learned. . . . Do you know, people who have been killed by a storm or in war, or who have died after a difficult confinement go to paradise. . . . This is not written anywhere in books, but it is true. My mother is now in paradise! I think the thunder will also kill me some day, and I shall go to paradise too. . . . Are you a cultivated man?'

'Yes.'

'Then you will not laugh. . . . This is how I should like to die: to dress in the most costly fashionable frock, like the one I saw the other day on our rich lady, the landowner Sheffer; to put bracelets on my arms. . . . Then to go to the very summit of the Stone Grave and allow myself to be killed by the lightning, so that all the people could see it. . . . A terrible peal of thunder, and then, you know, the end!'

'What an odd fancy!' I said, laughing and looking into her eyes that were full of holy horror at this terrible but dramatic death. 'Then you don't want to die in an ordinary dress?'

'No! . . .' Olenka shook her head. 'And so that everybody should see me.'

'The frock you are in is far better than any fashionable and expensive dress. . . . It suits you. In it you look like the red flower of the green woods.'

'No, that is not true!' And Olenka sighed ingenuously. 'This frock is a cheap one; it can't be pretty.'

The Count came up to our window with the evident intention of talking to pretty Olenka. My friend could speak three European languages, but he did not know how to talk to women. He stood near us awkwardly, smiling in an inane manner; then he mumbled inarticulately, 'Er – yes,' and retraced his steps to the decanter of vodka.

'You were singing "I love the thunder in early May," ' I said to Olenka. 'Have those verses been set to music?'

'No, I sing all the verses I know to my own melodies.'

I happened by chance to glance back. Urbenin was looking at

us. In his eyes I read hatred and animosity: passions that were not at all in keeping with his kind, meek face.

'Can he be jealous?' I thought.

The poor fellow caught my inquiring glance, rose from his chair and went into the lobby to look for something. . . . Even by his gait one could see that he was agitated. The peals of thunder became louder and louder, more prolonged, and oftener repeated. . . . The lightning unceasingly illuminated the sky, the pines and the wet earth with its pleasant but blinding light. . . . The rain was not likely to end soon. I left the window and went up to the bookshelves and began to examine Olenka's library. 'Tell me what you read, and I will tell you what you are,' I said. But from the books that were so symmetrically ranged on the shelves it was difficult to arrive at any estimate of Olenka's mental capacities or 'educational standard'. There was a strange medley on those shelves. Three anthologies, one book of Börne's, Evtushevsky's arithmetic, the second volume of Lermontov's works, Shklyarevsky, a number of the magazine *Work*, a cookery book, *Skladchina* . . . I might enumerate other books for you, but at the moment I took *Skladchina* from the shelf and began to turn over the pages. The door leading into the next room opened, and a person entered the drawing-room, who at once diverted my attention from Olenka's standard of culture. This person was a tall, muscular man in a print dressing-gown and torn slippers, with an extremely odd appearance. His face, covered all over with blue veins, was ornamented with a pair of sergeant's moustaches and whiskers, and had in general a strong resemblance to a bird. His whole face seemed to be drawn forwards, as if trying to concentrate itself in the tip of the nose. Such faces are like the spout of a pitcher. This person's small head was set on a long thin throat, with a large Adam's-apple, and shook about like the nesting-box of a starling in the wind. . . . This strange man looked round on us all with his dim green eyes, and then let them rest on the Count.

'Are the doors shut?' he asked in an imploring voice.

The Count looked at me and shrugged his shoulders.

'Don't trouble, papasha!' Olenka answered. 'They are all shut. . . . Go back to your room!'

'Is the barn door shut?'

'He's a little queer. . . . It takes him sometimes,' Urbenin whispered to me as he came in from the lobby. 'He's afraid of thieves, and always worrying about the doors, as you see.'

'Nikolai Efimych,' he continued, addressing this strange apparition, 'go back to your room and go to bed! Don't worry, everything is shut up!'

'And are the windows shut?'

Nikolai Efimych hastily looked to see if the windows were properly bolted, and then without taking any notice of us he shuffled off into his own room.

'The poor fellow has these attacks sometimes,' Urbenin began to explain as soon as he had left the room. 'He's a good, capable man; he has a family, too – such a misfortune! Almost every summer he is a little out of his mind. . . .'

I looked at Olenka. She became confused, and hiding her face from us began to put in order again her books that I had disarranged. She was evidently ashamed of her mad father.

'The carriage is here, your Excellency! Now you can drive home, if you wish!'

'Where has that carriage come from?' I asked.

'I sent for it. . . .'

A minute later I was sitting with the Count in the carriage, listening to the peals of thunder and feeling very angry.

'We've been nicely turned out of the little house by that Pëtr Egorych, the devil take him!' I grumbled, getting really angry. 'So he's prevented us from examining Olenka properly! I wouldn't have eaten her! . . . The old fool! The whole time he was bursting with jealousy. . . . He's in love with that girl. . . .'

'Yes, yes, yes. . . . Would you believe it, I noticed that, too! He wouldn't let us go into the house from jealousy. And he sent for the carriage out of jealousy too. . . . Ha, ha, ha!'

'The later love comes the more it burns. . . . Besides, brother, it'd be difficult not to fall in love with this girl in red, if one saw her every day as we saw her today! She's devilish pretty! But she's not for the likes of him. . . . He ought to understand it and not be so selfishly jealous of others. . . . Why can't he just love her and not stand in the way of others, especially as he must know she's not destined for him? . . . What an old blockhead!'

'Do you remember how enraged he was when Kuz'ma mentioned her name at tea-time?' the Count sniggered. 'I thought he was going to thrash us all. . . . A man does not defend the good fame of a woman so hotly if he's indifferent to her. . . .'

'Some men will, brother. . . . But this is not the question. . . . What's important is this. . . . If he can order us about in the way he has done today, what does he do with the lesser folk, with those who are under his thumb? Doubtless, the stewards, the butlers, the huntsmen and the rest of the small fry are prevented by him from even approaching her! Love and jealousy make a man unjust, heartless, misanthropical. . . . I don't mind betting that for the sake of this Olenka he's upset more than one of the people under his control. You'd be wise in future if you put less trust in his complaints of the people in your service and his demands for the dismissal of this person or that. In general, limit his power for a time. . . . Love will pass – well, and then there will be nothing to fear. He's a kind and honest fellow. . . .'

'And what do you think of her papa?' the Count asked, laughing.

'A madman. . . . He ought to be in a madhouse and not looking after forests. In general you won't be far from the truth if you put up a signboard "Madhouse" over the gate of your estate. . . . You have a real Bedlam here! This forester, the Scops-Owl, Franz, who is mad on cards, this old man in love, an excitable girl, a drunken Count. . . . What more do you want?'

'Why, this forester receives a salary! How can he do his work if he is mad?'

'Urbenin evidently only keeps him for his daughter's sake. . . . Urbenin says that Nikolai Efimych has these attacks every summer. . . . That's not likely. . . . This forester is ill, not every summer, but always. . . . By good luck, your Pëtr Egorych seldom lies, and he gives himself away when he does lie about anything. . . .'

'Last year Urbenin informed me that our old forester Akhmet'ev was going to become a monk on Mount Athos, and he recommended me to take the "experienced, honest and worthy Skvortsov" . . . I, of course, agreed as I always do. Letters are not faces: they do not give themselves away when they lie.'

The carriage drove into the courtyard and stopped at the front door. We alighted. The rain had stopped. The thunder cloud, scintillating with lightning and emitting angry grumbles, was hurrying towards the north-east and uncovering more and more of the dark blue star-spangled sky. It was like a heavily armed power which having ravaged the country and imposed a terrible tribute, was rushing on to new conquests. . . . The small clouds that remained behind were chasing after it as if fearing to be unable to catch it up. . . . Nature had its peace restored to it.

And that peace seemed astonished at the calm, aromatic air, so full of softness, of the melodies of nightingales, at the silence of the sleeping gardens and the caressing light of the rising moon. The lake awoke after the day's sleep, and by gentle murmurs brought memories of itself to man's hearing. . . .

At such a time it is good to drive through the fields in a comfortable calash or to be rowing on the lake. . . . But we went into the house. . . . There another sort of poetry was awaiting us.

V

A man who under the influence of mental pain or unbearably oppressive suffering sends a bullet through his own head is called a suicide; but for those who give freedom to their pitiful, soul-debasing passions in the holy days of spring and youth, there is no name in man's vocabulary. After the bullet follows the peace of the grave: ruined youth is followed by years of grief and painful recollections. He who has profaned his spring will understand the present condition of my soul. I am not yet old, or grey, but I no longer live. Psychologists tell us that a soldier, who was wounded at Waterloo, went mad, and afterwards assured everybody – and believed it himself – that he had died at Waterloo, and that what was now considered to be him was only his shadow, a reflection of the past. I am now experiencing something resembling this semi-death. . . .

'I am very glad that you ate nothing at the forester's and haven't spoilt your appetite,' the Count said to me as we entered the house. 'We shall have an excellent supper. . . . Like old times. . . . Serve supper!' He gave the order to Il'ya who was helping him to take off his coat and put on a dressing-gown.

We went into the dining-room. Here on the side-table life was already bubbling over. Bottles of every colour and of every imaginable size were standing in rows as on the shelves of a theatre refreshment-room, reflecting on their sides the light of the lamps while awaiting our attention. All sorts of salted and pickled viands and various *hors d'œuvres* stood on another table with a decanter of vodka and another of English bitters. Near the wine bottles there were two dishes, one of sucking pig and the other of cold sturgeon.

'Well, gentlemen,' the Count began as he poured out three glasses of vodka and shivered as if from cold. 'To our good health! Kaetan Kazimirovich, take your glass!'

I drank mine off, the Pole only shook his head in refusal. He moved the dish of sturgeon towards himself, smelt it, and began to eat.

I must apologize to the reader. I have now to describe something not at all 'romantic'.

'Well, come on . . . Let's have another,' the Count said, and filled the glasses again. 'Fire away, Lecoq!'

I took up my wineglass, looked at it and put it down again.

'The devil take it, it's so long since I drank,' I said. 'Shouldn't we drink to old times?'

Without further reflection, I filled five glasses and emptied them one after another down my throat. That was the only way I knew how to drink. Small schoolboys learn how to smoke cigarettes from big ones: the Count looked at me, poured out five glasses for himself, and, bending forwards in the form of an arch, frowning and shaking his head, he drank them off. My five glasses appeared to him to be bravado, but I drank them not at all to display my talent for drinking. . . . I wanted to get drunk, to get properly, thoroughly drunk. . . . Drunk as I had not been for a long time while living in my village. Having drunk them, I sat down to table and began to discuss the sucking pig.

Intoxication was not long in coming. I soon felt a slight giddiness. There was a pleasant feeling of coolness in my chest – and a happy, expansive condition set in. Without any visible transition I suddenly became very gay. The feeling of emptiness and dullness gave place to a sensation of thorough joy and gaiety. I smiled. I suddenly wanted chatter, laughter, people around me. As I chewed the sucking pig I began to feel the fullness of life, almost the self-sufficiency of life, almost happiness.

'Why don't you drink anything?' I asked the Pole.

'He never drinks,' the Count said. 'Don't force him to.'

'But surely you can drink something?'

The Pole put a large bit of sturgeon into his mouth and shook his head in refusal. His silence incensed me.

'I say, Kaetan – what's your patronymic? – why are you always silent?' I asked him. 'I have not had the pleasure of hearing your voice as yet.'

His two eyebrows that resembled the outstretched wings of a swallow were raised and he gazed at me.

'Do you wish me to speak?' he asked with a strong Polish accent.

'Very much.'

'Why do you wish it?'

'Why, indeed! On board steamers at dinner strangers and people who are not acquainted converse together, and here are we, who have known one another for several hours, looking at each other and not exchanging a single word! What does that look like?'

The Pole remained silent.

'Why are you silent?' I asked again after waiting a moment. 'Answer something, can't you?'

'I do not wish to answer you. I hear laughter in your voice, and I do not like derision.'

'He's not laughing at all,' the Count interposed in alarm. 'Where did you fish up that notion, Kaetan? He's quite friendly. . . .'

'Counts and Princes have never spoken to me in such a tone!' Kaetan said, frowning. 'I don't like that tone.'

'Consequently, you will not honour me with your conversation?' I continued to worry him as I emptied another glass and laughed.

'Do you know my real reason for coming here?' the Count broke in, desirous of changing the conversation. 'I haven't told you as yet? In Petersburg I went to the doctor who has always treated me, to consult him about my health. He listened to my chest, knocked and pressed me everywhere, and said: "You're not a coward!" Well, you know, though I'm no coward, I grew pale. "I'm not a coward," I replied.'

'Cut it short, brother. . . . This is tiresome.'

'He told me I should soon die if I did not go away from Petersburg! My liver is quite diseased from too much drink. . . . So I decided to come here. It would have been silly to remain there. This estate is so fine – so rich. . . . The climate alone is worth a fortune! . . . Here, at least, I can occupy myself with my own affairs. Work is the best, the most efficacious medicine. Kaetan, is that not true? I shall look after the estate and chuck drink. . . . The doctor did not allow me a single glass . . . not one!'

'Well, then, don't drink.'

'I don't drink. . . . Today is the last time, in honour of meeting you again' – the Count stretched towards me and gave me a smacking kiss on the cheek – 'my dear, good friend. Tomorrow – not a drop! Today, Bacchus takes leave of me for ever. . . . Serezha, let us have a farewell glass of cognac together?'

We drank a glass of cognac.

'I shall get well, Serezha, golubchek, and I shall look after the estate. . . . Rational agriculture! Urbenin – is good, kind . . . he understands everything, but is he the master? He sticks to routine! We must send for magazines, read, look into everything, take part in the agricultural and dairy exhibitions, but he is not educated for that! Is it possible he can be in love with Olenka? Ha-ha! I shall look into everything and keep him as my assistant. . . . I shall take part in the elections; I shall entertain society. . . . Eh? Even here one can live happily! What do you think? Now there you are, laughing again! Already laughing! One really can't talk with you about anything!'

I was gay, I was amused. The Count amused me; the candles, the bottles amused me; the stucco hares and ducks that ornamented the walls of the dining-room amused me. . . . The only thing that did not amuse me was the sober face of Kaetan Kazimirovich. The presence of this man irritated me.

'Can't you send that Polish nobleman to the devil?' I whispered to the Count.

'What? For God's sake! . . .' the Count murmured, seizing both my hands as if I had been about to beat his Pole. 'Let him sit there!'

'I can't look at him! I say,' I continued, addressing Pshekhotsky, 'you refused to talk to me; but forgive me. I have not yet given up hope of being more closely acquainted with your conversational capacities.'

'Leave him alone!' the Count said, pulling me by the sleeve. 'I implore you!'

'I shall not stop worrying you until you answer me,' I continued. 'Why are you frowning? Is it possible that you still hear laughter in my voice?'

'If I had drunk as much as you have, I would talk to you; but as it is we are not fairly matched,' the Pole replied.

'That we are not fairly matched is what was to be proved. . . . That is exactly what I wanted to say. A goose and a swine are no comrades; the drunkard and the sober man are no kin; the drunkard disturbs the sober man, the sober man the drunkard. In the adjoining drawing-room there is a soft and excellent sofa. It's a good thing to lie upon it after sturgeon with horse-radish. My voice will not be heard there. Do you not wish to retire to that room?'

The Count clasped his hands and walked about the dining-room with blinking eyes.

He is a coward and is always afraid of 'big' talk. I, on the contrary, when drunk, am amused by cross-purposes and discontentedness.

'I don't understand! I don't un-der-stand!' the Count groaned, not knowing what to say or what to do.

He knew it was difficult to stop me.

'I am only slightly acquainted with you,' I continued. 'Perhaps you are an excellent man, and therefore I don't wish to quarrel with you too soon. . . . I won't quarrel with you. I only invite you to understand that there is no place for a sober man among drunken ones. . . . The presence of a sober man has an irritating effect on the drunken organism! . . . Take that to heart!'

'Say whatever you like!' Pshekhotsky sighed. 'Nothing that you can say will provoke me, young man.'

'So nothing will provoke you? Will you also not be offended if I call you an obstinate swine?'

The Pole grew red in the face – but only that. The Count became pale, he came up to me, looked imploringly at me, and spread his arms.

'Come, I beg you! Restrain your tongue!'

I had now quite entered into my drunken part, and wanted to go on, but fortunately at that moment the Count and the Pole heard footsteps and Urbenin entered the dining-room.

'I wish you all a good appetite!' he began. 'I have come, your Excellency, to find out if you have any orders for me?'

'I have no orders so far, but a request,' the Count replied. 'I am very glad you have come, Pëtr Egorych. . . . Sit down and have supper with us, and let us talk about the business of the estate. . . .'

Urbenin sat down. The Count drank off a glass of cognac and began to explain his plans for the future rational management of the estate. He spoke very long and wearisomely, often repeating himself and changing the subject. Urbenin listened to him lazily and attentively as serious people listen to the prattle of children and women. He ate his fish-soup, and looked sadly at his plate.

'I have brought some remarkable plans with me!' the Count said among other things. 'Remarkable plans! I will show them to you if you wish?'

Karnéev jumped up and ran into his study for the plans. Urbenin took advantage of his absence to pour out half a tumbler of vodka, gulped it down, and did not even take anything to eat after it.

'Disgusting stuff this vodka is!' he said, looking with abhorrence at the decanter.

'Why didn't you drink while the Count was here, Pëtr Egorych?' I asked him. 'Is it possible that you were afraid to?'

'It is better to dissimulate, Sergey Petrovich, and drink in secret than to drink before the Count. You know what a strange character the Count has. . . . If I stole twenty thousand from him and he knew it, he would say nothing owing to his carelessness; but if I forgot to give him an account of ten kopecks that I had spent, or drank vodka in his presence, he would begin to lament that his bailiff was a robber. You know him well.'

Urbenin half-filled the tumbler again and swigged it off.

'I think you did not drink formerly, Pëtr Egorych,' I said.

'Yes, but now I drink . . . I drink terribly!' he whispered. 'Terribly, day and night, not giving myself a moment's respite! Even the Count never drank to such an extent as I do now. . . . It is dreadfully hard, Sergey Petrovich! God alone knows what a weight I have on my heart! It's just grief that makes me drink. . . . I always liked and honoured you, Sergey Petrovich, and I can tell you quite candidly . . . I'd often be glad to hang myself!'

'For what reason?'

'My own stupidity. . . . Not only children are stupid. . . . There are also fools at fifty. Don't ask the cause.'

The Count re-entered the room and put a stop to his effusions.

'A most excellent liqueur,' he said, placing a pot-bellied bottle with the seal of the Benedictine monks on the table instead of the 'remarkable plans'. 'When I passed through Moscow I got it at Depré's. Have a glass, Sergey?'

'I thought you had gone to fetch the plans,' I said.

'I? What plans? Oh, yes! But, brother, the devil himself couldn't find anything in my portmanteaux. . . . I rummaged and rummaged and gave it up as a bad job. . . . The liqueur is very nice. Won't you have some, Serezha?'

Urbenin remained a little longer, then he took leave and went away. When he left we began to drink claret. This wine quite finished me. I became intoxicated in the way I had wished while riding to the Count's. I became very bold, active and unusually gay. I wanted to do some extraordinary deed, something ludicrous, something that would astonish people. . . . In such moments I thought I could swim across the lake, unravel the most entangled case, conquer any woman. . . . The world and its life made me enthusiastic; I loved it, but at the same time I wanted to pick a quarrel with somebody, to consume him with venomous jests and ridicule. . . . It was necessary to scoff at the comical black-browed Pole and the Count, to attack them with biting sarcasm, to turn them to dust.

'Why are you silent?' I began again. 'Speak! I am listening to you! Ha-ha! I am awfully fond of hearing people with serious, sedate faces talk childish drivel! . . . It is such mockery, such mockery of the brains of man! . . . . The face does not correspond to the brains! In order not to lie, you ought to have the faces of idiots, and you have the countenances of Greek sages!'

I had not finished. . . . My tongue was entangled by the thought that I was talking to people who were nullities, who were unworthy of even half a word! I required a hall filled with people, brilliant women, thousands of lights. . . . I rose, took my glass and began walking about the rooms. When we indulge in debauchery, we do not limit ourselves to space. We do not restrict ourselves only to the dining-room, but take the whole house and sometimes even the whole estate.

I chose a Turkish divan in the 'mosaic hall', lay down on it and gave myself up to the power of my fantasy and to castles in the air. Drunken thoughts, one more grandiose, more limitless than the other, took possession of my young brain. A new world arose before me, full of stupefying delights and indescribable beauty.

It only remained for me to talk in rhyme and to see visions.

The Count came to me and sat down on a corner of the divan. . . . He wanted to say something to me. I had begun to read in his eyes the desire to communicate something special to me shortly after the five glasses of vodka described above. I knew of what he wanted to speak.

'What a lot I have drunk today!' he said to me. 'This is more harmful to me than any sort of poison. . . . But today it is for the last time. . . . Upon my honour, the very last time. . . . I have strength of will. . . .'

'All right, all right. . . .'

'For the last . . . Serezha, my dear friend, for the last time. . . . Shouldn't we send a telegram to town for the last time?'

'Why not? Send it. . . .'

'Let's have one last spree in the proper way. . . . Well, get up and write it.'

The Count himself did not know how to write telegrams. They always came out too long and insufficient with him. I rose and wrote:

S— Restaurant London. Karpov, manager of the chorus. Leave everything and come instantly by the two o'clock train
                                                        – The Count.

'It is now a quarter to eleven,' the Count said. 'The man will take three-quarters of an hour to ride to the station, maximum an hour. . . . Karpov will receive the telegram before one. . . . They should have time to catch the train . . . . If they don't catch it, they can come by the goods train. Yes!'

VI

The telegram was dispatched with one-eyed Kuz'ma. Il'ya was ordered to send carriages to the station in about an hour. In order to kill time, I began leisurely to light the lamps and candles in all the rooms, then I opened the piano and passed my fingers over the keys.

After that, I remember, I lay down on the same divan and thought of nothing, only waving away with my hand the Count, who came and pestered me with his chatter. I was in a state of drowsiness, half-asleep, conscious only of the brilliant light of the lamps and feeling in a gay and quiet mood. . . . The image of the girl in red, with her head bent towards her shoulder, and her eyes filled with horror at the thought of that dramatic death, stood before me and quietly shook its little finger at me . . . . The image of another girl, with a pale, proud face, in a black dress, flitted past. She looked at me half-entreatingly, half-reproachfully.

Later on I heard noise, laughter, running about. . . . Deep, dark eyes obscured the light. I saw their brilliancy, their laughter. . . . A joyful smile played about the luscious lips. . . . That was how my gipsy Tina smiled.

'Is it you?' her voice asked. 'You're asleep? Get up, darling. . . . How long it is since I saw you last!'

I silently pressed her hand and drew her towards me. . . .

'Let us go inside. . . . Everybody has come. . . .'

'Stay! . . . I'm all right here, Tina. . . .'

'But . . . there's too much light. . . . You're mad! . . . . Someone might come in. . . .'

'I'll wring the neck of anyone who does! . . . I'm so happy, Tina. . . . Two years have passed since last we met . . . .'

Somebody began to play the piano in the ballroom.

'Akh! Moskva, Moskva, Moskva, white-stoned Moskva!' . . . several voices sang in chorus.

'You see, they are all singing there. . . . Nobody will come in. . . .'

'Yes, yes. . . .'

The meeting with Tina took away my drowsiness. . . . Ten minutes later she led me into the ballroom, where the chorus was standing in a semi-circle. . . . The Count, sitting astride a chair, was beating time with his hands . . . . Pshekhotsky stood behind his chair, looking with astonished eyes at these singing birds. I tore the balalaika out of Karpov's hands, struck the chords, and –

'Down the Volga . . . down the mother Volga.'

'Down the Vo-o-olga!' the chorus chimed in.

'Ay, burn, speak . . . speak . . .'

I waved my hand, and in an instant with the rapidity of lightning there was another transition. . . .

'Nights of madness, nights of gladness . . .'

Nothing acts more irritatingly, more titillatingly on my nerves than such rapid transitions. I trembled with rapture, and embracing Tina with one arm and waving the balalaika in the air with the other hand, I sang 'Nights of madness' to the end. . . . The balalaika fell noisily on the floor and was shivered into tiny fragments. . . .

'Wine!'

After that my recollections are confused and chaotic. . . . Everything is mixed, confused, entangled; everything is dim, obscure. . . . I remember the grey sky of early morning. . . . We are in a boat. . . . The lake is slightly agitated, and seems to grumble at our debauchery. . . . I am standing up in the middle of the boat, shaking it. . . . Tina tries to convince me I may fall into the water, and implores me to sit down. . . . I deplore loudly that there are no waves on the lake as high as the Stone Grave, and frighten the martins that flit like white spots over the blue surface of the lake with my shouts. . . . Then follows a long, sultry day, with its endless lunches, its ten-year-old liqueurs, its punches . . . its debauches. . . . There are only a few moments I can remember of that day. . . . I remember swinging with Tina in the garden. I stand on one end of the board, she on the other. I work energetically, using my whole body as much as my strength permits, and I don't exactly know what I want: that Tina should fall from the swing and be killed, or that she should fly to the very clouds! Tina stands there, pale as death, but proud and determined; she has pressed her lips tightly together so as not to betray by a single sound the fear she feels. We fly ever higher and higher, and . . . I can't remember how it ended. Then there follows a walk with Tina in a distant avenue of the park, with green vaults above that protect it from the sun. A poetical twilight, black tresses, luscious lips, whispers. . . . Then the little contralto is walking beside me, a fair-haired girl with a sharp little nose, childlike eyes and a small waist. I walk about with her until Tina, having followed us, makes a scene. . . . The gipsy is pale and furious. . . . She calls me 'accursed', and, much offended, prepares to return to town. The Count, also pale and with trembling hands, runs along beside us, and, as usual, can't find the proper words to persuade Tina to remain. . . . In the end she boxes my ears. . . . Strange! I, who fly into a rage at the slightest insult offered me by a man, am quite indifferent to a box on the ear given me by a woman. . . . Again time is dragging heavily after dinner, again there is a snake on the steps, the sleeping figure of Franz with flies round his mouth, the gate. . . . The girl in red is standing on the Stone Grave, but perceiving us from afar, she disappears like a lizard.

By evening we had made it up with Tina and were again friends. The evening was succeeded by the same sort of wild night, with music, riotous singing, the same nerve-wracking succession of refrains . . . and not a moment's sleep!

'This is self-destruction!' Urbenin whispered to me. He had come in for a moment to listen to our singing.

He was certainly right. I remember next the Count and I standing in the garden face to face, and quarrelling. Black-browed Kaetan is walking about near us all the time, taking no part in our jollifications, but he had still not slept but had followed us about like a shadow. . . . The sky is already brightening, and on the very summits of the highest trees the golden rays of the rising sun are beginning to shine. Around us is the chatter of sparrows, the songs of the starlings, and the rustle and flapping of wings that had become heavy during the night. . . . The lowing of the herds and the cries of the shepherds can be heard. A table with a marble slab stands before us. On the table are candles that give out a faint light.

Ends of cigarettes, papers from sweets, broken wineglasses, orange peel. . . .

'You must take it!' I say, pressing on the Count a parcel of rouble notes. 'I will force you to take it!'

'But it was I who sent for them and not you!' the Count insisted, trying to catch hold of one of my buttons. 'I am the master here. . . . I treated you. Why should you pay? Can't you understand you even insult me by offering to do so?'

'I also engaged them, so I pay half. You won't take it? I don't understand such favours! Surely you don't think because you are as rich as the devil that you have the right to confer such favours on me? The devil take it! I engaged Karpov, and I will pay him! I want none of your halves! I wrote the telegram!'

'In a restaurant, Serezha, you may pay as much as you like, but my house is not a restaurant. . . . Besides, I really don't understand why you are making all this fuss. I can't understand your insistent prodigality. You have little money, while I am rolling in wealth. . . . Justice itself is on my side!'

'Then you will not take it? No? Well, then, you needn't! . . .'

I go up to the faintly burning candles and applying the banknotes to the flame set them on fire and fling them on the ground. Suddenly a groan is torn from Kaetan's breast. He opens his eyes wide, he grows pale, and falling with the whole weight of his heavy body on the ground tries to extinguish the money with the palms of his hands. . . . In this he succeeds.

'I don't understand!' he says, placing the slightly burnt notes in his pocket. 'To burn money? As if it were last year's chaff or love letters! . . . It's better that I should give it to the poor than let it be consumed by the flames.'

I go into the house. . . . There in every room on the sofas and the carpets the weary gipsies are lying, overcome by fatigue. My Tina is sleeping on the divan in the 'mosaic drawing-room'.

She lies stretched out and breathing heavily. Her teeth clenched, her face pale. . . . She is evidently dreaming of the swing. . . . The Scops-Owl is going through all the rooms, looking with her sharp eyes sardonically at the people who had so suddenly broken into the deadly quiet of this forgotten estate. . . . She is not doing all this without some purpose.

That is all that my memory retained after two wild nights; all the rest had escaped my drunken brain, or is not appropriate for description. . . . But it is enough!

At no other time had Zorka borne me with so much zest as on the morning after the burning of the banknotes. . . . She also wanted to go home. . . . The rippling waves glinted gently in the rays of the rising sun, as the lake gradually prepared for the sleep of the day. The woods and the willows that bordered the lake stood motionless as if in morning prayer. It is difficult to describe the feelings that filled my soul at the time. . . . Without entering into details, I will only say that I was unspeakably glad and at the same time almost consumed by shame when, turning out of the Count's homestead, I saw on the bank of the lake the holy old face, all wrinkled by honest work and illness, of venerable Mikhey. In appearance Mikhey resembles the fishermen of the Bible. His hair and beard are white as snow, and he gazes contemplatively at the sky. . . . When he stands motionless on the bank and his eyes follow the chasing clouds, you can imagine that he sees angels in the sky. . . . I like such faces! . . . .

When I saw him I reined in Zorka and gave him my hand as if I wanted to cleanse myself by the touch of his honest, horny palm. . . . He raised his small sagacious eyes on me and smiled.

'How do you do, good master!' he said, giving me his hand awkwardly. 'So you've ridden over again? Or has that old rake come back?'

'Yes, he's back.'

'I thought so. . . . I can see it by your face. . . . Here I stand and look. . . . The world's the world. Vanity of vanities. . . . Look there! That German ought to die, and he thinks only of vanities. . . . Do you see?'

The old man pointed with a stick at the Count's bathing-cabin. A boat was being rowed away quickly from it. A man in a jockey cap and a blue jacket was sitting in the boat. It was Franz, the gardener.

'Every morning he takes money to the island and hides it there. The stupid fellow can't understand that for him sand and money have much the same value. When he dies he can't take it with him. Barin,* give me a cigar!'

I offered him my cigar case. He took three cigarettes and put them into his breast pocket. . . .

'That's for my nephew. . . . He can smoke them.'

Zorka moved impatiently, and galloped off. I bowed to the old man in gratitude for having been allowed to rest my eyes on his face. For a long time he stood looking after me.

At home I was met by Polycarp. With a contemptuous, even a crushing glance, he measured my noble body as if he wanted to know whether this time I had bathed again in all my clothes, or not.

'Congratulations!' he grumbled. 'You've enjoyed yourself.'

'Hold your tongue, fool!' I said.

His stupid face angered me. I undressed quickly, covered myself up with the bedclothes and closed my eyes.

My head became giddy and the world was enveloped in mist. Familiar figures flitted through the mist. . . . The Count, snakes, Franz, flame-coloured dogs, 'the girl in red', mad Nikolai Efimych.

'The husband killed his wife! Oh, how stupid you are!'

The 'girl in red' shook her finger at me, Tina obscured the light with her black eyes, and . . . I fell asleep.

* Master, sir.

VII

'How sweetly and tranquilly he sleeps! When one gazes on this pale, tired face, on this childishly innocent smile, and listens to this regular breathing, one might think that it is not a magistrate who is lying here, but the personification of a quiet conscience! One might think that Count Karnéev had not yet arrived, that there had been neither drunkenness nor gipsies, nor trips on the lake. . . . Get up, you wretched man! You don't deserve to enjoy such a blessing as peaceful sleep! Get up!'

I opened my eyes and stretched myself voluptuously. . . . A broad sunbeam, in which countless white dust atoms were agitated and chased each other, streamed from the window on to my bed, causing the sunray itself to appear as if tinged with some dull whiteness. . . . The ray disappeared and reappeared before my eyes, as Pavel Ivanovich Voznesensky, our charming district doctor, who was walking about my bedroom, came into or went out of the stream of light. In the long, unbuttoned frock-coat that flapped around him, as if hanging on a clothes rack, with his hands thrust deep into the pockets of his unusually long trousers, the doctor went from corner to corner of my room, from chair to chair, from portrait to portrait, screwing up his short-sighted eyes as he examined whatever came in his way. In accordance with his habit of poking around and sticking his nose into everything, he either stooped down or stretched out, peeped into the washstand, into the folds of the closed blinds, into the chinks of the door, into the lamp . . . he seemed to be looking for something or wishing to assure himself that everything was in order. . . . When he looked attentively through his spectacles into a chink, or at a spot on the wallpaper, he frowned, assumed an anxious expression, and smelt it with his long nose. . . . All this he did quite mechanically, involuntarily, and from habit; but at the same time, as his eyes passed rapidly from one object to another, he had the appearance of a connoisseur making an evaluation.

'Get up, don't you hear!' he called to me in his melodious tenor voice, as he looked into the soap-dish and removed a hair from the soap with his nail.

'Ah, ah, ah! How do you do, Mr Screw!' I yawned, when I saw him bending over the washstand. 'We haven't met for ages!'

The whole district knew the doctor by the name of 'Screw' from the habit he had of constantly screwing up his eyes. I, too, called him by that nickname. Seeing that I was awake, Voznesensky came and sat down on a corner of my bed and at once took up a box of matches and lifted it close to his screwed-up eyes.

'Only lazy people and those with clear consciences sleep in that way,' he said, 'and as you are neither the one nor the other, it would be more seemly for you, my friend, to get up somewhat earlier. . . .'

'What o'clock is it?'

'Almost eleven.'

'The devil take you, Screwy! Nobody asked you to wake me so early. Do you know, I only got to sleep at past five today, and if not for you I would have slept on till evening.'

'Indeed!' I heard Polycarp's bass voice say in the next room. 'He hasn't slept long enough yet! It's the second day he's been sleeping, and it's still not enough! Do you know what day it is?' Polycarp asked, coming into the bedroom and looking at me in the way clever people look at fools.

'Wednesday,' I said.

'Of course, certainly! It's been specially arranged for you that the week shall have two Wednesdays. . . .'

'Today's Thursday!' the doctor said. 'So, my good fellow, you've been pleased to sleep through the whole of Wednesday. Fine! Very fine! Allow me to ask you how much you drank?'

'For twice twenty-four hours I had not slept, and I drank . . . I don't know how much I drank.'

Having sent Polycarp away, I began to dress and describe to the doctor what I had lately experienced of 'Nights of madness, nights of gladness' which are so delightful and sentimental in the songs and so unsightly in reality. In my description I tried to retain a casual air, to keep to facts and not to deviate into moralizing, although all this was contrary to the nature of a man who entertained a passion for inferences and results. . . . I spoke with the air of one discussing trifles that did not trouble him in the slightest degree. In order to spare the chaste ears of Pavel Ivanovich, and knowing his dislike of the Count, I suppressed much, touched lightly on a great deal but nevertheless, despite the playfulness of my tone and the style of caricature I gave to my narrative during the whole course of it, the doctor looked into my face seriously, shaking his head and shrugging his shoulders impatiently from time to time. He never once smiled. It was evident that my casual air had produced on him a far from casual effect.

'Why don't you laugh, Screwy?' I asked him when I had finished my description.

'If it had not been you who had told me all this, and if it had not been for certain circumstances, I would not have believed a word of it. It's all too bizarre, my friend!'

'Of what circumstances are you speaking?'

'Last evening the muzhik whom you had belaboured in such an indelicate way with an oar, came to me . . . Ivan Osipov. . . .'

'Ivan Osipov? . . .' I shrugged my shoulders. 'That's the first time I've heard his name!'

'A tall, red-haired man . . . with a freckled face. . . . Try to remember! You struck him on the head with an oar.'

'I can't remember anything! I don't know an Osipov. . . . I struck nobody with an oar . . . You've dreamed it all, uncle!'

'God grant that I dreamed it. . . . He came to me with a report from the Karnéev district administration and asked me for a medical certificate. . . . In the report it was stated that the wound was given him by you, and he does not lie . . . Can you remember now? The wound he had received was above the forehead, just where the hair begins. . . . You got to the bone, my dear sir!'

'I can't remember!' I murmured. . . . 'Who is he? What's his occupation?'

'He's an ordinary muzhik from the Karnéev village. He rowed the boat when you were having your spree on the lake.'

'Hm! Perhaps! I can't remember. . . . I was probably drunk, and somehow by chance . . .'

'No, sir, not by chance. . . . He said you got angry with him about something, you swore at him for a long time, and then getting furious you rushed at him and struck him before witnesses. . . . Besides, you shouted at him "I'll kill you, you rascal!" '

I got very red, and began walking about from corner to corner of the room.

'For the life of me, I can't remember!' I said, trying with all my might to recall what had happened. 'I can't remember! You say I "got furious". . . . When drunk I become unpardonably nasty!'

'So you admit it yourself?'

'The muzhik evidently wants to make a case of it, but that's not the important thing. . . . The important thing is the fact itself, the blows. . . . Is it possible that I'm capable of fighting? And why should I strike a poor muzhik?'

'Yes sir! Of course, I could not give him a certificate, but I told him to apply to you. . . . You'll manage to settle the matter with him somehow. . . . The wound is a slight one, but considering the case unofficially a wound in the head that goes as far as the skull is a serious affair. . . . There are often cases when an apparently trifling wound in the head which had been considered a slight one has ended with mortification of the bone of the skull and consequently with a journey *ad patres.*'

And, carried away by his subject, 'Screw' rose from his seat and, walking about the room along the walls and waving his hands, he began to unload all his knowledge of surgical pathology for my benefit. . . . Mortification of the bones of the skull, inflammation of the brain, death, and other horrors poured from his lips with endless explanations, macroscopic and microscopic processes, that accompany this misty and, for me, quite uninteresting *terra incognita.*

'Stop that drivel!' I cried, trying to check his medical chatter. 'Can't you understand how tiresome all this stuff is?'

'No matter that it's tiresome. . . . Pay heed, and take yourself in hand. . . . Perhaps another time you will be more careful. It may teach you not to do such stupidities. If you don't arrange matters with this scabby Osipov, it may cost you your position! The priest of Themis to be tried for thrashing a man! . . . What a scandal!'

Pavel Ivanovich is the only man whose judgments I listen to with a light heart, without frowning, whom I allow to gaze inquiringly into my eyes and to thrust his investigating hand into the depths of my soul. . . . We two are friends in the very best sense of the word; we respect each other, although we have between us accounts of the most unpleasant, the most delicate nature. . . . Like a black cat, a woman had passed between us. This eternal *casus belli* had been the cause of reckonings between us, but did not make us quarrel, and we continued to be at peace. 'Screw' is a very nice fellow. I like his impassive face, with its large nose, screwed-up eyes and thin, reddish beard. I like his tall, thin, narrow-shouldered figure, on which his frock-coat and paletot hung as on a clothes-horse.

His badly made trousers formed ugly creases at the knees, and his boots were terribly trodden down at the heels; his white tie was always in the wrong place. But do not think that he was slovenly. . . . You had only to look once at his calm, intense expression to understand that he had no time to trouble about his own appearance; besides, he did not know how to. . . . He was young, honest, not vain, and loved his medicine, and he was always on the move – this in itself is sufficient to explain to his advantage all the defects of his inelegant toilet. He, like an artist, did not know the value of money, and imperturbably sacrificed his own comfort and the blessings of life to one of his passions, and thus he gave the impression of being a man without means, who could scarcely make both ends meet. . . . He neither smoked nor drank, he spent no money on women, but nevertheless the two thousand roubles he earned by his appointment at the hospital and by private practice passed through his hands as quickly as my money does when I am out on a spree. Two passions drained him: the passion of lending money, and the passion of ordering things he saw advertised in the newspapers. . . . He lent money without demur to whoever asked for it, not uttering a single word about when it was to be returned. It was not possible either by hook or by crook to eradicate in him his heedless trust in people's conscientiousness, and this confidence was even more apparent in his constantly ordering things that were lauded in newspaper advertisements. . . . He wrote off for everything, the necessary and the unnecessary. He wrote for books, telescopes, humorous magazines, dinner services 'composed of 100 articles', chrono-meters. . . . And it was not surprising that the patients who came to Pavel Ivanovich mistook his room for an arsenal or for a museum. He had always been cheated, but his trust was as strong and unshakable as ever. He was a capital fellow, and we shall meet him more than once in the pages of this novel.

'Good gracious! What a time I have been sitting here!' he exclaimed suddenly, looking at the cheap half-hunter watch he had ordered from Moscow, and which was 'guaranteed for five years', but had already been repaired twice. 'I must be off, friend! Good-bye! And mark my words, these sprees of the Count's will lead to no good! To say nothing about your health. . . . Oh, by-the-by! Will you be going to Tenevo tomorrow?'

'What's up there tomorrow?'

'The church fête! Everybody will be there, so be sure you come too! I have promised that you will be there. Don't make me out a liar!'

It was not necessary to ask to whom he had given his word. We understood each other. The doctor then took leave, put on his well-worn overcoat, and went away.

I remained alone. . . . In order to drown the unpleasant thoughts that began to swarm in my head, I went to my writing-table and trying not to think nor to call myself to account, I began to open my post. The first envelope that caught my eye contained the following letter:

My Darling Serezha,

   Forgive me for troubling you, but I am so surprised that I don't know to whom to apply. . . . It is shameful! Of course, now it will be impossible to get it back, and I'm not sorry, but judge for yourself: if thieves are to enjoy indulgence, a respectable woman cannot feel safe anywhere. After you left I awoke on the divan and found many of my things were missing. Somebody had stolen my bracelet, my gold studs, ten pearls out of my necklace, and had taken about a hundred roubles out of my purse. I wanted to complain to the Count, but he was asleep, so I went away without doing so. This is very wrong! The Count's house – and they steal as in a tavern! Tell the Count. I send you much love and kisses.

Your loving
TINA.

That his Excellency's house was swarming with thieves was nothing new to me; and I added Tina's letter to the information I had already in my memory on this count. Sooner or later I would be obliged to use this intelligence in a case. . . . I knew who the thieves were.

VIII

Black-eyed Tina's letter, her large sprawling hand-writing, reminded me of the mosaic room and aroused in me desires such as a drunkard has for more drink; but I overcame them, and by the strength of my will I forced myself to work. At first I found it unspeakably dull to decipher the bold handwriting of the various commissaries, but gradually my attention became fixed on a burglary, and I began to work with delight. All day long I sat working at my table, and Polycarp passed behind me from time to time and looked suspiciously at my work. He had no confidence in my sobriety, and at any moment he expected to see me rise from the table and order Zorka to be saddled; but towards evening, seeing my persistence, he began to give credence to my good intentions, and the expression of moroseness on his face gave place to one of satisfaction. . . . He began to walk about on tiptoe and to speak in whispers. . . . When some young fellows passed my house, playing on the accordion, he went into the street and shouted:

'What do you young devils mean by making such a row here? Can't you go another way? Don't you know, you infidels, that the master is working?'

In the evening when he served the samovar in the dining-room, he quietly opened my door and called me graciously to come to tea.

'Will you please come to tea?' he said, sighing gently and smiling respectfully.

And while I was drinking my tea he came up behind me and kissed me on the shoulder.

'Now that's better, Sergey Petrovich,' he mumbled. 'Why don't you let that white-eyebrowed devil go hang. . . . How can you, with your great intelligence and your education, behave like this? You have a noble calling. . . . You must behave so that people will respect you. . . . But if you go around with that good-for-nothing

Count and bathe in the lake in your clothes, everyone will say: "He
has no sense! He's an empty-headed fellow!" And so that reputa-
tion will be noised about the whole world! Foolhardiness is suitable
for merchants, but not for noblemen. . . . Noblemen must have
regard to their place in the world. . . .'

'All right! Enough, enough. . . .'

'Sergey Petrovich, don't keep company with that Count. If you
want to have a friend, who could be better than Doctor Pavel
Ivanovich? He goes about shabbily dressed, but how clever he is!'

I was melted by Polycarp's sincerity. . . . I wanted to say an
affectionate word to him. . . .

'What novel are you reading now?' I asked.

'*The Count of Monte Cristo*. That's a Count for you! That's a real
Count! Not like that filthy Count you go around with.'

After tea I again sat down to work and worked until my eyelids
began to droop and my tired eyes to close. . . . When I went to
bed I ordered Polycarp to wake me at five o'clock.

The next morning, before six o'clock, whistling gaily and
knocking off the heads of the field flowers, I was walking towards
Tenevo, where the church fête to which my friend 'Screw' had
invited me to come was being celebrated that day. It was a glorious
morning. Happiness itself appeared to be hanging above the earth,
and, reflected in every dewdrop, enticed the soul of the passer-by
to itself. The woods enwrapped in morning light were quiet and
motionless as if listening to my footsteps, and the chirping
brotherhood of birds met me with expressions of mistrust and
alarm. . . . The air, filled with the verdancy of spring, caressed my
healthy lungs with its softness. I breathed it in, and casting my
enraptured eyes over the whole distant prospect, I felt the spring
and youth, and it seemed to me that the young birches, the grass at
the roadside, and the ceaselessly humming cockchafers shared
these feelings with me.

'Why is it that out there in the world men crowd together in
their miserable hovels, in their narrow and limited ideas,' I
thought, 'while here they have so much space for life and thought?
Why do they not come here?'

And my poetic imagination refused to be disturbed by thoughts
of winter and of bread, those two sorrows that drive poets into

cold, prosaic Petersburg and uncleanly Moscow, where fees are paid for verse, but no inspiration can be found.

Peasants' carts and landowners' britzkas hurrying to church or to market passed me constantly as I trudged along. All the time I had to take off my cap in answer to the courteous bows of the muzhiks and the landowners of my acquaintance. They all offered to give me a lift, but to walk was pleasanter than to drive, and I refused all their offers. Among others the Count's gardener, Franz, in a blue jacket and a jockey cap, passed me on a racing droshky. . . . He looked lazily at me with his sleepy, sour eyes and touched his cap in a still more lazy fashion. Behind him a twelve-gallon barrel with iron hoops, evidently for vodka, was tied to the droshky. . . . Franz's disagreeable phiz and his barrel somewhat disturbed my poetical mood, but very soon poetry triumphed again when I heard the sound of wheels behind me, and looking round I saw a heavy wagonette drawn by a pair of bays, and in the heavy wagonette, on a leathern cushion on a sort of box seat, was my new acquaintance, 'the girl in red', who two days before had spoken to me about the 'electricity that had killed her mother'. Olenka's pretty, freshly washed and somewhat sleepy face beamed and blushed slightly when she saw me striding along the footpath that separated the wood from the road. She nodded merrily to me and smiled in the affable manner of an old acquaintance.

'Good morning!' I shouted to her.

She kissed her hand to me and disappeared from my sight, together with her heavy wagonette, without giving me enough time to admire her fresh, pretty face. This day she was not dressed in red. She wore a sort of dark green costume with large buttons and a broad-brimmed straw hat, but even in this garb she pleased me no less than she had done before. I would have talked to her with pleasure, and I would gladly have heard her voice. I wanted to gaze into her deep eyes in the brilliancy of the sun, as I had gazed into them that night by the flashes of lightning. I wanted to take her down from the ugly wagonette and propose that she should walk beside me for the rest of the way, and I certainly would have done so if it had not been for the 'rules of society'. For some reason it appeared to me that she would have gladly agreed to this proposal. It was not without some cause that she had twice looked back at me as the wagonette disappeared behind some old alders! . . .

It was about six versts from the place of my abode to Tenevo – nothing of a distance for a young man on a fine morning. Shortly after six I was already making my way between loaded carts and the booths of the fair towards the Tenevo church. Notwithstanding the early hour and the fact that the liturgy in the church was not over as yet, the noise of trade was already in the air. The squeaking of cart wheels, the neighing of horses, the lowing of cattle, and the sounds of toy trumpets were intermixed with the cries of gipsy horse-dealers and the songs of muzhiks, who had already found time to get drunk. What numbers of gay, idle faces! What types! What beauty there was in the movements of these masses, bright with brilliant coloured dresses, on which the morning sun poured its light! All this many-thousand-headed crowd swarmed, moved, made a noise in order to finish the business they had to do in a few hours, and to disperse by the evening, leaving after them, on the market place as a sort of remembrance, refuse of hay, oats spilt here and there, and nutshells. . . . The people, in dense crowds, were going to and coming from the church.

The cross that surmounts the church emitted golden rays, bright as those of the sun. It glittered and seemed to be aflame with golden fire. Beneath it the cupola of the church was burning with the same fire, and the freshly painted green dome shone in the sun, and beyond the sparkling cross the clear blue sky stretched out in the far distance. I passed through the crowds in the churchyard and entered the church. The liturgy had only just begun and the Gospel was being read. The silence of the church was only broken by the voice of the reader and the footsteps of the incense-bearing deacon. The people stood silent and immovable, gazing with reverence through the wide-open holy gates of the altar and listening to the drawling voice of the reader. Village decorum, or, to speak more correctly, village propriety, strictly represses every inclination to violate the reverend quiet of the church. I always felt ashamed when in a church anything caused me to smile or speak. Unfortunately it is seldom that I do not meet some of my acquaintances who, I regret to say, are only too numerous, and it generally happens that I have hardly entered the church before I am accosted by one of the 'intelligentsia' who, after a long introduction about the weather, begins a conversation on his own trivial affairs. I answer 'yes' and 'no', but I am too considerate to refuse to give him any attention. While I talk I glance bashfully at my neighbours who are praying, fearing that my idle chatter may wound them.

This time, as usual, I did not escape from acquaintances. When I entered the church I saw my heroine standing close to the door – that same 'girl in red' whom I had met on the way to Tenevo.

Poor little thing! There she stood, red as a crawfish, and perspiring in the midst of the crowd, casting imploring glances on all those faces in the search for a deliverer. She had stuck fast in the densest crowd and, unable to move either forward or backward, looked like a bird who was being tightly squeezed in a fist. When she saw me she smiled bitterly and began nodding her pretty chin.

'For God's sake, escort me to the front!' she said, seizing hold of my sleeve. 'It is terribly stuffy here – and so crowded. . . . I beg you!'

'In front it will be as crowded,' I replied.

'But there, all the people are well dressed and respectable. . . . Here are only common people. A place is reserved for us in front. . . . You, too, ought to be there. . . .'

So she was red not because it was stuffy and crowded in the church. Her little head was troubled by the question of precedence. I granted the vain girl's prayer, and by carefully pressing aside the people I was able to conduct her to the very dais near the altar on which the flower of our district *beau-monde* was collected. Having placed Olenka in a position that was in accordance with her aristocratic desires, I took up a post at the back of the *beau-monde* and began an inspection.

As usual, the men and women were whispering and giggling. The Justice of the Peace, Kalinin, gesticulating with his hands and shaking his head, was telling the landowner, Deryaev, in an undertone all about his ailments. Deryaev was abusing the doctors almost aloud and advising the justice of the peace to be treated by a certain Evstrat Ivanych. The ladies, perceiving Olenka, pounced upon her as a good subject for their criticism and began whispering. There was only one girl who evidently was praying. . . . She was kneeling, with her black eyes fixed in front of her; she was moving her lips. She did not notice a curl of hair that had got loose under her hat and was hanging in disorder over her temple. . . . She did not notice that Olenka and I had stopped beside her.

She was Nadezhda Nikolaevna, Justice Kalinin's daughter. When I spoke above of the woman, who, like a black cat, had run between the doctor and me, I was speaking of her. . . . The doctor loved her as only such noble natures as my dear 'Screw's' are able to love. Now he was standing beside her, as stiff as a pikestaff, with his hands at his sides and his neck stretched out. From time to time his loving eyes glanced inquiringly at her concentrated face. He seemed to be watching her pray and in his eyes there shone a melancholy, passionate longing to be the object of her prayers. But, to his grief, he knew for whom she was praying. . . . It was not for him. . . .

I made a sign to Pavel Ivanovich when he looked round at me, and we both left the church.

'Let's stroll about the market,' I proposed.

We lighted our cigarettes and went towards the booths.

IX

'How is Nadezhda Nikolaevna?' I asked the doctor as we entered a tent where toys were being sold.

'Pretty well. . . . I think she's all right . . .' the doctor replied, frowning at a little soldier with a lilac face and a crimson uniform. 'She asked about you. . . .'

'What did she ask about me?'

'Things in general. . . . She is angry that you have not been to see them for so long . . . she wants to see you and to inquire the cause of your sudden coldness towards their household. . . . You used to go there nearly every day and then – dropped them! As if cut off. . . . You don't even acknowledge them in the street.'

'That's not true, Screw. . . . Want of leisure is really the cause of my ceasing to go to the Kalinins. What's true is true! My connection with that family is as excellent as formerly. . . . I always bow if I happen to meet any of them.'

'However, last Thursday, when you met her father, for some reason you did not return his bow.'

'I don't like that old blockhead of a Justice,' I said, 'and I can't look with equanimity at his phiz; but I still find myself able to bow to him and to press the hand he stretches out to me. Perhaps I didn't notice him on Thursday, or I didn't recognize him. You're not in a good humour today, Screwy, and are trying to pick a quarrel.'

'I love you, my dear boy,' Pavel Ivanovich sighed; 'but I don't believe you. . . . "Didn't notice, didn't recognize"! . . . I don't require your justifications nor your evasions. . . . What's the use of them when there's so little truth in them? You're an excellent, a good man, but there's a kind of a screw loose in your brain that makes you – forgive me for saying it – capable of anything.'

'I'm humbly obliged.'

'Don't be offended, golubchek. . . . God grant that I may be mistaken, but you appear to me to be something of a psychopath. Sometimes, quite in spite of your will and the dictates of your excellent nature, you have attacks of such desires and commit such acts that all who know you as a respectable man are quite nonplussed. You make one marvel how your highly moral principles, which I have the honour of knowing, can exist together with your sudden impulses, which, in the end, produce the most screaming abominations! . . . What animal is this?' Pavel Ivanovich asked the salesman abruptly in quite another tone, lifting close to his eyes a wooden animal with a man's nose, a mane, and a grey stripe down its back.

'A lion,' the salesman answered, yawning. 'Or perhaps some other sort of creature. The deuce only knows!'

From the toy booths we went to the shops where textiles were sold and trade was already very brisk.

'These toys only mislead children,' the doctor said. 'They give the falsest ideas of flora and fauna. For example, that lion . . . striped, purple, and squeaking. . . . Whoever heard of a lion that squeaks?'

'I say, Screwy,' I began, 'you evidently want to say something to me and you seem not to be able. . . . Go ahead! . . . I like to hear you, even when you tell me unpleasant things. . . .'

'Whether pleasant or unpleasant, friend, you must listen to me. There is much I want to talk to you about.'

'Begin. . . . I am transformed into one very large ear.'

'I have already mentioned to you my supposition that you are a psychopath. Now have the goodness to listen to the proofs. . . . I will speak quite frankly, perhaps sometimes sharply. . . . My words may jar on you, but don't be angry, friend. . . . You know my feelings for you: I like you better than anybody else in the district. . . . . I speak not to reprove, nor to blame, nor to upset you. Let us both be objective, friend. . . . Let us examine your psyche with an unprejudiced eye, as if it were a liver or a stomach. . . .'

'All right, let's be objective,' I agreed.

'Excellent! . . . Then let us begin with your connection with Kalinin. . . . If you consult your memory it will tell you that you began to visit the Kalinins immediately after your arrival in this district so favourably looked upon by the good Lord. Your acquaintance was not sought by them. At first you did not please the Justice of the Peace, owing to your arrogant manner, your sarcastic tone, and your friendship with the dissolute Count, and you would never have been in the Justice's house if you yourself had not paid him a visit. You remember? You became acquainted with Nadezhda Nikolaevna, and you began to frequent the Justice's house almost every day. . . . Whenever one came to the house you were sure to be there. . . . You were welcomed in the most cordial manner. You were shown all possible marks of friendship – by the father, the mother, and the little sister. . . . They became as much attached to you as if you were a relative. . . . They were enraptured by you . . . you were made much of, they were in fits of laughter over your slightest witticism. . . . You were for them the acme of wisdom, nobility, gentle manners. You appeared to understand all this, and you reciprocated their attachment with attachment – you went there every day, even on the eve of holidays – the days of cleaning and bustle. Lastly, the unhappy love that you aroused in Nadezhda's heart is no secret to you. . . . Is that not so? Well, then, you, knowing she was over head and ears in love with you, continued to go there day after day. . . . And what happened then, friend? A year ago, for no apparent reason, you suddenly ceased visiting the house. You were awaited for a week . . . a month. . . . They are still waiting for you, and you still don't appear . . . they write to you . . . you do not reply. . . . You end by not even bowing. . . . To you, who set so much store by decorum, such conduct must appear as the height of rudeness! Why did you break off your connection with the Kalinins in such a sharp and off-hand manner? Did they offend you? No. . . . Did they bore you? In that case you might have broken off gradually, and not in such a sharp and insulting manner, for which there was no cause. . . .'

'I stopped visiting a house and therefore have become a psychopath!' I laughed. 'How naive you are, Screwy! What difference is there if you suddenly cease an acquaintance or do so gradually? It's even more honest to do so suddenly – there's less hypocrisy in it. But what trifles all these are!'

'Let us admit that all this is trifling, or that the cause of your sudden rudeness is a secret that does not concern other people. But how can you explain your subsequent conduct?'

'For instance?'

'For instance, you appeared one day at a meeting of our Zemstvo Board – I don't know what your business was there – and in reply to the president, who asked you how it came that you were no longer to be met at Kalinin's, you said . . . Try to remember what you said! "I'm afraid they want to marry me!" Those were the words that came from your lips! And this you said during the meeting in a loud and distinct voice, so that every single man present could hear you! Pretty? In reply to your words laughter and various offensive witticisms about fishing for husbands could be heard on all sides. Your words were caught up by a certain scamp, who went to Kalinin's and repeated them to Nadenka during dinner. . . . Why such an insult, Sergey Petrovich?'

Pavel Ivanovich barred the way. He stood before me and continued looking at me with imploring, almost tearful eyes.

'Why such an insult? Why? Because this charming girl loves you? Let us admit that her father, like all fathers, had intentions on your person. . . . He is like all fathers, they all have an eye on you, on me, on Markuzin. . . . All parents are alike! . . . There's not the slightest doubt that she is over head and ears in love; perhaps she had hoped she would become your wife. . . . Is that a reason to give her such a sounding box on the ear? Dyadenka, dyadenka!* Was it not you yourself who encouraged these intentions on your person? You went there every day; ordinary guests never go so often. In the daytime you went out fishing with her, in the evening you walked about the garden with her, jealously guarding your tête-à-tête. . . . You learned that she loved you, and you made not the slightest change in your conduct. . . . Was it possible after that not to suspect you of having good intentions? I was convinced you would marry her! And you – you complained – you laughed! Why? What had she done to you?'

'Don't shout, Screwy, the people are staring at us,' I said, getting round Pavel Ivanovich. 'Let us change this conversation.

* Little uncle, a familiar form of affectionate address.

It's old women's chatter. I'll explain in a few words, and that must be enough for you. I went to the Kalinins' house because I was bored and also because Nadenka interested me. She's a very interesting girl. . . . Perhaps I might even have married her. But, finding out that you had preceded me as a candidate for her heart, that you were not indifferent to her, I decided to disappear. . . . It would have been cruel on my part to stand in the way of such a good fellow as yourself. . . .'

'Thanks for the favour! I never asked you for this gracious gift, and, as far as I can judge by the expression on your face, you are now not speaking the truth; you are talking nonsense, not reflecting on what you say. . . . And besides, the fact of my being a good fellow didn't hinder you on one of your last meetings with Nadenka from making her a proposal in the summer-house, which would have brought no good to the excellent young fellow if he had married her.'

'O-ho! Screwy, where did you find out about this? It seems that your affairs are not going on badly, if such secrets are confided to you! . . . However, you've grown white with rage and almost look as if you were going to strike me. . . . And just now we agreed to be objective! Screwy, what a funny fellow you are! Well, we've had about enough of all this nonsense. . . . Let's go to the post office. . . .'

X

We went to the post office, which looked out gaily with its three little windows on to the market place. Through the grey paling gleamed the many-coloured flower garden of our postmaster, Maxim Fedorovich, who was known in the whole district as a great connoisseur of all that concerned gardening and the art of laying out beds, borders, lawns, etc.

We found Maxim Fedorovich very pleasantly occupied. Smiling, and red with pleasure, he was seated at his green table, turning over hundred-rouble notes as if they were a book. Evidently even the sight of another man's money had a pleasing effect on his frame of mind.

'How do you do, Maxim Fedorovich?' I said to him. 'Where have you got such a pile of money?'

'It's to be sent to St Petersburg,' the postmaster replied, smiling sweetly, and he pointed his chin at the corner of the room where a dark figure was sitting on the only chair in the post office.

This dark figure rose when he saw me and came towards us. I recognized my new acquaintance, my new enemy, whom I had so grievously insulted when I had got drunk at the Count's.

'My best greetings!' he said.

'How are you, Kaetan Kazimirovich?' I answered, pretending not to notice his outstretched hand. 'How's the Count?'

'Thank God, he's quite well. . . . It's just that he's a little bored. . . . He's expecting you to come at any minute.'

I read on Pshekhotsky's face the desire to converse with me. How could that desire have arisen after the 'swine' to which I had treated him on that evening, and what caused this change of tone?

'What a lot of money you have!' I said, gazing at the packet of hundred-rouble notes he was sending away.

It seemed as if somebody had given a fillip to my brain! I noticed that one of the hundred-rouble notes had charred edges, and one corner had been quite burnt off. . . . It was the hundred-rouble note which I had wanted to burn in the flame of a Chandor candle, when the Count refused to accept it from me as my share of the payment for the gipsies, and which Pshekhotsky had picked up when I flung it on the ground.

'It's better that I should give it to the poor, than let it be consumed by the flames,' he had said then.

To what 'poor' was he sending it now?

'Seven thousand five hundred roubles,' Maxim Fedorovich counted in a drawling voice. 'Quite right!'

It is ill to pry into the secrets of other people, but I wanted terribly to find out whose this money was and to whom this black-browed Pole was sending it in Petersburg. This money was certainly not his, and the Count had nobody to whom he would send it.

'He has plundered the drunken Count,' I thought. 'If deaf and silly Scops-Owl knows how to plunder the Count, how much trouble will this clever fellow have in thrusting his paw into his pockets?'

'Oh, by-the-by, I'll also take this opportunity of sending some money,' Pavel Ivanovich said hastily. 'Do you know, gentlemen, it's quite incredible! For fifteen roubles you can get five things carriage-free! A telescope, a chronometer, a calendar, and something more. . . . Maxim Fedorovich, kindly let me have a sheet of paper and an envelope!'

Screw sent off his fifteen roubles, I received my newspaper and a letter, and we left the post office.

We went towards the church. Screwy paced after me, as pale and dismal as an autumn day. The conversation in which he had tried to show himself to be 'objective' had excited him quite beyond all expectation.

All the church bells were being rung. An apparently endless crowd was slowly descending the steps that led from the church porch.

Ancient banners and a dark cross were held high above the crowd, at the head of the procession. The sun played gaily on the vestments of the priests, and the icon of the Holy Virgin emitted blinding rays. . . .

'Ah, there are our people!' the doctor said, pointing to the *beau-monde* of our district which had separated itself from the crowd and was standing aside.

'Your people, but not mine,' I said.

'That's all the same. . . . Let us join them. . . .'

I approached my acquaintances and bowed. The Justice of the Peace, Kalinin, a tall, broad-shouldered man with a grey beard and crawfish-like eyes, was standing in front of all the others, whispering something in his daughter's ear. Trying to appear as if he had not noticed me, he made not the slightest movement in answer to my general salute that had been made in his direction.

'Good-bye, my angel,' he said in a lachrymose voice as he kissed his daughter on the forehead. 'Take the carriage on ahead. I shall be back by evening. My visits won't take very long.'

Having kissed his daughter again and smiled sweetly on the *beau-monde*, he frowned fiercely, and turning sharply round on one heel, towards a muzhik wearing the disc of a foreman, he said hoarsely to him:

'When will they bring up my carriage?'

The muzhik became excited and waved his arms.

'Look out!'

The crowd that was following the procession made way and the carriage of the Justice of the Peace drove up smartly and with the sound of bells to where Kalinin was standing. He sat down, bowed majestically, and alarming the crowd by his 'Look out!' he disappeared from sight without casting a single glance at me.

'What a supercilious swine!' I whispered in the doctor's ear. 'Come along!'

'Don't you want to say a word to Nadezhda Nikolaevna?' Pavel Ivanovich asked:

'It's time for me to go home. I'm in a hurry.'

The doctor looked at me angrily, sighed, and turned away. I made a general bow and went towards the booths. As I was making my way through the dense crowd, I turned to look back at the Justice's daughter. She was looking after me and appeared to be seeing whether I could bear her pure, searching gaze, so full of bitter injury and reproach.

Her eyes said: 'Why?'

Something stirred in my breast, and I felt remorse and shame for my silly conduct. I suddenly felt a wish to return and caress and fondle with all the strength of my soft, and not yet quite corrupt, soul this girl who loved me passionately, and who had been so grievously wronged by me; and tell her that it was not I who was at fault, but my accursed pride that prevented me from living, breathing or advancing a step. Silly, conceited, foppish pride, full of vanity. Could I, a frivolous man, stretch out the hand of reconciliation, when I knew and saw that every one of my movements was watched by the eyes of the district gossips and the 'ill-omened old women'? Sooner let them laugh her to scorn and cover her with derisive glances and smiles, than undeceive them of the 'inflexibility' of my character and the pride, which silly women admired so much in me.

Just before, when I had spoken with Pavel Ivanovich about the reasons that had caused me suddenly to cease my visits to the Kalinins, I had not been candid or accurate. . . . I had held back the real reason; I had concealed it because I was ashamed of its triviality. . . . The cause was as tiny as a grain of dust. . . . It was this. On the occasion of my last visit, after I had given up Zorka to the coachman and was entering the Kalinins' house, the following phrase reached my ears:

'Nadenka, where are you? . . . Your betrothed has come!'

These words were spoken by her father, the Justice of the Peace, who probably did not think that I might hear him. But I heard him, and my self-love was aroused.

'I her betrothed?' I thought. 'Who allowed you to call me her betrothed? On what basis?'

And something snapped in my breast. Pride rebelled within me, and I forgot all I had remembered when riding to Kalinin's. . . . I forgot that I had lured the young girl, and was myself attracted by her to such a degree that I was unable to pass a single evening without her company. . . . I forgot her lovely eyes that never left my memory either by night or day, her kind smile, her melodious voice. . . . I forgot the quiet summer evenings that will never return either for her or me. . . . Everything had crumbled away under the pressure of the devilish pride that had been aroused by the silly phrase of her simple-minded father. . . . I left the house in a rage, mounted Zorka, and galloped off, vowing to snub Kalinin, who without my permission had dared to consider me as his daughter's betrothed.

'Besides, Voznesensky is in love with her,' I thought, trying to justify my sudden departure, as I rode home. 'He began to pay court to her before I did, and they were considered to be engaged when I made her acquaintance. I won't interfere with him!'

From that day I never put a foot in Kalinin's house, though there were moments when I suffered from longing to see Nadia, and my soul yearned for the renewal of the past. . . . But the whole district knew of the rupture, knew that I had 'bolted' from marriage. . . . How could my pride make concessions?

Who can tell? If Kalinin had not said those words, and if I had not been so stupidly proud and touchy, perhaps I would not have had to look back, nor she to gaze at me with such eyes. . . . But even those eyes were better, even the feeling of being wronged and of reproach was better, than what I saw in those eyes a few months after our meeting in the Tenevo church! The grief that shone in the depths of those black eyes now was only the beginning of the terrible misfortune that, like the sudden onrush of a train, swept that girl from the earth. They were like little flowers compared to those berries that were then already ripening in order to pour terrible poison into her frail body and anguished heart.

XI

When I left Tenevo I took the same road by which I had come. The sun showed it was already midday. As in the morning, peasants' carts and landowners' britzkas beguiled my ears with their squeaking and the metallic rumble of their bells. Again, the gardener, Franz, drove past me with his vodka barrel, but this time it was probably full. Again his eyes gave me a sour look, and he touched his cap. His nasty face jarred on me, but this time again the disagreeable impression that the meeting with him had made on me was entirely wiped away by the forester's daughter, Olenka, whose heavy wagonette caught me up.

'Give me a lift!' I called to her.

She nodded gaily to me and stopped her vehicle. I sat down beside her, and the wagonette rattled on along the road, which cut like a light stripe through the three versts of the Tenevo forest. For about two minutes we looked at each other in silence.

'What a pretty girl she really is!' I thought as I looked at her throat and chubby chin. 'If I were told to choose between Nadenka and her, I would choose her. . . . She's more natural, fresher, her nature is more generous, bolder. . . . If she fell into good hands, much could be made of her! . . . The other is morose, visionary . . . clever.'

Lying at Olenka's feet there were two pieces of linen and several parcels.

'What a number of purchases you have made!' I said. 'What will you do with so much linen?'

'That's not all I need!' Olenka replied. 'I've bought other things too. Today I was a whole hour buying things in the market; tomorrow I must go to make purchases in the town. . . . And then all this has to be made up. . . . I say, don't you know any woman who would go out to sew?'

'No, I think not. . . . But why have you to buy so many things? Why have they to be sewn? God knows your family is not large. . . . One, two . . . there I've counted you all. . . .'

'How queer all you men are! You don't understand anything! Wait till you get married, you yourself will be angry then if after the wedding your wife comes to you all slovenly. I know Pëtr Egorych is not in want of anything. Still, it seems a bit awkward not to appear as a good housewife from the first. . . .'

'What has Pëtr Egorych to do with it?'

'Hm! . . . You are laughing at me, as if you don't know!' Olenka said and blushed slightly.

'Young lady, you are talking in riddles.'

'Have you really not heard? Why, I am going to marry Pëtr Egorych!'

'Marry?' I said in astonishment, my eyes growing large. 'What Pëtr Egorych?'

'Oh, good Lord! Urbenin, of course!'

I stared at her blushing and smiling face.

'You? Going to marry . . . Urbenin? What a joke!'

'It's not a joke at all . . . . I really can't understand where you see the joke. . . .'

'You to marry . . . Urbenin . . .' I repeated, turning pale, I really don't know why. 'If this is not a joke, what is it?'

'What joke! I can't understand what is so extraordinary – what is so strange in it?' Olenka said, pouting.

A minute passed in silence. . . . I gazed at the pretty girl, at her young, almost childish face, and was astonished that she could make such terrible jokes! I instantly pictured to myself Urbenin, elderly, fat, red-faced with his protruding ears and hard hands, whose very touch could only scratch that young female body which had scarcely begun to live . . . . Surely the thought of such a picture must frighten this pretty wood fay, who could see the poetry in the sky when it is reft by lightning and thunder growls angrily! I, even I, was frightened!

'It's true he's a little old,' Olenka sighed, 'but he loves me. . . . His love is trustworthy.'

'It's not a matter of trustworthy love, but of happiness. . . .'

'I shall be happy with him. . . . He has means, thank God, and he's no pauper, no beggar, but a nobleman. Of course, I'm not in love with him, but are only those who marry for love happy? Oh, I know those marriages for love!'

'My child, when have you had time to stuff your brain with this terrible worldly wisdom?' I asked. 'Admitted that you are joking with me, but where have you learned to joke in such a vulgar, adult way? . . . Where? When?'

Olenka looked at me with astonishment and shrugged her shoulders.

'I don't understand what you are saying,' she said. 'You don't like to see a young girl marry an old man? Is that so?'

Olenka suddenly blushed all over, her chin moved nervously, and without waiting for my answer she rattled on rapidly.

'This does not please you? Then perhaps you'd like to try living in the wood – with nothing to amuse you but a few sparrow-hawks and a mad father – and waiting until a young suitor comes along! You liked it the other evening, but if you saw it in winter, when one only wishes . . . that death might come – '

'Oh, all this is absurd, Olenka, it is childish, silly! If you are not joking . . . Truly I don't know what to say! You had better be silent and not offend the air with your tongue. I, in your place, would have hanged myself on the nearest tree, and you buy linen . . . and smile. Ach!'

'In any case, with his means he will be able to have father cured,' she whispered.

'How much do you need for your father's cure?' I cried. 'Take it from me – a hundred? Two hundred? . . . A thousand? Olenka, it's not your father's cure that you want!'

The news Olenka had communicated to me had excited me so much that I had not even noticed that the wagonette had driven past my village, or how it had turned into the Count's yard and stopped at the bailiff's porch. When I saw the children run out, and the smile on Urbenin's face, who also had rushed out to help Olenka down, I jumped out of the wagonette and ran into the Count's house without even taking leave. Here further news awaited me.

XII

'How opportune! How opportune!' the Count cried as he greeted me and scratched my cheek with his long, pointed moustache. 'You could not have chosen a happier time! We have only just sat down to luncheon. . . . Of course, you are acquainted. . . . You have doubtless often come across each other in your legal department. . . . Ha, ha!'

With both hands the Count pointed to two men who, seated in soft armchairs, were partaking of cold tongue. In one I had the vexation of recognizing the Justice of the Peace, Kalinin; the other, a little grey-haired man with a large moonlike bald pate, was my good friend, Babaev, a rich landowner who occupied the post of perpetual member of our district council. Having exchanged bows, I looked with astonishment at Kalinin. I knew how much he disliked the Count and what reports he had set in circulation in the district about the man at whose table he was now eating tongue and green peas with such appetite and drinking ten-year-old liqueur. How could a respectable man explain such a visit? The Justice of the Peace caught my glance and evidently understood it.

'I have devoted this day to visits,' he said to me. 'I am driving round the whole district. . . . And, as you see, I have also called upon his Excellency. . . .'

Il'ya brought a fourth cover. I sat down, drank a glass of vodka, and began to lunch.

'It's wrong, your Excellency, very wrong!' Kalinin said, continuing the conversation my entrance had interrupted. 'It's no sin for us little people, but you are an illustrious man, a rich man, a brilliant man. . . . It's a sin for you to fail.'

'That's quite true; it's a sin,' Babaev acquiesced.

'What's this all about?' I asked.

'Nikolai Ignat'ich has given me a good idea!' the Count said, nodding to the justice of the peace. 'He came to me. . . . We sat down to lunch, and I began complaining of being bored. . . .'

'And he complained to me of being bored,' Kalinin interrupted the Count. 'Boredom, melancholy . . . this and that. . . . In a word, disillusionment. A sort of Onegin. "Your Excellency," I said, "you're yourself to blame. . . ." "How so?" "Quite simply. . . . In order not to be bored," I said, "accept some office . . . occupy yourself with the management of your estate. . . . Farming is excellent, wonderful. . . ." He tells me he intends to occupy himself with farming, but still he is bored. . . . What fails him is, so to speak, the entertaining, the stimulating element. There is not the – how am I to express myself? – er – strong sensations . . .'

'Well, and what idea did you give him?'

'I really suggested no idea, I only reproached his Excellency. "How is it your Excellency," I said, "that you, a young, cultivated, brilliant man, can live in such seclusion? Is it not a sin?" I asked. "You go nowhere, you receive nobody, you are seen nowhere. . . . You live like an old man, or a hermit. . . . What would it cost you to arrange parties . . . so to speak, at homes?" '

'Why should he have at homes?' I asked.

'How can you ask? First, if his Excellency gave evening parties, he would become acquainted with society – study it, so to speak. . . . Secondly, society would have the honour of becoming more closely acquainted with one of the richest of our landowners. . . . There would be, so to speak, a mutual exchange of thoughts, conversation, gaiety. . . . And when one comes to think of it, how many cultivated young ladies and men we have among us! . . . What musical evenings, dances, picnics could be arranged! Only think! The reception rooms are huge, there are pavilions in the gardens, and so on, and so on. Nobody in the district could have dreamed of the private theatricals or the concerts that could be got up. . . . Yes, by God! Only imagine them! Now all this is lost, as if we're buried alive; but then . . . one must just know how to do things! If I had his Excellency's means, I would show them how to live! And he says: "Bored"! By God! it's laughable to listen to it. . . . It makes one feel ashamed. . . .'

And Kalinin began to blink his eyes, wishing to appear to be really ashamed. . . .

'All this is quite just,' the Count said, rising from his seat and thrusting his hands into his pockets. 'I could give excellent evening parties. . . . Concerts, private theatricals . . . all this could be arranged charmingly. Besides, these parties would not only enter-tain society, they would have an educational influence too! Don't you think so?'

'Well, yes,' I acquiesced. 'As soon as our young ladies see your moustachioed physiognomy they will at once be penetrated by the spirit of civilization. . . .'

'Serezha, you're always joking,' the Count said, somewhat offended, 'and you never give me any friendly advice! Everything is laughable for you! My friend, it is about time to drop these student habits!'

The Count began to pace about the room from corner to corner, and to explain to me in long and tiresome sentences the benefits that his evening parties might bring to humanity. Music, litera-ture, the drama, riding, shooting. The shooting alone might unite all the best forces of the district! . . .

'We shall revert to the subject,' the Count said to Kalinin in taking leave of him after lunch.

'Then, if I understand your Excellency, the district may hope?' the Justice of the Peace inquired.

'Certainly, certainly. . . . I will develop this idea and see what I can do. . . . I am happy . . . delighted. You can tell every-body. . . .'

It was a sight to note the look of beatitude that was imprinted on the face of the Justice of the Peace as he took his seat in his carriage and said to the coachman: 'Go!' He was so delighted that he even forgot our differences and in taking leave he called me 'golubchek' and pressed my hand warmly.

After the visitors had left, the Count and I sat down to table again and continued our lunch. We lunched till seven o'clock in the evening, when the crockery was removed from the table and dinner was served. Young drunkards know how to shorten the time between meals. The whole time we drank and ate tidbits, by which means we sustained the appetite which would have failed us if we had entirely ceased to eat.

'Did you send money to anybody today?' I asked the Count, remembering the packets of hundred-rouble notes I had seen in the morning in the Tenevo post-office.

'I sent no money.'

'Tell me, please, is your – what's his name? – new friend, Kazimir Kaetanych, or Kaetan Kazimirovich, a wealthy man?'

'No, Serezha. He's a poor beggar! But what a soul he has – what a heart! You are wrong in speaking so disdainfully of him . . . and you bully him. Brother, you must learn to discriminate between people. Let's have another glass?'

Pshekhotsky returned for dinner. When he saw me sitting at table and drinking, he frowned, and after turning about round our table for a time he seemed to think it best to retire to his own room. He refused to have any dinner, pleading a bad headache, but he expressed no objection when the Count advised him to go to bed and have his dinner there.

During the second course, Urbenin came in. I hardly recognized him. His broad red face beamed all over with pleasure. A happy smile seemed to be playing on his protruding ears and on the thick fingers with which he was arranging his smart new necktie all the time.

'One of the cows is ill, your Excellency,' he reported. 'I sent for the vet, but it appears he has gone away somewhere. Wouldn't it be a good thing to send to town for the veterinary surgeon? If I send to him he won't listen and won't come, but if you write to him it will be quite a different matter. Perhaps it is a mere trifle, but it may be something serious.'

'All right, I will write . . .' the Count grumbled.

'I congratulate you, Pëtr Egorych,' I said, rising and stretching out my hand to the bailiff.

'On what occasion?' he murmured.

'Why, you are about to get married!'

'Yes, yes, just fancy! He's going to get married!' the Count began, winking at the blushing Urbenin. 'What do you think of him? Ha, ha, ha! He was silent, never said a word, and then suddenly – this bombshell. And – do you know whom he is going to marry? We guessed it that evening! Pëtr Egorych, we thought then that that mischievous heart of yours was up to no good. When he looked at you and Olenka he said: "That fellow's bitten!" Ha, ha! Sit down and have dinner with us, Pëtr Egorych!'

Urbenin sat down carefully and respectfully and made a sign

with his eyes to Il'ya to bring him a plate of soup. I poured him out a glass of vodka.

'I don't drink, sir,' he said.

'Nonsense, you drink more than we do.'

'I used to drink, but now I don't,' the bailiff said, smiling. 'Now, I mustn't drink. . . . There's no cause. Thank God, everything is settled satisfactorily, everything is arranged, all exactly as my heart had desired, even better than I could have expected.'

'Well, then, to your happiness you can drink this,' I said, pouring him out a glass of sherry.

'This – why not? I really did drink hard. Now I can confess it to his Excellency. Sometimes from morning to night. When I rose in the morning I remembered it . . . well, naturally, I went to the cupboard at once. Now thank God, I have nothing to drown in vodka.'

Urbenin drank the glass of sherry. I poured out a second. He drank this one too, and imperceptibly got drunk. . . .

'I can scarcely believe it,' he said, laughing a happy childish laugh. 'I look at this ring and remember her words when she gave her consent – I can still scarcely believe it. . . . It seems laughable. . . . How could I, at my age, with my appearance, hope that this deserving girl would not disdain to become mine . . . the mother of my orphan children? Why, she's a beauty, as you have been pleased to notice; an angel personified! Wonders will never cease! You have filled my glass again? Why not, for the last time. . . . I drank to drown care, I will now drink to happiness. How I suffered, gentlemen! What grief I endured! I saw her first a year ago, and would you believe it – from that time I have not slept quietly a single night; there was not a single day on which I did not drown this – silly weakness with vodka . . . and scolded myself for this folly. . . . I sometimes looked at her through the window and admired her and . . . tore out the hair of my head. . . . At times I could have hanged myself. . . . But, thank God, I plucked up courage and proposed, and, do you know, it took me quite by surprise. Ha, ha! I heard, but I could not believe my own ears. She said: "I accept," and it appeared to me like: "Go to the devil, you old dotard!" . . . Afterwards, when she kissed me, I was convinced. . . .'

At the recollection of that first kiss received from the poetical Olenka, Urbenin closed his eyes and, despite his fifty years, he blushed like a boy . . . I found it quite disgusting.

'Gentlemen,' he said, looking at us with happy, kind eyes, 'why don't you get married? Why are you wasting your lives, throwing them out of the window? Why do you shun that which is the greatest blessing of all who live upon the earth? The delight that debauchery gives is not a hundredth part of what a quiet family life would give you! Young men, your Excellency and you, Sergey Petrovich . . . I am happy now, and . . . God knows how I love you both! Forgive me for giving stupid advice, but . . . I want you both to be happy! Why don't you get married? Family life is a blessing. . . . It's every man's duty! . . .'

The happy and fond look on the face of the old man, who was about to marry a young girl and was advising us to alter our dissolute existence for a quiet family life, became unbearable to me.

'Yes,' I said, 'family life is a duty. I agree with you. So you are discharging yourself of this duty for a second time?'

'Yes, for a second time. I am fond of family life in general. To be a bachelor or a widower is only half of a life for me. Whatever you may say, gentlemen, wedlock is a great thing!'

'Certainly . . . even when the husband is almost three times as old as his wife?'

Urbenin blushed. The hand that was lifting a spoonful of soup to his mouth trembled, and the soup spilled back into the plate.

'I understand what you mean, Sergey Petrovich,' he mumbled. 'I thank you for your frankness. I ask myself: Am I not being unfair? The thought torments me. But there seems no time to ask oneself such questions when every moment one feels happy, when one forgets one's age, ugliness . . . everything. *Homo sum*, Sergey Petrovich! And when for a second, thoughts about the inequalities of our ages come to me, I don't worry about finding an answer, but try to stay calm. I think I have made Olga happy. I have given her a father and my children a mother. Besides, all this is like a novel, and . . . my head feels giddy. It was wrong to make me drink sherry.'

Urbenin rose, wiped his face with his napkin, and sat down

again. A minute later he gulped down another glass of sherry and looked at me for a long time with an imploring glance as if he were begging me for mercy, and suddenly his shoulders began to shake, and quite unexpectedly he burst into sobs like a boy.

'It's nothing . . . nothing!' he mumbled, trying to master his sobs. 'Don't be uneasy. After your words my heart grew sick with a strange foreboding. But it is nothing.'

Urbenin's foreboding was realized, realized so soon that I have not time to change my pen and begin a new page. From the next chapter my calm muse will change the expression of calmness on her face for one of passion and affliction. The introduction is finished and the drama begins.

The criminal will of man enters upon its rights.

XIII

I remember a fine Sunday morning. Through the windows of the Count's church the diaphanous blue sky could be seen and the whole of the church, from its painted cupola to its floor, was flooded by soft sunrays in which little clouds of incense played about gaily. . . . The songs of swallows and starlings were borne in through the open doors and windows. . . . One sparrow, evidently a very bold little fellow, flew in at the door, and having circled, chirping, several times round and round above our heads, flew out again through one of the windows. . . . In the church itself there was also singing. . . . They sang sweetly, with feeling, and with the enthusiasm for which our Little Russian singers are so celebrated when they feel themselves the heroes of the moment, and that all eyes are bent upon them. . . . The melodies were all gay and playful, like the soft, bright sunspots that played upon the walls and the clothes of the congregation. . . . In the unschooled but soft and fresh notes of the tenor my ear seemed to catch, despite the gay wedding melodies, deep, melancholy chords. It appeared as if this tenor was sorry to see that next to young, pretty and poetical Olenka there stood Urbenin, heavy, bear-like, and getting on in years. . . . And it was not only the tenor who was sorry to see this ill-assorted pair. . . . On many of the faces that lay within my field of vision, notwithstanding all their efforts to appear gay and unconcerned, even an idiot could have read an expression of compassion.

Arrayed in a new dress suit, I stood behind Olenka, holding the crown over her head. I was pale and felt unwell. . . . I had a racking headache, the result of the previous night's carouse and a pleasure party on the lake, and the whole time I was looking to see if the hand that held the crown did not tremble. . . . My soul felt the disagreeable presentiment of dread that is felt in a forest on a rainy autumn night. I was vexed, disgusted, sorry. . . . Cats seemed to be scratching at my heart, somewhat resembling qualms of conscience. . . . There in the depths, at the very bottom of my heart, a little devil was seated who obstinately, persistently whispered to me that if Olenka's marriage with clumsy Urbenin was a sin, I was the cause of that sin. . . . Where did such thoughts come from? How could I have saved this little fool from the unknown risks of her indubitable mistake? . . .

'Who knows?' whispered the little devil. 'Who should know better than you?'

In my time I have known many ill-assorted marriages. I have often stood before Pukirev's picture.★ I have read countless novels based on disagreements between husband and wife; besides, I have known the physical differences that inevitably punish ill-assorted marriages, but never once in my whole life had I experienced that terrible spiritual condition from which I was unable to escape all the time I was standing behind Olenka, executing the functions of best man.

'If my soul is agitated only by commiseration, how is it that I never felt that compassion before when I assisted at other weddings? . . .'

'There is no commiseration here,' the little devil whispered, 'but jealousy. . . .'

One can only be jealous of those one loves, but do I love the girl in red? If I loved all the girls I met in the course of my life, my heart wouldn't be able to stand it; besides, it would be too much of a good thing. . . .

My friend Count Karnéev was standing right at the back near the door behind the churchwarden's counter, selling wax tapers. He was well groomed, with well smoothed hair, and exhaled a narcotic, suffocating odour of scents. That day he looked such a darling that when I greeted him in the morning I could not refrain from saying:

'Alexey, today you are looking like the perfect quadrille dancer!'

He greeted everybody who entered or left with the sweetest of smiles, and I heard the ponderous compliments with which he rewarded each lady who bought a candle from him. He, the spoilt child of Fortune, who never had copper coins, did not know how

★ A picture entitled 'The Misalliance' or 'The Ill-assorted Marriage'. – J.S.

to handle them, and was constantly dropping on the floor five and
three-kopeck pieces. Near him, leaning against the counter, Kalinin stood majestically with a Stanislav decoration on a ribbon
round his neck. His countenance shone and beamed. He was
pleased that his idea of 'at homes' had fallen on good soil, and was
already beginning to bear fruit. In the depths of his soul he was
showering on Urbenin a thousand thanks; his marriage was an
absurdity, but it was a good opportunity to get the first 'at home'
arranged.

Vain Olenka must have rejoiced. . . . From the nuptial lectern
to the doors of the high altar stretched out two rows of the most
representative ladies of our district flower garden. The guests were
decked out as smartly as they would have been if the Count himself
was being married: more elegant toilettes could not have been
desired. . . . . The assembly consisted almost exclusively of aristocrats . . . Not a single priest's wife, not a single tradesman's
wife. . . . There were even among them ladies to whom Olenka
would formerly never have considered herself entitled to bow. . . .
And Olenka's bridegroom – a bailiff, a privileged retainer; but
there was no threat to her vanity in this. He was a nobleman and
the possessor of a mortgaged estate in the neighbouring district. . . . His father had been marshal of the district and he himself
had for more than nine years been a magistrate in his own native
district. . . . What more could have been desired by the ambitious
daughter of a self-made nobleman? Even the fact that her best man
was known throughout the province as a *bon vivant* and a Don Juan
could tickle her pride. . . . All the women were looking at
him. . . . He was as resplendent as forty thousand best men
thrown into one, and what was not the least important, he had not
refused to be her best man, she, a simple little girl, when, as
everybody knew, he had even refused aristocrats when they had
asked him to be their best man. . . .

But vain Olenka did not rejoice. . . . She was as pale as the linen
she had lately brought home from the Tenevo market. The hand in
which she held the candle shook slightly and her chin trembled
from time to time. In her eyes there was a certain dullness, as if
something had suddenly astonished or frightened her. . . . There
was not a sign of that gaiety which had shone in her eyes even the

day before when she was running about the garden talking with enthusiasm of the sort of wallpaper she would have in her drawing-room, and saying on what day she would receive guests, and so on. Her face was now too serious, more serious than the solemn occasion demanded. . . .

Urbenin was in a new dress-suit. He was respectably dressed, but his hair was arranged as the orthodox Russians wore their hair in the year 'twelve. As usual, he was red in the face, and serious. His eyes prayed and the signs of the cross he made after every 'Lord have mercy upon us' were not made in a mechanical manner.

Urbenin's children by his first marriage – the schoolboy Grisha and the little fair-haired girl Sasha – were standing just behind me. They gazed at the back of their father's red head and his protruding ears, and their faces seemed to represent notes of interrogation. They could not understand why Aunt Olia had given herself to their father, and why he was taking her into his house. Sasha was only surprised, but the fourteen-year-old Grisha frowned and looked scowlingly at him. He would certainly have replied in the negative if his father had asked his permission to marry. . . .

The marriage service was performed with special solemnity. Three priests and two deacons officiated. The service lasted long, so long, indeed, that my arm was quite tired of holding the crown, and the ladies who love to see a wedding ceased looking at the bridal pair. The chief priest read the prayers, with pauses, without leaving out a single one. The choir sang something very long and complicated; the cantor took advantage of the occasion to display the compass of his voice, reading the Gospels with extra slowness. But at last the chief priest took the crown out of my hands . . . the young couple kissed each other. . . . The guests got excited, the straight lines were broken, congratulations, kisses and exclamations were heard. Urbenin, beaming and smiling, took his young wife on his arm, and we all went out into the air.

If anybody who was in the church with me finds this description incomplete and not quite accurate, let him set down these oversights to the headache from which I was suffering and the above-mentioned spiritual depression which prevented me from observing and noting. . . . Certainly, if I had known at the time that I would have to write a novel, I would not have looked at the floor as I did on that day, and I would not have paid attention to my headache!

Fate sometimes allows itself bitter and malignant jokes! The couple had scarcely had time to leave the church when they were met by an unexpected and unwished for surprise. When the wedding procession, bright with many tints and colours in the sunlight, was proceeding from the church to the Count's house, Olenka suddenly made a backward step, stopped, and gave her husband's elbow such a violent pull that he staggered.

'He's been let out!' she said aloud, looking at me with terror.

Poor little thing! Her insane father, the forester Skvortsov, was running down the avenue to meet the procession. Waving his hands and stumbling along with rolling, insane eyes, he presented a most unattractive picture. However, all this would possibly have looked less out of place if he had not been in his print dressing-gown and downtrodden slippers, the raggedness of which ill accorded with the elegant wedding finery of his daughter. His face looked sleepy, his dishevelled hair was blown about by the wind, his nightshirt was unbuttoned.

'Olenka!' he mumbled when he had come up to them. 'Why have you left me?'

Olenka blushed scarlet and looked askance at the smiling ladies. The poor little thing was consumed by shame.

'Mit'ka did not lock the door!' the forester continued, turning to us. 'It would not be difficult for robbers to get in! . . . The samovar was stolen out of the kitchen last summer, and now she wants us to be robbed again.'

'I don't know who can have let him out!' Urbenin whispered to me. 'I ordered him to be locked up. . . . Sergey Petrovich, golubchek, have pity on us; get us out of this awkward position somehow! Anyhow!'

'I know who stole your samovar,' I said to the forester. 'Come along, I'll show you where it is.'

Taking Skvortsov round the waist, I led him towards the church. I took him into the churchyard and talked to him until, by my calculation, I thought the wedding procession ought to be in the house, then I left him without having told him where his stolen samovar was to be found.

Although this meeting with the madman was quite unexpected and extraordinary, it was soon forgotten. . . . A further surprise that Fate had prepared for the newly-married pair was still more unusual.

XIV

An hour later we were all seated at long tables, dining.

To anybody who was accustomed to cobwebs, mildew and wild gipsy whoops in the Count's apartments it must have seemed strange to look on the workaday, prosaical crowd that now, by their habitual chatter, broke the usual silence of the ancient and deserted halls. This varied and noisy throng looked like a flight of starlings which in flying past had alighted to rest in a neglected churchyard or – may the noble bird forgive me such a comparison! – a flight of storks that on one of their migrations had settled down on the ruins of a deserted castle.

I sat there hating that crowd which frivolously examined the decaying wealth of the Counts Karnéev. The mosaic walls, the carved ceilings, the rich Persian carpets and the rococo furniture excited enthusiasm and astonishment. A self-satisfied smile never left the Count's moustachioed face. He received the enthusiastic flattery of his guests as something that he deserved, though in reality all the riches and luxuries of his deserted mansion were not acquired in any way thanks to him, but on the contrary, he merited the bitterest reproaches and contempt for the barbarously dull indifference with which he treated all the wealth that had been collected by his fathers and grandfathers, collected not in days, but in scores of years! It was only the mentally blind or the poor of spirit who could not see in every slab of damp marble, in every picture, in each dark corner of the Count's garden, the sweat, the tears and the callouses on the hands of the people whose children now swarmed in the little log huts of the Count's miserable villages. . . . Among all those people seated at the wedding feast, rich, independent people, people who might easily have told him the plainest truths, there was not one who would have told the Count that his self-satisfied grin was stupid and out of place. . . . Everybody found it necessary to smile flatteringly and to burn paltry incense before him. If this was ordinary politeness (with us, many love to attribute everything to politeness and propriety), I would prefer the churl who eats with his hands, who takes the bread from his neighbour's plate, and blows his nose between two fingers, to these dandies.

Urbenin smiled, but he had his own reasons for this. He smiled flatteringly, respectfully, and in a childlike, happy manner. His broad smiles were the result of a sort of dog's happiness. A devoted and loving dog, who had been fondled and petted, and now in sign of gratitude wagged its tail gaily and with sincerity.

Like Risler Père in Alphonse Daudet's novel, beaming and rubbing his hands with delight, he gazed at his young wife, and from the superabundance of his feelings could not refrain from asking question after question:

'Who could have thought that this young beauty would fall in love with an old man like myself? Is it possible she could not find anybody younger and more elegant? Women's hearts are incomprehensible!'

He even had the courage to turn to me and blurt out:

'When one looks around, what an age this is we live in! He, he! When an old man can carry off such a fairy from under the nose of youth! Where have you all had your eyes? He, he. . . . Young men are not what they used to be!'

Not knowing what to do or how to express the feelings of gratitude that were overflowing in his broad breast, he was constantly jumping up, stretching out his glass towards the Count's glass and saying in a voice that trembled with emotion:

'Your Excellency, my feelings toward you are well known. This day you have done so much for me that my affection for you appears like nothing. How have I merited such a great favour, your Excellency, or that you should take such an interest in my joy? It is only Counts and bankers who celebrate their weddings in such a way! What luxury, what a bevy of distinguished guests! . . . Oh what can I say! . . . Believe me, your Excellency, I shall never forget you, as I shall never forget this best and happiest day of my life.'

And so on. . . . Olenka was evidently not pleased with her husband's florid respectfulness. One could see she was annoyed at his speeches, that raised smiles on the faces of the guests and even caused them to feel ashamed for him. Notwithstanding the champagne she had drunk, she was still not gay, and morose as before. . . . She was as pale as she had been in church, and the same look of dread was in her eyes. . . . She was silent, she answered indifferently all the questions that were asked, scarcely smiled at the Count's witticisms, and she hardly touched the expensive dishes. . . . The more Urbenin became slightly intoxicated and accounted himself the happiest of mortals, the more unhappy her pretty face appeared. It made me sad to look at her, and in order not to see her face I tried to keep my eyes on my plate.

How could her sadness be explained? Was not regret beginning to gnaw at the poor girl's heart? Or perhaps her vanity had expected even greater pomp?

During the second course when I lifted my eyes and looked at her, I was painfully struck by her expression. The poor girl, in trying to answer some of the Count's silly remarks, was making strenuous efforts to swallow something; sobs were welling up in her throat. She did not remove her handkerchief from her mouth, and looked at us timidly, like a frightened little animal, to see whether we had noticed that she wanted to cry.

'Why are you looking so glum today?' the Count asked. 'Oh, ho! Pëtr Egorych, it's your fault! Have the goodness to cheer your wife up! Ladies and gentlemen, I demand a kiss! Ha, ha! . . . The kiss I demand is, of course, not for me, but only . . . that they should kiss each other!'

Urbenin, smiling all over his red face, rose and began to blink. Olenka, forced by the calls and the demands of the guests, rose slightly and offered her motionless, lifeless lips to Urbenin. He kissed her. . . . Olenka pressed her lips together as if she feared they would be kissed another time, and glanced at me. . . . Probably my look was an evil one. Catching my eye, she suddenly blushed, and taking up her handkerchief, she began to blow her nose, trying in that way to hide her terrible confusion. . . . The thought entered my mind that she was ashamed before me, ashamed of that kiss, ashamed of her marriage.

'What have I to do with you?' I thought, but at the same time I did not remove my eyes from her face, trying to discover the cause of her confusion.

The poor little thing could not stand my gaze. It is true the blush of shame soon left her face, but in place of it tears began to rise up in her eyes, real tears such as I had never before seen on her face. Pressing her handkerchief to her face, she rose and rushed out of the dining-room.

'Olga Nikolaevna has a bad headache,' I hastened to say in order to explain her departure. 'Already this morning she complained of her head. . . .'

'Not at all, brother,' the Count said jokingly. 'A headache has nothing to do with it. It's all caused by the kiss, it has confused her. Ladies and gentlemen, I announce a severe reprimand for the bridegroom! He has not taught his bride how to kiss! Ha, ha, ha!'

The guests, delighted with the Count's wit, began to laugh. . . . But they ought not to have laughed. . . .

Five minutes passed, ten minutes passed, and the bride did not return. . . . A silence fell on the party. . . . Even the Count ceased joking. . . . Olenka's absence was all the more striking as she had left suddenly without saying a word. . . . To say nothing about the etiquette of the matter, Olenka had left the table immediately after the kiss, so it was evident she was cross at having been forced to kiss her husband. . . . It was impossible to suppose she had gone away because she was confused. . . . One can be confused for a minute, for two, but not for an eternity, as the first ten minutes of her absence appeared to us all. What a number of evil thoughts entered into the half tipsy minds of the men, what scandals were being prepared by the charming ladies! The bride had risen and left the table! What a picturesque scene for a drama in the provincial *beau monde*!

Urbenin began to be uneasy and looked around.

'Nerves . . .' he muttered. 'Or perhaps something has gone wrong with her toilette. . . . Who can account for anything with these women? She'll come back directly – this very minute.'

But when another ten minutes had passed and she had not appeared, he looked at me with such unhappy, imploring eyes that I was sorry for him.

'Would it matter if I went to look for her?' his eyes asked. 'Won't you help me, golubchek, to get out of this horrible position? Of all here you are the cleverest, the boldest, the most ready-witted man. Do help me!'

I saw the entreaty in his unhappy eyes and decided to help him. How I helped him the reader will see farther on. . . . I will only say that the bear who assisted the hermit in Krylov's fable loses all its animal majesty, becomes pale, and turns into an innocent infusoria when I think of myself in the part of the 'obliging fool'. . . . The resemblance between me and the bear consists only in this that we both went to help quite sincerely without foreseeing any bad consequences from our help, but the difference between us is enormous. . . . The stone with which I struck Urbenin's forehead was many times more weighty. . . .

'Where is Olga Nikolaevna?' I asked the lackey who had brought round the salad.

'She went into the garden, sir,' he replied.

'This is becoming quite impossible, mesdames!' I said in a jocular tone, addressing myself to the ladies. 'The bride has gone away and my wine has become quite sour! . . . I must go to look for her and bring her back, even if all her teeth were aching! The best man is an official personage, and he is going to show his authority!'

I rose, amid the loud applause of my friend the Count, left the dining-room and went into the garden. The hot rays of the midday sun poured straight upon my head, which was already excited by wine. Suffocating heat and sultriness seemed to strike me in the face. I went along one of the side avenues at a venture, and, whistling some sort of melody, I gave full scope to my capacities as an ordinary detective. I examined all the bushes, summer-houses and caves, and when I began to be tormented by the regret that I had turned to the right instead of the left, I suddenly heard a strange sound. Somebody was laughing or crying. The sounds issued from one of the grottoes that I had left to examine last of all. Quickly entering it, I found the object of my search enveloped in dampness, the smell of mildew, mushrooms, and lime.

She stood there leaning against a wooden column that was covered with black moss, and lifting her eyes full of horror and despair on me, she tore at her hair. Tears poured from her eyes as from a sponge that is pressed.

'What have I done? What have I done?' she muttered.

'Yes, Olia, what have you done?' I said, standing before her with folded arms.

'Why did I marry him? Where were my eyes? Where was my sense?'

'Yes, Olia. . . . It is difficult to explain your action. To explain it by inexperience is too indulgent; to explain it by depravity – I would rather not. . . .'

'I only understood it today . . . only today! Why did I not understand it yesterday? Now all is irrevocable, all is lost! All, all! I might have married the man I love, the man who loves me!'

'Who is that, Olia?' I asked.

'You!' she said, looking me straight and openly in the eyes. 'But I was too hasty! I was foolish! You are clever, noble, young. . . . You are rich! You appeared to me unattainable!'

'Well, that's enough, Olia,' I said, taking her by the hand. 'Wipe your little eyes and come along. . . . They are waiting for you there. . . . Well, don't cry any more, don't cry. . . .' I kissed her hand. . . . 'That's enough, little girl! You have done a foolish thing and are now paying for it. . . . It was your fault. . . . Well, that's enough, be calm. . . .'

'But you love me? Yes? You are so big, so handsome! Don't you love me?'

'It's time to go, my darling. . . .' I said, noticing to my great horror that I was kissing her forehead, taking her round the waist, that she was scorching me with her hot breath and that she was hanging round my neck.

'Enough!' I mumbled. 'That must satisfy you!'

Five minutes later, when I carried her out of the grotto in my arms and troubled by new impressions put her on her feet, I saw Pshekhotsky standing almost at the entrance. . . . He stood there, looking at me maliciously, and silently applauding. . . . I measured him with my glance, and giving Olga my arm, walked off towards the house.

'We'll see the last of you here today,' I said, looking back at Pshekhotsky. 'You will have to pay for this, spying!'

My kisses had probably been ardent because Olga's face was

burning as if ablaze. There were no traces of the recently shed tears to be seen on it.

'Now I have no fear, I feel everything is possible,' she murmured as we went together towards the house and she pressed my elbow convulsively. 'This morning I did not know where to hide myself from terror, and now . . . now, my good giant, I don't know what to do from happiness! My husband is sitting and waiting for me there. . . . Ha, ha! . . . . What's that to me? If he were even a crocodile, a terrible serpent . . . I'm afraid of nothing! I love you, and that's all I want to know!'

I looked at her face, radiant with happiness, at her eyes, brimful of joyful, satisfied love, and my heart sank with fear for the future of this pretty, happy creature: her love for me was but an extra impulse towards the abyss. . . . How will this laughing woman with no thought for the future end? . . . My heart misgave me and sank with a feeling that cannot be called either pity or sympathy, because it was stronger than these feelings. I stopped and laid my hand on Olga's shoulder. . . . I had never before seen anything more beautiful, graceful and at the same time more pitiful. . . . There was no time for reasoning, deliberation or thought, and, carried away by my feelings, I exclaimed:

'Olga, come home with me at once! This instant!'

'How? What did you say?' she asked, unable to understand my somewhat solemn tone.

'Let us drive to my house immediately!'

Olga smiled and pointed to the house. . . .

'Well, and what of that?' I said. 'Isn't it all the same if I take you tomorrow or today? But the sooner the better. . . . Come!'

'But . . . won't it look strange? . . .'

'What, girl, you're afraid of the scandal? Yes, there'll be a tremendous, an almighty scandal, but a thousand scandals are better than that you should remain here! I won't leave you here! I can't leave you here! Olga, do you understand? Cast aside your faint-heartedness, your womanly logic, and obey me! Obey me if you do not desire your own ruin!'

Olga's eyes said that she did not understand me. . . . Meanwhile time did not stop but went its course, and it was impossible for us to remain standing in the avenue while they were expecting us *there*. We had to decide. . . . I pressed to my heart 'the girl in red', who actually was my wife now, and at that moment it appeared to me that I really loved her . . . loved her with a husband's love, that she was mine, and that her fate rested on my conscience. . . . I saw that I was united with this creature for ever, irrevocably.

'Listen, my darling, my treasure!' I said. 'It's a bold step. . . . It will separate us from our nearest friends; it will call down upon our heads a thousand reproaches and tearful lamentations. Perhaps it will even spoil my career; it will cause me a thousand insurmountable unpleasantnesses, but, my darling, it is settled! You will be my wife! . . . I want no better wife. God preserve me from all other women! I will make you happy; I will take care of you like the apple of my eye, as long as I live; I will educate you – make a woman of you! I promise you this, and here is my honest hand on it!'

I spoke with sincere passion, with feeling, like a stage lover acting the most pathetic scene of his part. I spoke very well, I seemed to be inspired by the touch of an eagle's wing that was soaring over our heads. My Olia took my outstretched hand, held it in her own small hands, and kissed it tenderly. But this was not a sign of assent. On the silly little face of an inexperienced woman who had never before heard such speech, there appeared a look of perplexity. . . . She still could not understand me.

'You say I am to go to you?' she said reflectively. 'I don't quite understand you. . . . Don't you know what *he* would say?'

'What have you to do with what he would say?'

'How so? No, Serezha! Better say no more. . . . Please don't mention it again. . . . You love me, and I want nothing more. With your love I'm ready for anything.'

'But, little fool, how will you manage it?'

'I shall live here, and you – why, you will come every day. . . . I will come to meet you.'

'But I can't imagine such a life for you without a shudder! At night – him; in the day – me. . . . No, that is impossible! Olia, I love you so much at the present moment that . . . I am madly jealous. . . . I never suspected that I had the capacity for such feelings.'

But what imprudence! I had my arm round her waist, and she

was stroking my hand tenderly even though at any moment someone might pass along the avenue and see us.

'Come,' I said, removing my arm. 'Put on your cloak and let us be off!'

'How quickly you want to do things,' she murmured in a tearful voice. 'You hurry as if to a fire. God only knows what you're dreaming of! To run away immediately after the marriage! What will people say?'

And Olenka shrugged her shoulders. Her face wore such a look of perplexity, astonishment and incomprehension that I only waved my hand and postponed discussion of her emotional problems to another moment. Besides, there was no time to continue our conversation: we were going up the stone stairs that led to the terrace and could hear the sound of voices. At the dining-room door Olia arranged her hair, saw that her dress was in order, and went into the room. No signs of confusion could be noticed on her face. She entered the room much more boldly than I had expected.

'Ladies and gentlemen, I have brought back the fugitive,' I said as I sat down in my place. 'I found her with difficulty. . . . I'm quite tired out by this search. I went into the garden, I looked around, and there she was walking about in the avenue. . . . "Why are you here?" I asked her. "I just felt like it," she answered. "It's so stuffy." '

Olia looked at me, at the guests, at her husband, and began to laugh. Something amused her, and she became gay. I read on her face the wish to share with all that crowd of diners the sudden happiness that she had experienced; and not being able to give expression to it in words, she poured it out in her laughter.

'What a funny person I am!' she said. 'I am laughing, and I don't know why I am laughing. . . . Count, laugh!'

'Sweeten the wine,' cried Kalinin.

Urbenin coughed and looked inquiringly at Olia.

'Well?' she said, with a momentary frown.

'They are calling for us to sweeten the wine,' Urbenin smiled, and rising, he wiped his lips with his napkin.

Olga rose too and allowed him to kiss her immovable lips. . . .

The kiss was a cold one, but it served to increase the fire that was smouldering in my breast and threatened every moment to burst into flame. . . . I turned away and with compressed lips awaited the end of the dinner. . . . Fortunately the end was soon reached, otherwise I would not have been able to endure it.

XV

'Come here!' I said to the Count rudely, going up to him after dinner.

The Count looked at me with astonishment and followed me into the empty room to which I led him.

'What do you want, my dear friend?' he asked as he unbuttoned his waistcoat and hiccuped.

'Choose one of us . . .' I said, scarcely able to stand on my feet from the rage that had mastered me. 'Either me or Pshekhotsky! If you don't promise me that in an hour that scoundrel shall leave your estate, I will never set foot here again! . . . I give you half a minute to make your choice!'

The Count dropped the cigar out of his mouth and spread his arms. . . .

'What's the matter with you, Serezha?' he asked, opening his eyes wide. 'You look quite wild!'

'No useless words, if you please! I cannot endure that spy, scoundrel, rogue, your friend Pshekhotsky, and in the name of our close friendship I demand that he leave this place, and instantly, too!'

'But what has he done to you?' the Count asked, much agitated. 'Why are you attacking him?'

'I ask you again: me or him?'

'But, golubchek, you are placing me in a horribly awkward position. . . . Stop! There's a feather on your dress coat! . . . You are demanding the impossible from me!'

'Good-bye!' I said. 'I am no longer acquainted with you.'

And turning sharply on my heel, I went into the ante-room, put on my overcoat, and hastened out of the house. When crossing the garden towards the servants' quarters, where I wanted to give the order to have my horse put to, I was stopped. Coming towards me with a small cup of coffee in her hand, I was met by Nadia Kalinin. She was also at Urbenin's wedding, but a sort of undefined fear had forced me to avoid speaking to her, and during the whole day I had not gone up to her, nor said a word to her.

'Sergey Petrovich!' she said in an unnaturally deep voice when in passing her I slightly raised my hat. 'Stop!'

'What may your commands be?' I asked, as I came up to her.

'I have nothing to command. . . . Besides, you are no lackey,' she said, gazing straight into my eyes and becoming terribly pale. 'You are hurrying somewhere, but if you have time might I detain you for a moment?'

'Certainly! . . . There was no need to ask.'

'In that case let us sit down. . . . Sergey Petrovich,' she continued, after we had seated ourselves. 'All this day you have tried to avoid seeing me, and have skirted me as if on purpose, as if you were afraid of meeting me. So I decided to speak to you. . . . I am proud and egoistical. . . . I do not know how to obtrude myself . . . but once in a lifetime one can sacrifice pride.'

'To what do you refer?'

'I had decided to ask you . . . the question is humiliating, it is difficult for me. . . . I don't know how I shall stand it. . . . Answer me without looking at me. . . . Sergey Petrovich, is it possible you are not sorry for me?'

Nadia looked at me and slightly shook her head. Her face became paler. Her upper lip trembled and was drawn to one side.

'Sergey Petrovich! I always think that . . . you have been separated from me by some misunderstanding, some caprice. . . . I think if we had an explanation, all would go on as formerly. If I did not think it, I would not have strength to put you the question you are about to hear. Sergey Petrovich, I am unhappy. . . . You must see it. . . . My life is no life. . . . All is dried up. . . . And chiefly . . . this uncertainty . . . one does not know, whether to hope or not. . . . Your conduct towards me is so incomprehensible that it is impossible to arrive at any certain conclusion. . . . Tell me, and I shall know what to do. . . . My life will then have an aim. . . . I shall then decide on something.'

'Nadezhda Nikolaevna, you wish to ask me about something?' I said, preparing in my mind an answer to the question I had a presentiment was coming.

'Yes, I want to ask . . . the question is humiliating. . . . If anybody were listening to us they might think I was obtruding myself – in a word, was behaving like Pushkin's Tatiana. . . . But this question has been tortured from me. . . .'

The question was really forced from her by torture. When Nadia turned her face towards me to put that question, I became frightened: she trembled, pressed her fingers together convulsively, and uttered with melancholy sadness the fatal words. Her pallor was terrible.

'May I hope?' she whispered at last. 'Do not be afraid to tell me candidly. . . . Whatever the answer may be, it will be better than uncertainty. What is it? May I hope?'

She waited for an answer, but the state of my soul was such that I was incapable of making a sensible response. Drunk, excited by the occurrence in the grotto, enraged by Pshekhotsky's spying, and Olga's indecision, and the stupid conversation I had had with the Count, I scarcely heard Nadia.

'May I hope?' she repeated. 'Answer me!'

'Ach, I can't answer now, Nadezhda Nikolaevna!' I said with a wave of the hand as I rose. 'I am incapable at the present moment of giving any sort of answer. Forgive me, I neither heard nor understood you. I am stupid and excited. . . . It's really a pity you took the trouble.'

I again waved my hand and left Nadia. It was only afterwards, when I became calm again, that I understood how stupid and cruel I had been in not giving the girl an answer to her simple and ingenuous question. Why did I not answer her?

Now when I can look back dispassionately at the past, I do not explain my cruelty by the condition of my soul. It appears to me that in not giving a straightforward answer I was coquetting and playing the fool. It is difficult to understand the human soul, but it is still more difficult to understand one's own soul. If I really was playing the fool, may God forgive me. Although to make game of another's suffering ought not to be forgiven.

XVI

For three days I wandered about my rooms from corner to corner like a wolf in a cage, trying with all the strength of my unstable will to prevent myself from leaving the house. I did not touch the pile of papers that were lying on the table patiently awaiting my attention; I received nobody; I quarrelled with Polycarp; I was irritable. . . . I did not allow myself to go to the Count's estate, and this obstinacy cost me much nervous exertion. A thousand times I took up my hat and as often threw it down again. . . . Sometimes I decided to defy the whole world and go to Olga, whatever it might cost; at others I took a cold douche of common sense and decided to remain at home. . . .

My reason told me not to go to the Count's estate. Since I had sworn to the Count never to set foot in his house again, could I sacrifice my self-love and pride? What would that moustachioed coxcomb think if, after our stupid conversation, I went to him as if nothing had happened? Would it not be a confession that I had been in the wrong?

Besides, as an honest man I ought to break off all connection with Olga. All further intercourse with her would only lead to her ruin. She had made a mistake in marrying Urbenin; in falling in love with me she had made another mistake. If she had a secret lover while living with her old husband, would she not be like a depraved doll? To say nothing about how abominable, in principle, such a life is, it was necessary also to think of the consequences.

What a coward I am! I was afraid of the consequences, of the present, of the past. . . . An ordinary man will laugh at my reasoning. He would not have paced from corner to corner, he would not have seized his head in both hands, he would not have made all sorts of plans, but he would have left all to life which grinds into flour even mill-stones. Life would have digested everything without asking for his aid or permission. . . . But I am fearful almost to cowardice. Pacing from corner to corner, I suffered from compassion for Olga, and at the same time I feared she would understand the proposal I had made her in a moment of passion, and would appear in my house to stay as I had promised her, *for ever*. What would have happened if she had listened to me and had come home with me? How long would that *for ever* have lasted, and what would life with me have given poor Olga? I would not have given her family life and would consequently not have given her happiness. No, I ought not go to Olga!

At the same time my soul was drawn frantically towards her. I was as melancholy as a boy, in love for the first time, who is refused a rendezvous. Tempted by what had occurred in the grotto, I yearned for another meeting, and the alluring vision of Olga, who, as I well knew, was also expecting me, and was pining away from longing, never left my mind for a moment.

The Count sent me letter after letter, each one more rueful and humbler than the last . . . . He implored me to 'forget everything!' and come to him; he apologized for Pshekhotsky, he begged me to forgive that 'kind, simple, but somewhat shallow man', he was surprised that owing to trifles I had decided to break off old and friendly connections. In one of his last letters he promised to come to me and, if I wished it, to bring Pshekhotsky with him, who would ask my pardon, 'although he did not feel that he was at all at fault'. I read the letters and in answer begged each messenger to leave me in peace. I knew well how to be capricious!

At the very height of my nervous agitation, when I, standing at the window, was deciding to go away somewhere – anywhere except to the Count's estate – when I was tormenting myself with arguments, self-reproaches, and visions of love that awaited me with Olga, my door opened quietly, I heard light footsteps behind me, and soon my neck was encircled by two pretty little arms.

'Olga, is that you?' I asked and looked round.

I recognized her by her hot breath, by the manner in which she hung on my neck, and even by her scent. Pressing her head to my cheek, she appeared to me extraordinarily happy. . . . From happiness she could not say a word. . . . I pressed her to my breast and – where had the melancholy, and all the questions with which I had been tormenting myself during the whole of three days, disappeared? I laughed and jumped about with joy like the veriest schoolboy.

Olga was in a blue silk dress, which suited her pale face and splendid flaxen hair very well. The dress was in the latest fashion and must have been very expensive. It probably cost Urbenin a quarter of his yearly salary.

'How lovely you are today!' I said, lifting Olga up in my arms and kissing her neck. 'How are you? Quite well?'

'Why, you haven't much of a place here!' she said, casting her eyes round my study. 'You're a rich man, you receive a high salary, and yet . . . you live quite poorly.'

'Not everybody can live as luxuriously as the Count, my darling,' I said. 'But let us leave my wealth in peace. What good genius has brought you into my den?'

'Stop, Serezha! You'll crumple my frock. . . . Put me down. . . . I've only come to you for a moment, darling! I told everybody at home I was going to Akat'ikha, the Count's washerwoman, who lives here only three doors off. Let me go, darling! . . . It's awkward. Why haven't you been to see me for so long?'

I answered something, placed her on a chair opposite me, and began to contemplate her beauty. For a minute we looked at each other in silence.

'You are very pretty, Olia!' I sighed. 'It's a pity and a shame that you're so pretty!'

'Why is it a pity?'

'The devil only knows who's got you.'

'But what more do you want? Am I not yours? Here I am. . . . Listen, Serezha! . . . Will you tell me the truth if I ask you?'

'Of course, only the truth.'

'Would you have married me if I had not married Pëtr Egorych?'

'Probably not,' I wanted to say, but why should I probe the painful wound in poor Olia's heart that was already so troubled?

'Certainly,' I said in the tone of a man speaking the truth.

Olia sighed and cast her eyes down.

'What a mistake I've made! What a mistake! And what's worst

of all it can't be rectified! I suppose I can't get divorced from him?'

'You can't.'

'I can't understand why I was in such a hurry! We girls are so silly and giddy. . . . There's nobody to whip us! However, one can't undo the past, and to reason about it is useless. . . . Neither reasoning nor tears are of any good. Serezha, I cried all last night! He was there . . . lying next to me, and I was thinking of you. . . . I couldn't sleep. . . . I wanted to run away in the night, even into the wood to father. . . . It is better to live with a mad father than with this – what's his name.'

'Reasoning won't help. . . . Olia, you ought to have reasoned when you drove home with me from Tenevo, and were so happy at getting married to a rich man. . . . It's too late to practise eloquence now. . . .'

'Too late. . . . Then let it be so!' Olga said with a decisive wave of the hand. 'It will be possible to live, if it is no worse. . . . Good-bye, I must be off. . . .'

'No, not good-bye. . . .'

I drew Olia towards me and covered her face with kisses, as if I were trying to reward myself for the lost three days. She pressed close against me like a lamb sheltering from the cold and warmed my face with her hot breath. . . . There was stillness in the room. . . .

'The husband killed his wife!' bawled my parrot.

Olia shivered, released herself from my embraces, and looked inquiringly at me.

'It's only the parrot, my soul,' I said. 'Calm yourself.'

'The husband killed his wife!' Ivan Dem'yanych repeated again.

Olia rose, put on her hat in silence, and gave me her hand. Dread was written on her face.

'What if Urbenin gets to know?' she asked, looking at me with wide-open eyes. 'He is capable of killing me.'

'What nonsense!' I said, laughing. 'What sort of a fellow would I be if I allowed him to kill you? He's hardly capable of anything as extravagant as murder. . . . Are you going? Well, then, good-bye, my child! . . . I will wait . . . Tomorrow, in the wood, near the house where you lived. . . . Shall we meet there . . . ?'

After seeing Olia off, I returned to my study, where I found

Polycarp. He was standing in the middle of the room, he looked sternly at me and shook his head contemptuously.

'Sergey Petrovich, see that this sort of thing does not happen here again: I won't have it,' he said in the tone of a severe parent. 'I don't like it. . . .'

'What's "it"?'

'That thing. . . . You think I did not see? I saw everything. . . . See that she doesn't dare come here again. This is no house for that sort of philandering. There are other places for that. . . .'

I was in the best of humours, so Polycarp's spying and his censorious tone did not make me angry. I only laughed and sent him to the kitchen.

I had hardly had time to collect my thoughts after Olga's visit when another guest arrived. A carriage rattled up to my door and Polycarp, spitting to each side and mumbling abuse, announced the arrival of 'that there fellow, may he be . . .!' etc., etc. It was the Count, whom he hated with the whole strength of his soul. The Count entered, looked tearfully at me, and shook his head.

'You turn away. . . . You don't want to speak . . .'

'I don't turn away,' I said.

'I am so fond of you, Serezha, and you . . . for a trifle! Why do you wound me? Why?'

The Count sat down, sighed, and shook his head.

'Well, you've played the fool long enough!' I said. 'All right!'

I had a strong influence upon this weak, puny little man; it was as strong as my contempt for him. . . . My contemptuous tone never offended him; on the contrary. . . . When he heard my 'All right!' he jumped up and embraced me.

'I have brought him with me. . . . He is sitting in the carriage. . . . Do you wish him to apologize?'

'Do you know his fault?'

'No. . . .'

'So much the better. He needn't apologize, but you had better warn him that if ever a similar thing occurs, I'll not get excited, but I will take my own measures.'

'Then, Serezha, it's peace? Excellent! It ought to have been so long ago; the deuce only knows what you quarrelled about! Like two schoolgirls! Oh, by-the-by, golubchek, haven't you got half a glass of vodka? My throat is terribly dry!'

I ordered vodka to be served. The Count drank two glasses, sprawled himself out on the sofa, and began to chatter.

'I say, brother, I just met Olia. . . . A fine girl! I must tell you, I'm beginning to detest Urbenin. . . . That means that Olenka is beginning to please me. . . . She's devilish pretty! I'm thinking of making up to her.'

'One ought not to touch the married ones!' I said with a sigh.

'Come now, he's an old man. . . . It's no sin to cheat Pëtr Egorych out of his wife. . . . She's no mate for him. . . . He's like a dog; he can't eat it himself and won't let others have it. . . . I'm going to begin my siege today; I'll begin systematically. . . . She's such a sweet little duck – h'm! – quite chic, brother! One licks one's chops!'

The Count drank a third glass and continued:

'Of the girls here, do you know who else pleases me? Nadenka, that fool Kalinin's daughter. . . . A burning brunette, you know the sort, pale, with wonderful eyes. . . . I must also cast my line there. . . . I'm giving a party at Whitsuntide, a musical, vocal, literary evening on purpose to invite her. . . . As it turns out, it's not so bad here; quite jolly! There's society, and women . . . and . . . May I have forty winks here . . . only a moment?'

'You may. . . . But how about Pshekhotsky in the carriage?'

'He may wait, the devil take him! . . . Brother, I myself don't like him.'

The Count raised himself on his elbow and said mysteriously:

'I keep him only from necessity . . . because I must. . . . May the devil take him!'

The Count's elbow gave way, his head sank on the cushion. A minute later snores were heard.

In the evening after the Count had left, I had another visitor; the doctor, Pavel Ivanovich. He came to inform me of Nadezhda Nikolaevna's illness and also that she had definitely refused him her hand. The poor fellow was downhearted and went about like a drenched hen.

XVII

The poetical month of May had passed. . . .
The lilacs and tulips were over, and fate decreed that with
them the ecstasies of love, which, notwithstanding their guiltiness
and painfulness, had yet occasionally afforded us sweet moments
that can never be effaced from our memory, should likewise
wither. There are moments for which one would give months,
yea, even years!

On a June evening when the sun was already set, but its broad
track in purple and gold still glowed in the distant West, foretelling
a calm and clear day for the morrow, I rode on Zorka up to the
house where Urbenin lived. On that evening the Count was giving
a musical party. The guests were already arriving, but the Count
was not at home; he had gone for a ride and had left word he would
return soon.

A little later I was standing at the porch, holding my horse by
the bridle and chatting with Urbenin's little daughter, Sasha.
Urbenin himself was sitting on the steps with his head supported
on his fists, looking into the distance, which could be seen through
the open gates. He was gloomy and answered my questions
reluctantly. I left him in peace and occupied myself with Sasha.

'Where is your new mama?' I asked her.

'She has gone riding with the Count. She rides with him every
day.'

'Every day!' Urbenin grumbled with a sigh.

Much could be heard in that sigh. The same feelings could be
heard in it that were agitating my soul and that I was trying to
explain to myself, but was unable to do so, and therefore became
lost in conjecture.

Every day Olga went out for rides with the Count. But that was
a trifle. Olga could not fall in love with the Count, and Urbenin's
jealousy was groundless. We ought not to have been jealous of the
Count, but of something else which, however, I could not

understand for a long time. This 'something else' built up a whole wall between Olga and me. She continued to love me, but after the visit which has been described in the last chapter, she had not been to my house more than twice, and when we met in other places she flared up in a strange way and obstinately refused to answer my questions. She returned my caresses with passion, but her movements were sudden and startled, so that our short rendezvous only left a feeling of painful perplexity in my mind. Her conscience was not clean; this was clear, but what was the real cause? Nothing could be read on Olga's guilty face.

'I hope your new mama is well?' I asked Sasha.

'She's quite well. Only in the night she had toothache. She cried.'

'She cried,' Urbenin repeated, looking at Sasha. 'Did you see it? My darling, you only dreamed it.'

Olga had not had toothache. If she had cried it was not with pain, but for something else. . . . I wanted to continue talking to Sasha, but I did not succeed in this, as at that moment the noise of horses' hoofs was heard and we soon saw the riders – a man inelegantly jumping about in his saddle, and a graceful lady rider. In order to hide my joy from Olga, I took Sasha into my arms and, smoothing her fair hair with my hand, I kissed her on the forehead.

'Sasha, how pretty you are!' I said. 'And what nice curls you have!'

Olga cast a rapid glance at me, returned my bow in silence, and leaning on the Count's arm, entered the house. Urbenin rose and followed her.

Five minutes later the Count came out of the house. He was gay. I had never seen him so gay before. Even his face had a fresher look.

'Congratulate me,' he said, giggling, as he took my arm.

'What on?'

'On my conquest. . . . One more ride like this, and I swear by the ashes of my noble ancestors I shall tear the petals from this flower.'

'You have not torn them off yet?'

'As yet? . . . Almost! During ten minutes, "Thy hand in my hand," ' the Count sang, 'and . . . not once did she draw it

away. . . . I kissed it! Wait for tomorrow. Now let us go. They
are expecting me. Oh, by-the-by, golubchek, I want to talk to you
about something. Tell me, old man, is it true what people say –
that you are . . . that you entertain evil intentions with regard to
Nadenka Kalinin?'

'Why?'

'If that were true, I won't come in your way. It's not in my
principles to put a spoke in another's wheels. If, however, you
have no sort of intentions, then of course – '

'I have none.'

'*Merci*, my soul!'

The Count thought of killing two hares at the same time, and
was firmly convinced that he would succeed. On the evening I am
describing I watched the chase of these two hares. The chase was
stupid and as comical as a good caricature. When watching it one
could only laugh or be revolted at the Count's vulgarity, but
nobody could have thought that this schoolboy chase would end
with the moral fall of some, the ruin and the crimes of others!

The Count not only killed two hares, but more! He killed them,
but he did not get their skins and their flesh.

I saw him secretly press Olga's hand, who received him each
time with a friendly smile and looked after him with a contemptuous grimace. Once, evidently wishing to show that there were
no secrets between us, he even kissed her hand in my presence.

'What a blockhead!' she whispered into my ear, and wiped her
hand.

'I say, Olga,' I asked, when the Count had gone away, 'I think
there is something you want to tell me. What is it?'

I looked searchingly into her face. She blushed scarlet and began
to blink in a frightened manner, like a cat who has been caught
stealing.

'Olga,' I said sternly, 'you must tell me! I demand it!'

'Yes, there is something I want to tell you,' she whispered. 'I
love you – I can't live without you – but . . . my darling, don't
come to see me any more. Don't love me any more, and don't call
me Olia. It can't go on. . . . It's impossible. . . . And don't let
anybody see that you love me.'

'But why is this?'

'I want it. The reasons you need not know, and I won't tell you. Go. . . . Leave me!'

I did not leave her, and she herself was obliged to bring our conversation to an end. Taking the arm of her husband, who was passing us at that moment, she nodded to me with a hypocritical smile, and went away.

The Count's other hare – Nadenka Kalinin – was honoured that evening by the Count's special attention. The whole evening he hovered around her, he told her anecdotes, he was witty, he flirted with her, and she, pale and exhausted, drew her lips to one side in a forced smile. The Justice of the Peace, Kalinin, watched them all the time, stroking his beard and coughing importantly. That the Count was paying court to his daughter was agreeable to him. 'He has a Count as son-in-law!' What thought could be sweeter for a provincial *bon vivant*? From the moment that the Count began to pay court to his daughter he had grown at least three feet in height in his own estimation. And with what stately glances he measured me, how maliciously he coughed when he talked to me! 'So you stood on ceremonies and went away – it was all one to us! Now we have a Count!'

The day after the party I was again at the Count's estate. This time I did not talk with Sasha but with her brother, the schoolboy. The boy led me into the garden and poured out his whole soul to me. These confidences were the result of my questions as to how he got on with his 'new mother'.

'She's a friend of yours,' he began, nervously unbuttoning his uniform. 'You will repeat it to her; but I don't care. You may tell her whatever you like! She's spiteful, she's base!'

He told me that Olga had taken his room from him, she had sent away their old nurse who had served at Urbenin's for ten years, she was always screaming about something and always angry.

'Yesterday you admired sister Sasha's hair. . . . Hadn't she pretty hair? Just like flax! This morning she cut it all off!'

'That was jealousy,' I thus explained to myself Olga's invasion into the hairdresser's domain.

'She was evidently envious that you had praised Sasha's hair and not her own,' the boy said in confirmation of my thought. 'She worries papasha, too. Papasha is spending a terrible lot of money on her, and is neglecting his work. . . . He has begun to drink again! Again! She's a little fool. . . . She cries all day that she has to live in poverty in such a small house. Is it papasha's fault that he has little money?'

The boy told me many sad things. He saw that which his blinded father did not see or did not want to see. In the poor boy's opinion his father was wronged, his sister was wronged, his old nurse had been wronged. He had been deprived of his little den where he had been used to occupy himself with his books, and feed the goldfinches he had caught. Everybody had been wronged, everybody was scorned by his stupid and all-powerful stepmother! But the poor boy could not have imagined the terrible wrong that his young stepmother would inflict on his family, and which I was to witness that very evening after my talk with him. Everything else grew dim before that wrong, the cropping of Sasha's hair appeared as a mere trifle in comparison with it.

XVIII

Late at night I was sitting with the Count. As usual, we were drinking. The Count was quite drunk, I only slightly.

'Today I was allowed accidentally to touch her waist,' he mumbled. 'Tomorrow, therefore, we can begin to go further.'

'Well, and Nadia? How do things stand with Nadia?'

'We are progressing! I've only just begun with her as yet. So far, we are passing through the period of conversations with the eyes. I love to gaze into her sad black eyes, brother. Something is written there that words are unable to express, that only the soul can understand. Let's have another drink!'

'It seems that you must please her since she has the patience to listen to you for hours at a time. You also please her papa!'

'Her papa? Are you talking about that blockhead? Ha, ha! The simpleton suspects me of honourable intentions.'

The Count coughed and drank.

'He thinks I'll marry her! To say nothing of my not being able to marry, when one considers the question honestly it would be more honest in me to seduce a girl than to marry her. . . . A life spent in perpetuity with a drunken, coughing, semi-old man . . . br-r-r! My wife would pine away, or else run off the following day. . . . What noise is that?'

The Count and I jumped up. . . . Several doors were slammed to, and almost at the same moment Olga rushed into the room. She was as white as snow, and trembled like a chord that had been struck violently. Her hair was falling loose around her. The pupils of her eyes were dilated. She was out of breath and was crumpling in her hand the front pleats of her dressing-gown.

'Olga, what is the matter with you?' I asked, seizing her by the hand and turning pale.

The Count ought to have been surprised at this familiar form of address, but he did not hear it. His whole person was turned into one large note of interrogation, and with open mouth and staring eyes he stood looking at Olga as if she were an apparition.

'What has happened?' I asked.

'He beats me!' Olga said, and fell sobbing on to an armchair. 'He beats me!'

'Who is he?'

'My husband! I can't live with him! I have left him!'

'This is disgraceful!' the Count exclaimed, and he struck the table with his fist. 'What right has he? This is tyranny! This . . . the devil only knows what it is! Beating his wife? Beating her! What did he do it for?'

'For nothing, for nothing at all,' Olga said, wiping away her tears. 'I pulled my handkerchief out of my pocket, and the letter you sent me yesterday fell on the floor. . . . He seized it and read it . . . and began to beat me. . . . He clutched my hand and crushed it – look, there are still red marks on it – and demanded an explanation. . . . Instead of explaining, I ran here. . . . Can't you defend me? He has no right to treat his wife so roughly! I'm no cook! I'm a noblewoman!'

The Count paced about the room and jabbered with his drunken, muddling tongue some sort of nonsense which when rendered into sober language was intended to mean something about 'the status of women in Russia'.

'This is barbarous! This is like New Zealand! Does this muzhik also think that his wife is going to cut her throat at his funeral – like savages going into the next world and taking their wives with them!'

I could not recover from my surprise. . . . How was this sudden visit of Olga's in a nightdress to be understood? What was I to think – what to decide? If she had been beaten, if her dignity had been wounded, why had she not run away to her father or to the housekeeper? . . . Lastly why not to me, who was certainly near to her? And had she really been insulted? My heart told me of the innocence of simple-minded Urbenin, and understanding the truth, it sank with the pain that the stupefied husband must have been feeling at that time. Without asking any questions, not knowing where to commence, I began to soothe Olga and offered her wine.

'What a mistake I made! What a mistake!' she sighed between

her tears, lifting the wineglass to her lips. 'How sanctimonious he pretended to be when he was courting me! I thought he was an angel and not a man!'

'So you wanted him to be pleased with the letter that fell out of your pocket?' I asked. 'You wanted him to burst out laughing?'

'Don't let us talk about it!' the Count interrupted. 'Whatever the case, his action was dastardly all the same! That's no way to treat women. I'll challenge him! I'll teach him! Olga Nikolaevna, believe me he'll have to suffer for this!'

The Count gobbled like a young turkey cock, although he had no authority to come between husband and wife. I kept silent and did not contradict him, because I knew that taking vengeance for another man's wife was limited to drunken ebullitions of words between four walls, and that everything about the duel would be forgotten the next day. But why was Olga silent? . . . I did not want to think that she would readily accept the Count's favours. I did not wish to think that this stupid, beautiful little cat had so little sense of her own worth that she would willingly consent to the drunken Count being judge between man and wife.

'I'll drag him through the dirt!' piped her new knight-errant. 'And then I'll box his ears! I'll do it tomorrow!'

And she did not stop the mouth of that blackguard, who in his drunken mood was insulting a man whose only blame was that he had made a mistake and was now being duped. Urbenin had seized and pressed her hand very roughly, and this had caused her scandalous flight to the Count's house, and now, when before her eyes this drunken and morally degenerate creature was defaming the honest name and pouring abuse on a man, who at that time must have been languishing in melancholy and uncertainty, knowing that he was deceived, she did not so much as bat an eyelid!

While the Count was venting his wrath and Olga was wiping her eyes, the manservant brought in some roast partridges. The Count put half a partridge on his guest's plate. She shook her head negatively and then mechanically took up her knife and fork and began to eat. The partridge was followed by a large glass of wine, and soon there were no more signs of tears with the exception of red rims round her eyes and occasional deep sighs.

Soon we heard laughter. . . . Olga laughed like a consoled child who had forgotten its injury. And the Count looking at her laughed too.

'Do you know what I have thought of?' he began, sitting down next to her. 'I want to arrange private theatricals. We shall act plays in which there are good women's parts. Eh? What do you say to that?'

They began to talk about the private theatricals. How ill this silly chatter accorded with the terror that had but lately been depicted on Olga's face, when only an hour before she had rushed into the room, pale and weeping, with flowing hair! How cheap were those terrors, those tears!

Meanwhile time went on. The clock struck twelve. Respectable women go to bed at that time. Olga ought to have gone away long since. But the clock struck half-past twelve; it struck one, and she was still sitting there chatting with the Count.

'It's time to go to bed,' I said, looking at my watch. 'I'm off! . . . Olga Nikolaevna, will you permit me to escort you?'

Olga looked at me and then at the Count.

'Where am I to go?' she murmured. 'I can't go to him!'

'Yes, yes; of course, you can't go to him,' the Count said. 'Who can answer for his not beating you again? No, no!'

I walked about the room. All was quiet. I paced from corner to corner and my friend and my mistress followed my steps with their eyes. I seemed to understand this quiet and these glances. There was something expectant and impatient in them. I put my hat on the table and sat down on the sofa.

'So, sir,' the Count mumbled and rubbed his hands impatiently. 'So, sir. . . . Things are like this. . . .'

The clock struck half-past one. The Count looked quickly at the clock, frowned and began to walk about the room. I could see by the glances he cast on me that he wanted to say something, something important but ticklish and unpleasant.

'I say, Serezha!' he at last picked up courage, sat down next to me, and whispered in my ear. 'Golubchek, don't be offended. . . . Of course, you will understand my position, and you won't find my request strange or rude.'

'Tell me quickly. No need to mince matters.'

'You see how things stand . . . how . . . Go away, golubchek!

You are interfering with *us*. . . . She will remain with me . . . .
Forgive me for sending you away, but . . . you will understand
my impatience!'

'All right!'

My friend was loathsome. If I had not been fastidious, perhaps I
would have crushed him like a beetle, when he, shivering as if with
fever, asked me to leave him alone with Urbenin's wife. He, the
debilitated anchorite, steeped through and through with spirits and
disease, wanted to take the poetic 'girl in red' who dreamed of a
dramatic death and had been nurtured by the forests and the angry
lake! Surely not, she must be miles above him!

I went up to her.

'I am going,' I said.

She nodded her head.

'Am I to go away? Yes?' I asked, trying to read the truth in her
lovely, blushing little face. 'Yes?'

With the very slightest movement of her long black eyelashes
she answered 'Yes.'

'You have considered well?'

She turned away from me, as one turns away from an annoying
wind. She did not want to speak. Why should she speak? It is
impossible to answer a difficult question briefly, and there was
neither time nor place for long speeches.

I took up my hat and left the room without taking leave.
Afterwards, Olga told me that immediately after my departure, as
soon as the sound of my steps became mingled with the noise of
the wind in the garden, the drunken Count was pressing her in his
embrace. And she, closing her eyes and stopping up her mouth and
nostrils, was scarcely able to keep her feet from a feeling of disgust.
There was even a moment when she had almost torn herself away
from his embraces and rushed into the lake. There were moments
when she tore her hair and wept. It is not easy to sell oneself.

When I left the house and went towards the stables, I had to pass
the bailiff's house. I looked in at the window. Pëtr Egorych was
seated at a table by the dim light of a smoking oil lamp that had
been turned up too high. I did not see his face. It was covered by
his hands. But the whole of his robust, awkward figure displayed
so much sorrow, anguish and despair that it was not necessary to

see the face to understand the condition of his soul. Two bottles stood before him; one was empty, the other only just begun. They were both vodka bottles. The poor devil was seeking peace not in himself, nor in other people, but in alcohol.

Five minutes later I was riding home. The darkness was terrible. The lake blustered wrathfully and seemed to be angry that I, such a sinner, who had just been the witness of a sinful deed, should dare to infringe its austere peace. I could not see the lake for the darkness. It seemed as if an unseen monster was roaring, that the very darkness which enveloped me was roaring too.

I pulled up Zorka, closed my eyes, and meditated to the roaring of the monster.

'What if I returned at once and destroyed them?'

Terrible anger raged in my soul. . . . All the little of goodness and honesty that remained in me after long years of a depraved life, all that corruption had left, all that I guarded and cherished, that I was proud of, was insulted, spat upon, splashed with filth!

I had known venal women before, I had bought them, studied them, but they had not had the innocent rosy cheeks and sincere blue eyes that I had seen on the May morning when I walked through the wood to the Tenevo fair. . . . I myself, corrupt to the marrow of my bones, had forgiven, had preached tolerance of everything vicious, and I was indulgent to weakness. . . . I was convinced that it was impossible to demand of dirt that it should not be dirt, and that one cannot blame those ducats which from the force of circumstances have fallen into the mire. But I had not known before that ducats could melt in the mire and be blended with it into a single mass. So gold too could dissolve!

A strong gust of wind blew off my hat and bore it into the surrounding darkness. In its flight my hat touched Zorka's head. She took fright, reared on her hind legs and galloped off along the familiar road.

When I reached home I threw myself on the bed. Polycarp suggested that I should undress, and he got sworn at and called a 'devil' for no earthly reason.

'Devil yourself!' Polycarp grumbled as he went away from my bed.

'What did you say? What did you say?' I shouted.

'None so deaf as those who will not hear!'

'Oh, ho! . . . . You dare to be impudent!' I thundered and poured out all my bile on my poor lackey. 'Get out! Let me see no more of you, scoundrel! Out with you!'

And without waiting for my man to leave the room, I fell on the bed and began to sob like a boy. My overstrained nerves could bear no more. Powerless wrath, wounded feelings, jealousy – all found vent in one way or another.

'The husband killed his wife!' squalled my parrot, raising his yellow feathers.

Under the influence of this cry the thought entered my head that Urbenin might really kill his wife.

Falling asleep, I dreamed of murders. My nightmare was suffocating and painful. . . . It appeared to me that my hands were stroking something cold, and I had only to open my eyes to see a corpse. I dreamed that Urbenin was standing at the head of my bed, looking at me with imploring eyes.

XIX

After the night that is described above a calm set in. I remained at home, only allowing myself to leave the house or ride about on business. Heaps of work had accumulated, so it was impossible for me to be idle. From morning till night I sat at my writing-table scribbling, or examining people who had fallen into my magisterial claws. I was no longer drawn to Karnéevka, the Count's estate.

I thought no more of Olga. That which falls from the load is lost; and she it was who had fallen from my load and was, as I thought, irrecoverably lost. I thought no more about her and did not want to think about her.

'Silly, vicious trash!' I said to myself whenever her memory arose in my mind in the midst of my strenuous labours.

Occasionally, however, when I lay down to sleep or when I awoke in the morning, I remembered various moments of our acquaintance, and the short connection I had had with Olga. I remembered the 'Stone Grave', the little house in the wood in which 'the girl in red' lived, the road to Tenevo, the meeting in the grotto . . . and my heart began to beat faster. . . . I experienced bitter heartache. . . . But it was not for long. The bright memories were soon obliterated under the weight of the gloomy ones. What poetry of the past could withstand the filth of the present? And now, when I had finished with Olga, I looked upon this 'poetry' quite differently. . . . Now I looked upon it as an optical illusion, a lie, hypocrisy . . . and it lost half its charm in my eyes.

The Count had become quite repugnant to me. I was glad not to see him, and I was always angry when his moustachioed face returned vaguely to my mind. Every day he sent me letters in which he implored me not to sulk but to come to see the no longer 'solitary hermit'. Had I listened to his letters, I would have been doing a displeasure to myself.

'It's finished!' I thought. 'Thank God! . . . . It bored me. . . .'

I decided to break off all connection with the Count, and this decision did not cost me the slightest struggle. Now I was not at all the same man that I had been three weeks before, when after the quarrel about Pshekhotsky I could scarcely bring myself to stay at home. There was no attraction now.

Staying always at home at last seemed unendurable, and I wrote to Doctor Pavel Ivanovich, asking him to come and have a chat. For some reason I received no reply to this letter, so I wrote another. But the second received the same answer as the first. Evidently dear 'Screw' was pretending to be angry. . . . The poor fellow, having received a refusal from Nadenka Kalinin, looked upon me as the cause of his misfortune. He had the right to be angry, and if he had never been angry before it was merely because he did not know how to.

'When did he have time to learn?' I thought, being perplexed at not receiving answers to my letters.

In the third week of obstinate seclusion in my own house the Count paid me a visit. Having scolded me for not riding over to see him nor sending him answers to his letters, he stretched himself out on the sofa and before he began to snore he spoke on his favourite theme – women.

'I understand,' he began languidly, screwing up his eyes and placing his hands under his head, 'that you are delicate and susceptible. You don't come to me from fear of breaking into our duet . . . interfering. . . . An unwelcome guest is worse than a Tartar, a guest during the honeymoon is worse than a horned devil. I understand you. But, my dear friend, you forget that you are a friend and not a guest, that you are loved, esteemed. By your presence you would only complete the harmony. . . . And what harmony, my dear brother! A harmony that I am unable to describe to you!'

The Count pulled his hands out from under his head and began to wave them about.

'I myself am unable to understand if I am living happily or not. The devil himself wouldn't be able to understand it. There are certainly moments when one would give half one's life for an encore, but on the other hand there are days when one paces

the rooms from corner to corner, as if beside oneself and ready
to cry. . . .'

'For what reason?'

'Brother, I can't understand that Olga. She's like an ague not a
woman. With the ague one has either fever or shivering fits. That's
how she is; five changes every day. She is either gay or so lifeless
that she is choking back tears and praying. . . . Sometimes she
loves me, sometimes she doesn't. There are moments when she
caresses me as no woman has ever caressed me in my whole life.
But sometimes it is like this: You awake unexpectedly, you open
your eyes, and you see a face turned on you . . . such a terrible,
such a savage face . . . a face that is all distorted with malignancy
and aversion. . . . When one sees such a thing all the enchantment
vanishes. . . . And she often looks at me in that way. . . .'

'With aversion?'

'Well, yes! . . . I can't understand it. . . . She swears that she
came to me only for love, and still hardly a night passes that I do
not see that face. How is it to be explained? I begin to think,
though of course I don't want to believe it, that she can't bear me
and has given herself to me for those rags which I buy for her now.
She's terribly fond of rags! She's capable of standing before the
mirror from morning to evening in a new frock; she is capable of
crying for days and nights about a spoilt flounce. . . . She's
terribly vain! What chiefly pleases her in me is that I'm a Count.
She would never have loved me had I not been a Count. Never a
dinner or supper passes that she does not reproach me with tears in
her eyes, for not surrounding myself with aristocratic society.
You see, she would like to reign in that society. . . . A strange
girl!'

The Count fixed his dim eyes on the ceiling and became pensive.
I noticed, to my great astonishment, that this time, as an exception, he was sober. This struck and even touched me.

'You are quite normal today,' I said. 'You are not drunk, and
you don't ask for vodka. What's the meaning of this transforma-
tion?'

'Yes, so it is! I had no time to drink, I've been thinking. . . . I
must tell you, Serezha, I'm seriously in love; it's no joke. I am
terribly fond of her. It's quite natural, too. . . . She's a rare

woman, not of the ordinary sort, to say nothing of her appearance. Not much intellect, to be sure, but what feeling, elegance, freshness! She can't be compared with my former Amalias, Angelicas, and Grushas, whose love I have enjoyed till now. She's something from another world, a world I do not know.'

'Philosophizing!' I laughed.

'I'm captivated, I've almost fallen in love! But now I see the square of nought is nought. Her behaviour – she wore a mask that deceived me. The pink cheeks of innocence proved to be rouge, the kiss of love – the request to buy a new frock. . . . I took her into my house like a wife, and she behaves like a mistress who is paid in cash. But it's enough now. I am keeping a check on my soul's aspirations, and beginning to see Olga as a mistress. . . . Enough!'

'Well, why not? How about the husband?'

'The husband? Hm! . . . What do you think he's about?'

'I think it is impossible to imagine a more unhappy man.'

'You think that? Quite uselessly. . . . He's such a scoundrel, such a rascal, that I am not at all sorry for him. . . . A rascal can never be unhappy, he'll always find a way out.'

'Why do you abuse him in that way?'

'Because he's a rogue. You know that I esteemed him, that I trusted him as a friend . . . I and you too – in general everybody considered him an honest, respectable man who was incapable of cheating. Meanwhile he has been robbing, plundering me! Taking advantage of his position of bailiff, he has dealt with my property as he liked. The only things he didn't take were those that couldn't be moved from their places.'

I, who knew Urbenin to be a man in the highest degree honest and disinterested, jumped up as if I had been stung when I heard these words spoken by the Count, and went up to him.

'Have you caught him in the act of stealing?' I asked.

'No, but I know of his thievish tricks from trustworthy sources.'

'May I ask from what sources?'

'You needn't be uneasy. I would not accuse a man without cause. Olga has told me all about him. Even before she became his wife she saw with her own eyes what loads of slaughtered fowls and geese he sent to town. She saw how my geese and fowls were sent as presents to a certain benefactor where his son, the school-boy, lodged. More than that, she saw flour, millet and lard being dispatched there. Admitted that all these are trifles, but did these trifles belong to him? Here we have not a question of value but of principle. Principles were trespassed against. There's more, sir! She saw in his cupboard a whole cache of money. When she asked him whose money it was and where he had got it, he begged her not to mention to anybody that he had money. My dear fellow, you know he's as poor as a church mouse! His salary is scarcely sufficient for his board. Can you explain to me where this money came from?'

'And you, stupid fool, believe this little vermin?' I cried, stirred to the depths of my soul. 'She is not satisfied with having run away from him and disgraced him in the eyes of the whole district. She must now betray him! What an amount of meanness is contained in that small and fragile body! Fowls, geese, millet. . . . Master, master! You, with your political economy and your agricultural stupidity, are offended that he should have sent a present at holiday-time of a slaughtered bird which the foxes or polecats would have eaten, if it hadn't been killed and given away, but have you once checked the huge accounts that Urbenin has handed in? Have you ever counted up the thousands and the tens of thousands? No? Then what is the use of talking to you? You are stupid and a beast. You would be glad to incriminate the husband of your mistress, but you don't know how!'

'My connection with Olga has nothing to do with the matter. Whether or not he's her husband is all one, but since he has robbed me, I must be plain, and call him a thief. But let us leave this roguery alone. Tell me, is it honest or dishonest to receive a salary and for whole days to lie about dead drunk? He is drunk every day. There wasn't a single day that I did not see him reeling about! Low and disgusting! Decent people don't act in that way.'

'It's just because he's decent that he gets drunk,' I said.

'You have a kind of passion for taking the part of such gentlemen. But I have decided to be unmerciful. I paid him off today and told him to clear out and make room for another. My patience is exhausted!'

I considered it unnecessary to try to convince the Count that he was unjust, impractical and stupid. It was not for me to defend Urbenin against the Count.

Five days later I heard that Urbenin with his schoolboy son and his little daughter had gone to live in the town. I was told that he drove to town drunk, half-dead, and that he had twice fallen out of the cart. The schoolboy and Sasha had cried all the way.

XX

Shortly after Urbenin had left, I was obliged to go to the Count's estate, quite against my will. One of the Count's stables had been broken into at night and several valuable saddles had been carried off by the thieves. The examining magistrate, that is I, had been informed and *nolens-volens*, I was obliged to go there.

I found the Count drunk and angry. He was wandering about the rooms seeking a refuge from his melancholy but could not find one.

'I am worried by that Olga!' he said waving his hand. 'She got angry with me this morning and she left the house threatening to drown herself! And, as you see, there are no signs of her yet. I know she won't drown herself. Still, it is very unpleasant of her. Yesterday, all day long, she was rubbing her eyes and breaking crockery; the day before she over-ate herself with chocolate. The devil only knows what such natures are!'

I comforted the Count as well as I could and sat down to dinner with him.

'No, it's time to give up such childishness,' he kept mumbling during dinner. 'It's high time, for it is all stupid and ridiculous. Besides, I must also confess she is beginning to bore me with her sudden changes and tantrums. I want something quiet, orderly, modest, you know – something like Nadenka Kalinin . . . a splendid girl!'

After dinner when I was walking in the garden I met the 'drowned girl'. When she saw me she became very red and (strange woman) she began to laugh with joy. The shame on her face was mingled with pleasure, sorrow with happiness. For a moment she looked at me askance, then she rushed towards me and hung on my neck without saying a word.

'I love you!' she whispered, clinging to my neck. 'I have been so sad without you. I should have died if you had not come.'

I embraced her and silently led her to one of the summer-houses.

Ten minutes later when parting from her, I took out of my pocket a twenty-five-rouble note and handed it to her. She opened her eyes wide.

'What is that for?'

'I am paying you for today's love.'

Olga did not understand and continued to look at me with astonishment.

'You see, there are women who make love for money,' I explained. 'They are venal. They must be paid for with money. Take it! If you take money from others, why don't you want to take anything from me? I wish for no favours!'

Olga did not understand my cynicism in insulting her in this way. She did not know life as yet, and she did not understand the meaning of 'venal women'.

XXI

It was a fine August day.

The sun warmed as in summer, and the blue sky fondly enticed you to wander far afield, but the air already bore presages of autumn. In the green foliage of the pensive forest the worn-out leaves were already assuming golden tints and the darkening fields looked melancholy and sad.

A dull presentiment of inevitable autumn weighed heavily on us all. It was not difficult to foresee the nearness of a catastrophe. The roll of thunder and the rain must soon come to refresh the sultry atmosphere. It is sultry before a thunderstorm when dark leaden clouds approach in the sky, and moral sultriness was oppressing us all. It was apparent in everything – in our movements, in our smiles, in our speech.

I was driving in a light wagonette. The daughter of the Justice of the Peace, Nadenka, was sitting beside me. She was white as snow, her chin and lips trembled as they do before tears, her deep eyes were full of sorrow, while all the time she laughed and tried to appear very gay.

In front and behind us a number of vehicles of all sorts, of all ages and all sizes were moving in the same direction. Ladies and men on horseback were riding on either side. Count Karnéev, clad in a green shooting costume that looked more like a buffoon's than a sportsman's, bending slightly forward and to one side, galloped about relentlessly on his black horse. Looking at his bent body and at the expression of pain that constantly appeared on his lean face, one could have thought that he was riding for the first time. A new double-barrelled gun was slung across his back, and at his side he had a game-bag in which a wounded woodcock tossed about.

Olga Urbenin was the ornament of the cavalcade. Seated on a black horse, which the Count had given her, dressed in a black riding-habit, with a white feather in her hat, she no longer resembled that 'girl in red' who had met us in the wood only a few months before. Now there was something majestic, something of the *grande dame* in her figure. Each flourish of her whip, each smile was calculated to look aristocratic and majestic. In her movements, in her smiles there was something provocative, something incendiary. She held her head high in a foppishly arrogant manner, and from the height of her mount poured contempt on the whole company, as if in disdain of the loud remarks that were sent after her by our virtuous ladies. Coquetting with her impudence and her position 'at the Count's', she seemed to defy everybody, just as if she did not know that the Count was already tired of her, and was only awaiting the moment when he could disentangle himself from her.

'The Count wants to send me away!' she said to me with a loud laugh when the cavalcade rode out of the yard. It was clear she knew her position and understood it.

But why that loud laugh? I looked at her and was perplexed. Where could this dweller in the forests have found so much arrogance? When had she found time to sit her horse with so much grace, to move her nostrils proudly, and to show off with such commanding gestures?

'A depraved woman is like a swine,' Doctor Pavel Ivanovich said to me. 'If you set her down to table she puts her legs on it.'

But his explanation was too simple. Nobody could be more infatuated with Olga than I was, and I was the first to be ready to throw stones at her; still, the uneasy voice of truth whispered to me that this was not arrogance nor the swagger of a prosperous and satisfied woman, but the despairing presentiment of the near and inevitable catastrophe.

We were returning from the shoot to which we had gone early in the morning. The sport had been bad. Near the marshes, on which we had set great hopes, we met a party of sportsmen, who told us the game was wild. Three woodcocks and one duckling was all the game we were able to send to the other world as the net result of ten guns. At last one of the lady riders had an attack of toothache and we were obliged to hurry back. We returned along a good road that passed through the fields on which the sheaves of newly reaped rye were looking yellow against the background of the dark, gloomy forests. . . . Near the horizon the church and houses of the Count's estate gleamed white. To their right the mirror-like surface of the lake stretched out wide, and to the left the 'Stone Grave' rose darkly. . . .

'What a terrible woman!' Nadenka whispered to me every time Olga came up to our wagonette. 'What a terrible woman! She's as bad as she's pretty! . . . How long ago is it since you were best man at her wedding? She has not had time to wear out her wedding shoes, and she is already wearing another man's silk and is flaunting in another man's diamonds. If she has such instincts it would have been more tactful had she waited a year or two. . . .'

'She's in a hurry to live! She has no time to wait!' I sighed.

'Do you know what has become of her husband?'

'I hear he is drinking. . . .'

'Yes. . . . The day before yesterday father was in town and saw him driving in a droshky. His head was hanging to one side, he was without a hat, and his face was dirty. . . . He's a lost man! He's terribly poor, I hear; they have nothing to eat, the flat is not paid for. Poor little Sasha is for days without food. Father described all this to the Count. . . . You know the Count! He is honest, kind, but he is not fond of thinking about anything, or reasoning. "I'll send him a hundred roubles," he said. And he did it at once. I don't think he could have insulted Urbenin more than by sending this money. . . . He'll feel insulted by the Count's gift and will drink all the more.'

'Yes, the Count is stupid,' I said. 'He might have sent him the money through me, and in my name.'

'He had no right to send him money! Have I the right to feed you if I am strangling you, and you hate me?'

'That is quite true. . . .'

We were silent and pensive. . . . The thought of Urbenin's fate was always very painful to me; now when the woman who had ruined him was parading herself before me, this thought aroused in me a whole train of sad reflections. . . . What would become of him and of his children? In what way would she end? In what moral puddle would this pitiful, puny Count end his days?

The woman seated next to me was the only one who was respectable and worthy of esteem. There were only two people in our district whom I was capable of liking and respecting, and who alone had the right of turning from me because they stood higher than I did. . . . These were Nadezhda Kalinin and Doctor Pavel Ivanovich. . . . What awaited them?

'Nadezhda Nikolaevna,' I said to her, 'quite without wishing it, I have caused you no little sorrow, and less than anybody else have I the right to expect your confidence. But I swear to you nobody will understand you as well as I can. Your sorrow is my sorrow, your joy is my joy. If I ask you a question, don't suspect it is from idle curiosity. Tell me, my dear, why do you allow this pigmy Count to approach you? What prevents you from sending him away and not listening to his abominable amiabilities? His courting is no honour to a respectable woman! Why do you give these scandalmongers the right to couple your name with his?'

Nadenka looked at me with her bright eyes, and evidently reading sincerity in my face, she smiled gaily.

'What do they say?' she asked.

'They say your papa and you are trying to catch the Count, and that in the end you'll find the Count is only playing with you.'

'They speak so because they don't know the Count!' Nadenka flared up. 'The shameless slanderers! They are used to seeing only the bad side of people. . . . The good is inaccessible to their understanding.'

'And have you found the good in him?'

'Yes, I have found it! You are the first who ought to know. I would not have let him approach me if I had not been certain of his honourable intentions!'

'So your affairs have already reached the stage of "honourable intentions",' I said with astonishment. 'So soon! . . . And on what are they based – these honourable intentions?'

'Do you wish to know?' she asked, and her eyes sparkled. 'Those scandalmongers do not lie: I wish to marry him! Don't look so surprised, and don't laugh! You will say that to get married without love is dishonest and so on. It has already been said a thousand times, but . . . what am I to do? To feel that one is a useless bit of furniture in this world is very hard. . . . It's hard to live without an object. . . . When this man, whom you dislike so much, will have made me his wife, I shall have an object in life. . . . I will improve him, I will teach him to leave off drinking,

I will teach him to work. . . . Look at him! He does not look like a man now, and I will make a man of him.'

'Et cetera, et cetera,' I said. 'You will take care of his enormous fortune, you will do acts of charity. . . . The whole of the district will bless you, and will look upon you as a good angel sent down to comfort the miserable. . . . You will be the mother and the educator of his children. . . . Yes, a great work indeed! You are a clever girl, but you reason like a schoolgirl!'

'My idea may be worthless, it may be ludicrous and naive, but I live by it. . . . Under its influence I have become well and gay. . . . Do not disenchant me! Let me disenchant myself, but not now, at some other time . . . afterwards, in the distant future. . . . Let us change the subject!'

'Just one more indiscreet question! Do you expect him to propose?'

'Yes. . . . To judge by the note I received from him today, my fate will be decided this evening . . . today. . . . He writes that he has something very important to say to me. . . . The happiness of the whole of his life depends upon my answer.'

'Thank you for your frankness,' I said.

The meaning of the note that Nadia had received was quite clear to me. A base proposal awaited the poor girl. I decided to save her from that ordeal.

'We have already arrived at our wood,' the Count said, coming up to our wagonette. 'Nadezhda Nikolaevna, would you not wish to make a halt here?'

And without waiting for an answer he clapped his hands and ordered in a loud, shaky voice:

'Ha-a-lt!'

We settled ourselves down on the outskirts of the wood. The sun had sunk behind the trees, illuminating with purple and gold only the summits of the very highest alders and playing on the golden cross of the Count's church that could be seen in the distance. Flocks of frightened orioles and sparrow hawks soared over our heads. One of the men fired into them, alarming this feathered kingdom still more, and setting up an incessant concert of twitterings. This sort of concert has its charms in the spring and summer, but when you feel the approach of the cold autumn in the air, it only irritates the nerves and reminds one of their near migration.

The coolness of evening spread from the dense forest. The ladies' noses became blue and the Count began rubbing his hands against the chill. Nothing at that moment could have been more appropriate than the odour of charcoal in the samovars and the clatter of the tea service. One-eyed Kuz'ma, puffing and panting and stumbling about in the long grass, dragged forward a case of cognac. We began to warm ourselves.

A long outing in the fresh cool air acts on the appetite better than any appetising drops, and after it the balyk*, the caviar, the roast partridge and the other viands were as caressing to the sight as roses are on an early spring morning.

'You are wise today,' I said to the Count as I helped myself to a slice of balyk. 'Wise as you have never been before. It would have been difficult to arrange things better. . . .'

'We have arranged it together, the Count and I,' Kalinin said with a giggle as he winked towards the coachmen, who were getting the hampers and baskets of provisions, wines and crockery out of the vehicles. 'The little picnic will be a great success. . . . Towards the end there will be champagne!'

On this occasion the face of the Justice of the Peace shone with satisfaction as it had never shone before. Did he not expect that in the evening his Nadenka would have a proposal made to her? Did he not have the champagne prepared in order to drink the health of the young couple? I looked attentively at his face and, as usual, I could read nothing there but careless satisfaction, satiety, and the stupid self-importance that was suffused over the whole of his portly figure.

We fell upon the *hors d'œuvres* gaily. Only two of the guests looked with indifference on the luxurious viands that were spread out on carpets before us: these two were Olga and Nadezhda Kalinin. The first was standing to one side leaning against the back of a wagonette, motionless and silently gazing at the game-bag that the Count had thrown on the ground. In the game-bag a wounded woodcock was moving about. Olga watched the movements

* Salted and smoked sturgeon.

of the unfortunate bird and seemed to be expecting its death.

Nadia was sitting next to me and looked with indifference on the boisterous, cheerful company.

'When will all this be over?' her tired eyes said.

I offered her a sandwich with caviar. She thanked me and put it to one side. She evidently did not wish to eat.

'Olga Nikolaevna, why don't you sit down?' the Count called to Olga.

Olga did not answer but continued to stare as immovable as a statue, looking at the bird.

'What heartless people there are,' I said, going up to Olga. 'Is it possible that you, a woman, are capable of watching with indifference the suffering of this woodcock? Instead of looking at his contortions, it would be better if you ordered it to be dispatched.'

'Others suffer; let him suffer too,' Olga answered, frowning, without looking at me.

'Who else is suffering?'

'Leave me in peace!' she said hoarsely. 'I am not disposed to speak to you today . . . nor with your friend, that fool the Count! Go away from me!'

She glanced at me with eyes that were full of wrath and tears. Her face was pale, her lips trembled.

'What a change!' I said as I lifted up the game-bag and wrung the woodcock's neck. 'What a tone! I am astounded! Quite astounded!'

'Leave me in peace, I tell you! I'm not in the humour for jokes!'

'What's the matter with you, my enchantress?'

Olga looked at me from head to foot and turned her back on me.

'Only depraved and venal women are spoken to in that tone,' she continued. 'You consider me such a one . . . well, then, go to those saints! . . . I am worse and baser than anybody here. . . . When you were driving with that virtuous Nadenka you were afraid to look at me. . . . Well then, go to her! What are you waiting for? Go!'

'Yes, you are worse and baser than anybody else here,' I said, feeling that I was gradually being mastered by rage. 'Yes, you are depraved and venal.'

'Yes, I remember how you offered me money, damn you. . . . Then I did not know its meaning; now I understand. . . .'

Rage mastered me completely. And this rage was as strong as the love had been that at one time was beginning to be born in me for 'the girl in red'. . . . And who could – what stone could have remained indifferent? I saw before me beauty that had been cast by merciless fate into the mire. No mercy was shown to either youth, beauty or grace. . . . Now, when this woman appeared to me more beautiful than ever, I felt what a loss nature had sustained in her person, and my soul was filled with painful anger at the injustice of fate and the order of things. . . .

In moments of anger I am unable to control myself. I do not know what more Olga would have had to hear from me if she had not turned her back upon me and gone away. She walked slowly towards the trees and soon disappeared behind them. . . . It appeared to me that she was crying. . . .

'Ladies and gentlemen,' I heard Kalinin making a speech. 'On this day when we all have met for . . . for . . . in order to unite . . . we are assembled here, we are all acquainted with each other, we are all enjoying ourselves and this long desired union we owe to nobody else but to our luminary, to the star of our province. . . . Count, don't get confused. . . . The ladies will understand of whom I am speaking. . . . He, he, he! Well, ladies and gentlemen, let us continue. As we owe all this to our enlightened, to our youthful . . . youthful . . . Count Karnéev, I propose that we drink this glass to . . . But who is driving this way? Who is it?'

A calash was driving from the direction of the Count's house towards the clearing where we were seated.

'Who can it be?' the Count said in astonishment, turning his field glass on the calash. 'Hm! . . . strange! . . . It must be someone passing by. . . . Oh, no! I see Kaetan Kazimirovich's face. . . . And who is that with him?'

Suddenly the Count sprang up as if he had been stung. His face became deadly pale, and the field glass fell from his hand. His eyes strayed around like the eyes of a trapped mouse, and they rested sometimes on me, sometimes on Nadia, as if looking for aid. Not everybody noticed his confusion as the attention of most was directed on the approaching calash.

'Serezha, come here for a minute!' he whispered to me, seizing

hold of my arm and leading me to one side. 'Golubchek, I implore
you as a friend, as the best of men! . . . No questions, no
interrogating glances, no astonishment! I will tell you all afterwards! I swear that not an iota will remain a secret from you! . . . It
is such a misfortune in my life, such a misfortune, that I am unable
to find words to express it! You will know all, but no questions
now! Help me!'

Meanwhile the calash came nearer and nearer. . . . At last it
stopped, and the Count's stupid secret became the property of the
whole district. Pshekhotsky, clad in a new unbleached silk suit,
panting and smiling, crawled out of the calash. After him a young
lady of about three-and-twenty stepped out coolly. She was a tall,
graceful, fair woman with regular but not sympathetic features,
and with dark blue eyes. I only remember those dark blue
expressionless eyes, a powdered nose, a heavy, luxurious dress
and several massive bracelets on each arm. . . . I remember
that the scent of the evening dampness and the split cognac had to
give way before the penetrating odour of some sort of
perfume.

'What a big party!' the stranger said in broken Russian. 'It must
be very gay! How do you do, Alexis?'

She went up to Alexis and offered him her cheek, which the
Count smacked hastily and glanced uneasily at his guests.

'My wife, let me introduce her!' he mumbled. 'And these,
Zosia, are my good friends. . . . Hm, hm! . . . I've a cough!'

'And I have only just arrived! Kaetan advised me to rest! But I
said: "Why should I rest since I slept the whole way here! I would
sooner go to the shooting party!" I dressed and here I am. . . .
Kaetan, where are my cigarettes?'

Pshekhotsky sprang forward and handed the fair lady her golden
cigarette-case.

'And this is my wife's brother . . .' the Count continued to
mumble, pointing at Pshekhotsky. 'Why don't you help me?' and
he gave me a poke in the ribs. 'Help me out, for God's sake!'

I have been told that Kalinin fainted, and that Nadia, who
wished to help him, could not rise from her seat. I have been told
many got into their vehicles and drove away. All this I did not see.
I remember that I went into the wood, and searching for a

footpath, without looking in front, I went where my feet led me.★

When I came out of the wood, bits of clay were hanging to my feet, and I was covered with dirt. I had probably been obliged to jump over brooks, but I could not remember this fact. It seemed to me as though I had been severely beaten with sticks; I felt so weary and exhausted. I ought to have gone to the Count's stable yard, mounted my Zorka and ridden away. But I did not do so, and went home on foot. I could not bring myself to see the Count or his accursed estate. . . .†

My road led along the banks of the lake. That watery monster was already beginning to roar out its evening song. High waves with white crests covered the whole of its vast extent. In the air there was noise and rumbling. A cold, damp wind penetrated to my very bones. To the left lay the angry lake; from the right came the monotonous noise of the austere forest. I felt myself alone with nature as if I had been confronted with it. It appeared as if the whole of its wrath, the whole of these noises and roars, was directed only at my head. In other circumstances I might have felt timidity, but now I scarcely noticed the giants that surrounded me. What was the wrath of nature compared with the storm that was raging within me?'‡

★ At this point in Kamyshev's manuscript a hundred and forty lines have been effaced. – A. Ch.

† At this point of the manuscript, a pretty girl's face, with an expression of horror on it, is drawn in pen and ink. All that is written below it has been carefully blotted out. The upper half of the next page is also scratched out and only one word: 'temple', can be deciphered through the dense ink blots. – A. Ch.

‡ Here again there are erasures. – A. Ch.

XXII

When I reached home I fell upon my bed without undressing. 'He has no shame, again he's gone swimming with all his clothes on!' grumbled Polycarp as he pulled off my wet and dirty garments. 'Again I have to suffer for it! Again we have the noble, the educated, behaving worse than any chimney-sweep. . . . I don't know what they taught you in the 'versity!'

I, who could not bear the human voice or man's face, wanted to shout at Polycarp to leave me in peace, but the words died on my lips. My tongue was as enfeebled and powerless as the rest of my body. Though it was painful for me, I was obliged to let Polycarp pull off all my clothes, even to my wet underlinen.

'He might turn round at least,' my servant grumbled as he rolled me over from side to side like a doll. 'Tomorrow I'll give notice! Never again . . . for no amount of money! I, old fool, have had enough of this! May the devil take me if I remain any longer!'

The fresh warm linen did not warm or calm me. I trembled so much with rage and fear that my very teeth chattered. My fear was inexplicable. I was not frightened by apparitions or by spectres risen from the grave, not even by the portrait of Pospelov, my predecessor, which was hanging just above my head. He never took his lifeless eyes off my face, and seemed to wink at me. But I was quite unaffected when I looked at him. My future was not brilliant, but all the same I could say with great probability that there was nothing that threatened me, that there were no black clouds near. I was not expecting to die yet; illness held no terrors for me, and I took no heed of personal misfortunes. . . . What did I fear, then, and why did my teeth chatter?

I could not even understand my wrath. . . . .

The Count's 'secret' could not have enraged me so greatly. I had nothing to do with the Count, nor with the marriage, which he had concealed from me.

It only remains to explain the condition of my soul at that time by fatigue and nervous derangement. That is the only explanation I can find.

When Polycarp left the room I pulled the blankets up to my head and wanted to sleep. It was dark and quiet. The parrot moved restlessly about its cage, and the regular ticking of the hanging clock in Polycarp's room could be heard through the wall. Peace and quiet reigned everywhere else. Physical and moral exhaustion overpowered me, and I began to doze. . . . I felt a certain weight gradually fall from me, and hateful images melt into mist. . . . I remember I even began to dream. I dreamed that on a bright winter morning I was walking along the Nevsky in Petersburg, and, having nothing to do, looked into the shop windows. My heart was light and gay. . . . I had no reason to hurry. I had nothing to do, I was absolutely free. The consciousness that I was far from my village, far from the Count's estate and from the cold and sullen lake, made me feel all the more peaceful and gay. I stopped before one of the largest windows and began to examine ladies' hats. The hats were familiar to me. . . . I had seen Olga in one of them, Nadia in another: a third I had seen on the day of the shooting party on the fair-haired head of that Zosia, who had arrived so unexpectedly. . . . Familiar faces smiled at me under the hats. . . . When I wanted to say something to them they all three blended together into one large red face. This face moved its eyes angrily and stuck out its tongue. . . . Somebody pressed my neck from behind. . . .

'The husband killed his wife!' the red face shouted.

I shuddered, cried out, and jumped out of my bed as if I had been stung. I had terrible palpitations of the heart, a cold sweat came out on my brow.

'The husband killed his wife!' the parrot repeated again. 'Give me some sugar! How stupid you are! Fool!'

'It was only the parrot,' I said to calm myself as I got into bed again. 'Thank God!'

I heard a monotonous murmur. . . . It was the rain pattering on the roof. . . . The clouds I had seen when walking on the banks of the lake had now covered the whole sky. There were slight flashes of lightning that lighted up the portrait of the late Pospelov. . . . The thunder rumbled just over my bed. . . .

'The last thunderstorm of this summer,' I thought.

I remembered one of the first storms. . . . Just the same sort of thunder had rumbled overhead in the forest the first time I was in the forester's house. . . . The 'girl in red' and I were standing at the window then, looking out at the pine trees that were illuminated by the lightning. Dread shone in the eyes of that beautiful creature. She told me her mother had been killed by lightning, and that she herself was thirsting for a dramatic death. . . . She wanted to be dressed like the richest lady of the district. She knew that luxurious dress suited her beauty. And, proudly conscious of her splendour, she wanted to mount to the top of the 'Stone Grave' and there meet a sensational end.

Her wish had . . . though not on the sto . . .★

Losing all hope of falling asleep, I rose and sat down on the bed. The quiet murmur of the rain gradually changed into the angry roar I was so fond of hearing when my soul was free from dread and wrath. . . . Now this roar appeared to me to be ominous. One clap of thunder succeeded the other without intermission.

'The husband killed his wife!' croaked the parrot.

Those were its last words. . . . Closing my eyes in miserable fear, I groped my way in the dark to the cage and hurled it into a corner. . . .

'May the devil take you!' I cried when I heard the clatter of the falling cage and the squeak of the parrot.

Poor, noble bird! That flight into the corner cost it dear. The next day the cage contained only a cold corpse. Why did I kill it? If its favourite phrase about a husband who killed his wife remin . . .†

My predecessor's mother when she gave up the lodging to me made me pay for the whole of the furniture, not excepting the photographs of people I did not know. But she did not take a kopeck from me for the expensive parrot. On the eve of her departure for Finland she passed the whole night taking leave of her noble bird. I remember the sobs and the lamentations that

---

★ Here nearly a whole page is carelessly deleted. Only a few words survive, which give no clue to the meaning of what is obliterated. – A. Ch.

† It is evident Kamyshev made these deletions not at the time of writing but afterwards. At the end of the novel I will draw special attention to these passages. – A. Ch.

accompanied this leave-taking. I remember the tears she shed when asking me to take care of her friend until her return. I gave her my word of honour that her parrot would not regret having made my acquaintance. And I had not kept that word! I had killed the bird. I can imagine what the old woman would say if she knew of the fate of her squawking pet!

XXIII

Somebody tapped gently at my window. The little house in which I lived stood on the high road, and was one of the first houses in the village, and I often heard a tap at my window, especially in bad weather when a wayfarer sought a night's lodging. This time it was no wayfarer who knocked at my window. I went up to the window and waited there for a flash of lightning, when I saw the dark silhouette of a tall thin man. He was standing before the window and seemed to be shivering with cold. I opened the window.

'Who is there? What do you want?' I asked.

'Sergey Petrovich, it's me!' I heard a plaintive voice, such as people have who are starved with cold and fright. 'It's me! I've come to you, dear friend!'

To my great astonishment, I recognized in the plaintive voice of the dark silhouette the voice of my friend Doctor Pavel Ivanovich. This visit from 'Screw', who led a regular life and went to bed before twelve, was quite incomprehensible. What could have caused him to change his rules and appear at my house at two o'clock in the night, and in such weather too?

'What do you want?' I asked, at the same time in the bottom of my heart sending this unexpected guest to the devil.

'Forgive me, golubchek. . . . I wanted to knock at the door, but your Polycarp is sure to be sleeping like a dead man now, so I decided to tap at the window.'

'But what do you want?'

Pavel Ivanovich came close up to my window and mumbled something incomprehensible. He was trembling, and looked like a drunken man.

'I am listening!' I said, losing my patience.

'You . . . you are angry, I see; but . . . if you only knew all that has happened you would cease to be angry at your sleep being disturbed by visitors at an unseemly hour. It's no time for sleep now. Oh, my God, my God! I have lived in the world for thirty years, and today is the first time I've ever been so terribly unhappy! I am unhappy, Sergey Petrovich!'

'Ach! but what has happened? And what have I to do with it? I myself can scarcely stand on my legs. . . . I can't be bothered about others!'

'Sergey Petrovich!' Screw said in a plaintive voice, stretching out towards my head his hand wet with rain. 'Honest man! My friend!'

And then I heard a man crying. The doctor wept.

'Pavel Ivanovich, go home!' I said after a short silence. 'I can't talk with you now. . . . I am afraid of my own mood, and of yours. We won't understand each other. . . .'

'My dear friend!' the doctor said in an imploring voice. 'Marry her!'

'You've gone mad!' I said, and banged the window to. . . .

First the parrot, then the doctor suffered from my mood. I did not ask him to come in, and I slammed the window in his face. Two rude and indecorous sallies for which I would have challenged anybody, even a woman, to a duel.★ But meek and good-natured 'Screw' had no ideas about duels. He did not know what it is to be angry.

About two minutes later there was a flash of lightning, and glancing out of the window I saw the bent figure of my guest. His pose this time was one of supplication, of expectancy, the pose of a beggar watching for alms. He was probably waiting for me to pardon him, and to allow him to say what he had to communicate.

Fortunately my conscience was moved; I was sorry for myself, sorry that nature had implanted in me so much violence and meanness. My base soul as well as my healthy body were as hard as flint.†

★ The last sentence is written above some erased lines in which, however, one can decipher: 'would have torn his head from his shoulders and broken all the windows'. – A. Ch.

† Here follows a pretentious, pseudo-psychological explanation of the spiritual endurance of the author. The sight of human affliction, blood, post-mortem examinations, etc., etc., he maintains, produce no effect on him. The whole of this passage bears the imprint of boastful *naïveté* and insincerity. It astonishes by its coarseness, and I have deleted it. As a characterization of Kamyshev it has no importance. – A. Ch.

I went to the window and opened it.

'Come into the room!' I said.

'Never! . . . Every minute is precious! Poor Nadia has poisoned herself, and the doctor cannot leave her side. . . . With difficulty we saved the poor thing. . . . Such a misfortune! And you don't want to hear it and slam the window to!'

'Still she is alive?'

' "Still"! . . . My good friend, that is not the way to speak about misfortunes! Who could have supposed that such a clever, honest nature would want to depart this life on account of such a creature as that Count? No, my friend, it is a misfortune for men that women cannot be perfect! However clever a woman may be, with whatever perfections she may be endowed, she has still something contrary about her that prevents her and other people from living easily. . . . For instance, let us take Nadia. . . . Why did she do it? Self-love, nothing but self-love! Unhealthy self-love! In order to wound you she conceived the idea of marrying this Count. . . . She neither wanted his money nor his title . . . she only wanted to satisfy her monstrous self-love. . . . Suddenly a failure! You know that *his* wife has arrived. . . . It appears that this debauchee is married. . . . And people say that women are more long-suffering, that they know how to endure things better than men! Where is there endurance here, when such a miserable cause makes them snatch up sulphur matches? This is not endurance, it is vanity!'

'You will catch cold. . . .'

'What I have just seen is worse than any cold. . . . Those eyes, that pallor. . . . Oh! To unsuccessful love, to the unsuccessful attempt to humiliate you is now added unsuccessful suicide. . . . It is difficult to imagine greater misfortunes! . . . My dear fellow, if you have but a drop of compassion, if . . . if you would see her . . . Well, why should you not go to her? You love her! Even if you do not love her, why should you not give up a little of your time to her? Human life is precious, and for it one can give . . . all! Save her life!'

Somebody knocked loudly at my door. I shuddered. . . . My heart bled. . . . I do not believe in presentiments, but this time my alarm was not without cause. . . . Somebody was knocking at my door from without. . . .

'Who is there?' I cried out of the window.

'A message, your Honour!'

'What do you want?'

'A letter from the Count, your Honour! There has been a murder!'

A dark figure muffled up in a sheepskin coat came to the window and, swearing at the weather, handed me a letter. . . . I hurried away from the window, lit a candle, and read the following:

> For God's sake forget everything in the world and come at once! Olga has been murdered. I have lost my head and am going mad. –
>
> Yours, A. K.

Olga murdered! My head grew dizzy, and it was black before my eyes from this short phrase. . . . I sat down on the bed and my hands fell at my sides. I was unable to reason!

'Is that you, Pavel Ivanovich?' I heard the voice of the muzhik who had been sent to me ask. 'I was just going to drive on to you. . . . I have a letter for you, too.'

Five minutes later 'Screw' and I were driving in a closed carriage towards the Count's estate. The rain rattled on the roof of the carriage, and throughout our journey the path was lit by blinding flashes of lightning.

XXIV

We heard the roar of the lake. . . .

The last act of the drama was just beginning, and two of the actors were driving to see a harrowing sight.

'Well, and what do you think awaits us?' I asked dear Pavel Ivanovich.

'I can't imagine. . . . I don't know. . . .'

'I also don't know. . . .'

'Hamlet once regretted that the Lord of heaven and earth had forbidden the sin of suicide; in like manner I regret that fate has made me a doctor. . . . I regret it deeply!'

'I fear that, in my turn, I must regret that I am an examining magistrate,' I said. 'If the Count has not made a mistake and confounded murder with suicide, and if Olga has really been murdered, my poor nerves will have much to suffer!'

'You could always refuse the case!'

I looked inquiringly at Pavel Ivanovich, but, of course, owing to the darkness, I could see nothing. . . . How did he know that I could refuse the case? I was Olga's lover, but who knew it, with the exception of Olga herself and perhaps also Pshekhotsky, who had favoured me once with his silent applause?

'What makes you think I can refuse?' I asked 'Screw'.

'You could fall ill, or tender your resignation. There is no disgrace in that, because somebody else can take your place. A doctor is placed in quite a different position.'

'Only that?' I thought.

Our carriage, after a long, wearisome drive over the muddy roads stopped at last before the porch. Two windows just above the porch were brightly illuminated. Through the one on the right side, which was in Olga's room, a dim light issued. All the other windows looked like black spots. On the stairs we met the Scops-Owl. She looked at me with her piercing little eyes, and her wrinkled face became more wrinkled in an evil, mocking smile.

Her eyes seemed to say 'You'll have a great surprise!'

She probably thought we had come to carouse, and that we did not know there was grief in the house.

'Let me draw your attention to this,' I said to Pavel Ivanovich, as I pulled the cap off the old woman's head and exposed her completely bare pate. 'This old witch is ninety years old, my good soul. If some day you and I had to make a post-mortem examination of her, we should arrive at very different conclusions. You would find senile atrophy of the brain, and I would assure you that she was the cleverest and the most cunning creature in the whole district. . . . The devil in petticoats!'

I was astounded when I entered the ballroom. The picture I saw there was quite unexpected. All the chairs and sofas were occupied by people. . . . Groups of people were standing about in the corners and near the windows. . . . Where had they all come from? If anybody had told me I would meet these people there, I would have laughed at him. Their presence was so improbable and out of place in the Count's house at that time, when in one of the rooms Olga was either dying or already lying dead. They were the gipsy chorus of the chief gipsy Karpov from the Restaurant London; the same chorus which is known to the reader from one of the first chapters of this book.

When I entered the room my old friend Tina, having recognized me, left one of the groups and came towards me with a cry of joy. A smile spread over her pale and dark complexioned cheeks when I gave her my hand, and tears rose to her eyes when she wanted to tell me something. . . . Tears prevented her from speaking, and I was not able to obtain a single word from her. I turned to the other gipsies, and they explained their presence in the house in this way. In the morning the Count had sent them a telegram demanding that the whole chorus should be at the Count's estate without fail by nine o'clock that evening. In execution of this order they had taken the train and had been in this hall by eight o'clock.

'We had thought to afford pleasure to his Excellency and his guests. . . . We know so many new songs! . . . And suddenly . . .'

'And suddenly a muzhik arrived on horseback, with the news that a brutal murder had been committed at the shooting party and with the order to prepare a bed for Olga Nikolaevna. The muzhik was not believed, because he was as drunk as a swine, but when a noise was heard on the stairs and a black figure was borne through the dancing hall, it was no longer possible to doubt. . . .'

'And now we don't know what to do! We can't remain here. . . . When the priest arrives it is time for the entertainers to depart. . . . Besides, all the chorus girls are frightened and crying. . . . They can't be in the same house with a corpse. . . . We must go away, but they won't give us horses! His Excellency the Count is lying ill in bed and will not see anybody, and the servants only laugh at us when we ask for horses. . . . How can we go on foot in such weather and on such a dark night? The servants are in general terribly rude! When we asked for a samovar for our ladies they told us to go to the devil. . . .'

All these complaints ended in tearful requests to my magnanimity. Could I not obtain vehicles to enable them to depart from this 'accursed' house?

'If all the horses are not in the paddocks, and the coachmen have not been sent somewhere, you shall get away,' I said. 'I'll give the order. . . .'

The poor people, dressed out in their burlesque costumes, and accustomed to flaunt about in a swaggering manner, looked very awkward with their sober countenances and undecided poses. My promise to have them taken to the station somewhat encouraged them. The whispers of the men turned into loud talk, and the women ceased crying.

XXV

Then I went to the Count's study, and as I passed through a whole suite of dark, unlighted rooms, I looked into one of the numerous doors. I saw a touching picture. At a table near a boiling samovar Zosia and her brother Pshekhotsky were seated. . . . Zosia, dressed in a light blouse but still wearing the same bracelets and rings, was smelling at a scent bottle and sipping tea from her cup with fastidious languor. Her eyes were red with weeping. . . . Probably the occurrences at the shooting party had shaken her nerves very much, and had spoilt her frame of mind for a long time to come. Pshekhotsky, with his usual wooden face, was lapping up his tea in large gulps from the saucer and saying something to his sister. To judge from his admonitory expression, he was trying to calm her and persuade her not to cry.

It goes without saying that I found the Count with entirely shattered nerves. This puny and flabby man looked thinner and more dejected than ever. . . . He was pale, and his lips trembled as if with ague. His head was tied up in a white pocket-handkerchief, which exhaled a strong odour of vinegar that filled the whole room. When I entered the room he jumped up from the sofa, on which he was lying, and rushed towards me wrapped up in the folds of his dressing-gown.

'Oh! oh!' he began, trembling and in a choking voice. 'Well?'

And uttering some inarticulate sounds, he pulled me by the sleeve to the sofa and, waiting till I was seated, he pressed against me like a frightened dog and began to pour out all his grievances.

'Who could have expected it? Eh? Wait a moment, golubchek, I'll cover myself up with the plaid. . . . I have a fever. . . . Murdered, poor thing! And how brutally murdered! She's still alive, but the village doctor says she'll not last the night. . . . A terrible day! . . . She arrived without rhyme or reason, that . . . wife of mine . . . may the devil take her! . . . That was my most unfortunate mistake, Serezha; I was married in Petersburg when drunk. I hid it from you. I was ashamed of it, but there – she has arrived, and you can see her for yourself. . . . I look at her, and blame myself. . . . Oh, the accursed weakness! Under the influence of the moment and vodka, I'm capable of doing anything you like! The arrival of my wife is the first lovely surprise, the scandal with Olga the second. . . . I'm expecting a third. . . . I know what will happen next. . . . I know! I'll go mad! . . .'

Having drunk three glasses of vodka and called himself an ass, a scoundrel and a drunkard, the Count began in a whimpering voice and a confused manner to describe the drama that had taken place at the shooting party. . . . What he told me was approximately the following: About twenty or thirty minutes after I had left, when the astonishment at Zosia's arrival had somewhat subsided, and when Zosia herself, having made acquaintance with the guests, began to play the part of hostess, the company suddenly heard a piercing, heartrending shriek. This shriek came from the forest and was repeated four times. It was so extraordinary that the people who heard it sprang to their feet, the dogs began to bark, and the horses pricked up their ears. The shriek was unnatural, but the Count was able to recognize in it a woman's voice. . . . There were notes of despair and terror in it. . . .

Women must shriek in that way when they see a ghost, or at the sudden death of a child. . . . The alarmed guests looked at the Count; the Count looked at them. . . . For what seemed like minutes there was the silence of the grave.

While the ladies and gentlemen looked at each other, the coachmen and lackeys rushed towards the place from which the cry had come. The first messenger of grief was the old manservant, Il'ya. He ran back to the clearing from the forest, with a pale face, dilated pupils, and wanted to say something, but breathlessness and excitement prevented him from speaking. At last, overcoming his agitation, he crossed himself and said:

'The missis has been murdered!'

'What missis? Who has murdered her?'

But Il'ya made no reply to these questions. . . . The part of the second messenger fell to the lot of a man who was not expected and whose appearance caused general surprise. Both the sudden appearance and the look of this man were astonishing. . . . When the Count saw him, and remembered that Olga was walking about in the forest, his heart sank, and from a terrible presentiment his legs gave way under him.

It was Pëtr Egorych Urbenin, the Count's former bailiff and Olga's husband. At first the company heard heavy footsteps and the cracking of brushwood. . . . It seemed as if a bear was making his way from the forest to the clearing. Then the heavy form of the unfortunate Pëtr Egorych came in sight. When he came out of the forest and saw the company assembled on the clearing, he stepped back and stopped as if he were rooted to the ground. For some while he remained silent and motionless, and in this way gave the people time to examine him properly. He had his usual grey jacket on and trousers that were already well worn. He was without a hat, and his matted hair stuck to his sweaty brow and temples. . . . His face, which was usually purple and often almost blue, was now quite pale. . . . His eyes looked around senselessly, staring wildly. . . . His hands and lips trembled. . . .

But what was the most astonishing and what instantly attracted the attention of the stupefied spectators were his blood-stained hands. . . . Both his hands and shirt cuffs were thickly covered with blood, as if they had been washed in a bath of blood.

For several minutes Urbenin remained dumbstruck, and then, as if awakening from a dream, he sat down on the grass cross-legged and groaned. The dogs, scenting something unwonted, surrounded him and raised a bark. . . . Having glanced round the assembly company with dim eyes, Urbenin covered his face with both hands and again there was silence. . . .

'Olga, Olga, what have you done!' he groaned.

Heartrending sobs were torn from his breast and shook his broad shoulders. . . . When he removed the hands from his face the whole company saw the marks of blood that they had left on his cheeks and forehead.

When he reached this point in his narrative the Count waved his hands convulsively, seized a glass of vodka, drank it off, and continued:

'From that point my recollections become mixed. You can well understand all these events had so stunned me that I had lost the power of thinking. . . . I can remember nothing that happened afterwards! I only remember that the men brought some sort of a body in a torn, blood-stained dress out of the wood. . . . I could not look at it! They put it into a calash and drove off. . . . I did not hear either groans or weeping. . . . They say that the small dagger which she always carried about with her had been thrust into her side. . . . You remember it? I had given it to her. It was a blunt dagger – blunter than the edge of this glass. . . . What strength must have been necessary to plunge it in! Brother, I was fond of all those Caucasian weapons, but now may the deuce take the lot of them! Tomorrow I will have them all thrown away.'

The Count drank another glass of vodka and continued:

'But what a disgrace! What an abomination! We brought her to the house. . . . You can understand our despair, our horror, when suddenly, may the devil take them, we heard the gipsies gaily singing! . . . There they were, all ranged in a row, singing at the top of their voices! . . . You see, they wanted to make a show of receiving us, but it turned out to be quite misplaced. . . . It was like Ivanushka-the-fool, who, meeting a funeral, became excited and shouted: "Pull away, you can't pull it over!" Yes, brother! I wanted to entertain my guests and had ordered the gipsies, and what a muddle came of it! It was not gipsies who should have been sent for but doctors and priests. And now I don't know what to do! What am I to do? I don't know any of these formalities and customs. I don't know who to call in, who to send for. . . . Perhaps the police ought to come, the Public Prosecutor. . . . How the devil should I know? Thank goodness, Father Jeremiah, having heard about the scandal, came to give her the Communion. I should never have thought of sending for him. I implore you, dear friend, make all the necessary arrangements! By God, I'm going mad! The arrival of my wife, the murder . . . Brrr! . . . Where is my wife now? Have you seen her?'

'I've seen her. She's drinking tea with Pshekhotsky.'

'With her brother, you say. . . . Pshekhotsky, he's a rogue! When I ran away from Petersburg secretly, he found out about my flight and has stuck to me ever since. What an amount of money he has been able to squeeze out of me during the whole of this time no one can calculate!'

I had not time to talk long to the Count. I rose and went to the door.

'Listen,' the Count stopped me. 'I say, Serezha . . . that Urbenin won't stab me?'

'Did he stab Olga, then?'

'To be sure, he . . . I can't understand, however, how he came there! What the deuce brought him to the forest? And why to that part of the forest in particular? Admitting that he hid himself there and waited for us, how could he know that I wanted to stop just in that place and not in any other?'

'You don't understand anything,' I said. 'By-the-by, once for all I must beg you . . . If I undertake this case, please don't tell me your opinions. Have the goodness to answer my questions and nothing more.'

XXVI

When I left the Count I went to the room where Olga was lying. . . .*

A little blue lamp was burning in the room and faintly lighted up her face. . . . It was impossible either to read or write by its light. Olga was lying on her bed, her head bandaged up. One could only see her pale sharp nose and the eyelids that closed her eyes. At the moment I entered the room her bosom was bared and the doctors were placing a bag of ice on it.† Olga, it seemed, was still alive. Two doctors were attending on her. When I entered, Pavel Ivanovich, screwing up his eyes, was auscultating her heart with much panting and puffing.

The district doctor, who looked a worn-out and sickly man, was sitting pensively near the bed in an armchair and seemed to be feeling her pulse. Father Jeremiah, who had just finished his work, was wrapping up the cross in his stole and preparing to depart.

'Pëtr Egorych, do not grieve!' he said with a sigh and looked towards the corner of the room. 'Everything is God's will. Turn for protection to God.'

Urbenin was seated on a stool in a corner of the room. He was so much changed that I hardly recognized him. Want of work and drink during the last month had told as much on his clothes as on his appearance; his clothes were worn out, his face too.

The poor fellow sat there motionless, supporting his head on his fists and never taking his eyes off the bed. . . . His hands and face were still stained with blood. . . . He had forgotten to wash them. . . .

---

* Here two lines are erased. – A. Ch.

† I draw the reader's attention to a certain circumstance. Kamyshev, who loved on every occasion, even in his disputes with Polycarp, to descant on the condition of his soul, says not a word of the impression made on him by the sight of the dying Olga. I think this omission was intentional. – A. Ch.

Oh, that fatal presentiment of my soul and of my poor bird!

Whenever the noble bird which I had killed screamed out his phrase about the husband who killed his wife, Urbenin's figure always arose before my mind's eye. Why? . . . I knew that jealous husbands often kill their unfaithful wives; at the same time I knew that such men as Urbenin do not kill people. . . . And I drove away the thought of the possibility of Olga being killed by her husband as something absurd.

'Was it he or not he?' I asked myself as I looked at his unhappy face.

And to speak candidly I did not give myself an affirmative answer, despite the Count's story and the blood I saw on his hands and face.

'If he had killed her he would have washed off that blood long ago,' I said to myself, remembering the proposition of a magistrate of my acquaintance: 'A murderer cannot bear the blood of his victim.'

If I had wished to tax my memory I could have remembered many aphorisms of a similar nature, but I must not anticipate or fill my mind with premature conclusions.

'My respects!' the district doctor said to me. 'I am very glad you have come. . . . Can you tell me who is master here?'

'There is no master. . . . Chaos reigns here,' I answered.

'A very good apophthegm, but it does not assist me,' the district doctor answered with bitterness. 'For the last three hours I have been asking, imploring to have a bottle of port or champagne sent here and not a soul has deigned to listen to my prayer! They are all as deaf as posts! They have only just brought the ice I ordered three hours ago. What does it mean? A woman is dying here, and they only seem to laugh! The Count is pleased to sit in his study drinking liqueurs, and they can't bring even a wineglass here! I wanted to send to the chemist in the town, and I was told all the horses are worn out, and there's nobody who can go as they are all drunk. . . . I wanted to send to my hospital for medicines and bandages and they favoured me with a fellow who could hardly stand on his legs. I sent him two hours ago, and what do you think? They tell me he has only just started! Is that not disgusting? They're all drunk, rude, ill-bred! . . . They all seem idiots! By

God, it is the first time in my life I've come across such heartless people!'

The doctor's indignation was justifiable. He had not exaggerated, rather the contrary. . . . A whole night would have been too short a time for pouring out one's gall on all the disorders and malpractices that could be found on the Count's estate. The servants were all abominable, having been demoralized by the want of work and supervision. There was not a single manservant among them who could not have served as a model for the type of servant who had lived long and feathered his nest at the Count's expense.

I went off to get some wine. After dealing a few blows here and there, I succeeded in obtaining both champagne and Valerian drops, to the unspeakable delight of the doctors. An hour later* the doctor's assistant came from the hospital bringing with him all that was necessary.

Pavel Ivanovich succeeded in pouring into Olga's mouth a tablespoon of champagne. She made an effort to swallow and groaned. Then they injected some sort of drops under the skin.

'Olga Nikolaevna!' the district doctor shouted into her ear. 'Olga Ni-ko-la-evna!'

'I doubt if she will regain consciousness!' Pavel Ivanovich said with a sigh. 'The loss of blood has been too great; besides the blow she received on the head with some blunt instrument must have caused concussion of the brain.'

It is not my business to decide if there had been concussion of the brain or not, but Olga opened her eyes and asked for something to drink. . . . The stimulants had had effect.

'Now you can ask her whatever you require . . .' Pavel Ivanovich said, nudging my elbow. 'Ask.'

---

* I must draw the reader's attention to a very important circumstance. For two or three hours M. Kamyshev only walks about from room to room, shares the doctor's indignation about the servants, boxes their ears to right and left, and so on. Can you recognize in him an examining magistrate? He evidently was in no hurry, and was only trying to kill time. Evidently he knew who the murderer was. Besides, there are the quite unnecessary searches made in the Scops-Owl's room and the examination of the gipsies, described in the next chapter, that appear more like mockery than cross-questioning, and could only have been undertaken to pass the time. – A. Ch.

I went up to the bed. Olga's eyes were turned on me.

'Where am I?' she asked.

'Olga Nikolaevna!' I began, 'do you know me?'

During several seconds Olga looked at me and then closed her eyes.

'Yes!' she groaned. 'Yes!'

'I am Zinov'ev, the examining magistrate. I had the honour of being acquainted with you, and if you remember, I was best man at your wedding. . . .'

'Is it thou?' Olga whispered, stretching out her left arm. 'Sit down. . . .'

'She is delirious!' Screw sighed.

'I am Zinov'ev, the magistrate,' I continued. 'If you remember, I was at the shooting party. How do you feel?'

'Ask essential questions!' the district doctor whispered to me. 'I cannot answer for the consciousness being lasting. . . .'

'I beg you not to lecture me!' I said in an offended tone. 'I know what I have to say. . . . Olga Nikolaevna,' I continued, turning to her. 'I beg you to remember the events of the past day. I will help you. . . . At one o'clock you mounted your horse and rode out with a large party to a shoot. . . . The shoot lasted for about four hours. . . . Then there was a halt at a clearing in the forest. . . . Do you remember?'

'And thou . . . and thou didst . . . kill . . .'

'The woodcock? After I had killed the wounded woodcock you frowned and went away from the rest of the party. . . . You went into the forest. . . .* Now try to collect all your strength and remember. During your walk in the wood you were assaulted by a person unknown to us. I ask you, as the examining magistrate, who was it?'

Olga opened her eyes and looked at me.

'Tell us the name of that man! There are three other persons in the room besides me. . . .'

Olga shook her head.

---

* This avoidance of an issue of primary importance could only have had one object, to gain time and to wait until Olga lost consciousness and could not name the murderer. It is astonishing that the doctors did not interpret this action correctly. – A. Ch.

'You must name him,' I continued. 'He will suffer a severe punishment. The law will make him pay dearly for his brutality! He will be sent to penal servitude.★ . . . . I am waiting.'

Olga smiled and again shook her head. The further examination produced no results. I was not able to obtain another word from Olga, not a single movement. At a quarter to five she passed away.

★ At first glance all this may appear naive. It is evident Kamyshev wanted to make Olga understand what serious consequences her declaration would have for the murderer. If the murderer was dear to her, *ergo* – she must remain silent. – A. Ch.

XXVII

About seven o'clock in the morning the village elder and his assistants, whom I had sent for, arrived. It was impossible to drive to the scene of the crime: the rain that had begun in the night was still pouring down in buckets. Little puddles had become lakes. The grey sky looked gloomy, and there was no promise of sunlight. The soaked trees appeared dejected with their drooping branches, and sprinkled a whole shower of large drops at every gust of wind. It was impossible to go there. Besides, it might have been useless. The trace of the crime, such as bloodstains, human footprints, etc., had probably been washed away during the night. But the formalities demanded that the scene of the crime should be examined, and I deferred this visit until the arrival of the police, and in the meantime I made out a draft of the official report of the case, and occupied myself with the examination of witnesses. First of all I examined the gipsies. The poor singers had passed the whole night sitting up in the ballrooms expecting horses to be sent round to convey them to the station. But horses were not provided; the servants, when asked, only sent them to the devil, warning them at the same time that his Excellency had forbidden anybody to be admitted to him. They were also not given the samovar they asked for in the morning. The perplexing and ambiguous situation in which they found themselves in a strange house in which a corpse was lying, the uncertainty as to when they could get away, and the damp melancholy weather had driven the gipsies, both men and women, into such a state of distress that in one night they had become thin and pale. They wandered about from room to room, evidently much alarmed and expecting some serious issue. By my examination I only increased their anxiety. First because my lengthy examination delayed their departure from the accursed house indefinitely, and secondly because it alarmed them. The simple people, imagining that they were seriously suspected of the murder, began to assure me with tears in their eyes, that they were not guilty and knew nothing about the matter. Tina, seeing me as an official personage, quite forgot our former connection, and while speaking to me trembled and almost fainted with fright like a little girl about to be whipped. In reply to my request not to be excited, and my assurance that I saw in them nothing but witnesses, the assistants of justice, they informed me in one voice that they had never been witnesses, that they knew nothing, and that they trusted that in future God would deliver them from all close acquaintance with ministers of the law.

I asked them by what road they had driven from the station, had they not passed through that part of the forest where the murder had been committed, had any member of their party quitted it for even a short time, and had they not heard Olga's heartrending shriek.* This examination led to nothing. The gipsies, alarmed by it, only sent two members of the chorus to the village to hire vehicles. The poor people wanted terribly to get away. Unfortunately for them there was already much talk in the village about the murder in the forest, and these swarthy messengers were looked at with suspicion; they were arrested and brought to me. It was only towards evening that the harassed chorus was able to get free from this nightmare and breathe freely, as having hired five peasants' carts at three times the proper fare, they drove away from the Count's house. Afterwards they were paid for their visit, but nobody paid them for the moral suffering that they had endured in the Count's apartments. . . .

Having examined them, I made a search in the Scops-Owl's room.† In her trunks I found quantities of all sorts of old woman's rubbish, but although I looked through all the old caps and darned stockings, I found neither money nor valuables that the old woman had stolen from the Count or his guests. . . . Nor did I find the things that had been stolen from Tina some time before. . . . Evidently the old witch had another hiding-place only known to herself.

---

* If all this was necessary for M. Kamyshev, would it not have been easier to question the coachmen who had driven the gipsies? – A. Ch.
† Why? Even if we concede that all this was done by the examining magistrate in a drunken or sleepy condition, why write about it? Would it not have been better to hide from the reader these gross mistakes? – A. Ch.

I will not give here the preliminary report I drafted about the information I had obtained or the searches I had made. . . . It was long; besides, I have forgotten most of it. I will only give a general idea of it. First of all I described the condition in which I found Olga, and I gave an account of every detail of my examination of her. By this examination it was evident that Olga was quite conscious when she answered me and purposely concealed the name of the murderer. She clearly did not *want* the murderer to suffer the penalty, and this inevitably led to the supposition that the criminal was near and dear to her.

The examination of her clothes, which I made together with the commissary of the rural police who had arrived post-haste, was highly revealing. . . . The jacket of her riding habit, made of velvet with a silk lining, was still moist. The right side in which there was the hole made by the dagger was saturated with blood and in places bore marks of clotted blood. . . . The loss of blood had been very great, and it was astonishing that Olga had not died on the spot. The left side was also blood-stained. The left sleeve was torn at the shoulder and at the wrist. . . . The two upper buttons were torn off, and at our examination we did not find them. The skirt of the riding habit, made of black cashmere, was found to be terribly crumpled; it had been crumpled when they had carried Olga out of the wood to the vehicle and from the vehicle to her bed. Then it had been pulled off, rolled into a disorderly heap, and flung under the bed. It was torn at the waistband. This tear was about ten inches in length, and had probably been made while she was being carried or when it was pulled off; it might also have been made during her lifetime. Olga, who did not like mending, and not knowing to whom to give the habit to be mended, might have hidden away the tear under her bodice. I don't think any signs could be seen in this of the savage rage of the criminal, on which the assistant public prosecutor laid such special emphasis in his speech at the trial. The right side of the belt and the right-hand pocket were saturated with blood. The pocket-handkerchief and the gloves, that were in this pocket, were like two formless lumps of a rusty colour. The whole of the riding-habit, to the very end of the skirt, was bespattered with spots of blood of various forms and sizes. . . . Most of them, as it was afterwards explained, were the impressions of the blood-stained fingers and palms belonging to the coachmen and lackeys who had carried Olga. . . . The chemise was bloody, especially on the right side on which there was a hole produced by the cut of an instrument. There, as also on the left shoulder of the bodice, and near the wrists there were rents, and the wristband was almost torn off.

The things that Olga had worn, such as her gold watch, a long gold chain, a diamond brooch, ear-rings, rings and a purse containing silver coins, were found with the clothes. It was clear the crime had not been committed with the intent of robbery.

The results of the post-mortem examination, made by 'Screw' and the district doctor in my presence on the day after Olga's death, were set down in a very long report, of which I give here only a general outline. The doctors found that the external injuries were as follows: on the left side of the head, at the juncture of the temporal and the parietal bones, there was a wound of about one and a half inches in length that went as far as the bone. The edges of the wound were not smooth or rectilinear. . . . It had been inflicted by a blunt instrument, probably as we subsequently decided by the haft of the dagger. On the neck at the level of the lower cervical vertebrae a red line was visible that had the form of a semicircle and extended across the back half of the neck. On the whole length of this line there were injuries to the skin and slight bruises. On the left arm, an inch and a half above the wrist, four blue spots were found. One was on the back of the hand and the three others on the lower side. They were caused by pressure, probably of fingers. . . . This was confirmed by the little scratch made by a nail that was visible on one spot. The reader will remember that the place where these spots were found corresponds with the place where the left sleeve and the left cuff of the bodice of the riding-habit were torn. . . . Between the fourth and fifth ribs on an imaginary vertical line drawn from the centre of the armpit there was a large gaping wound of an inch in length. The edges were smooth, as if cut and steeped with liquid and clotted blood. . . . The wound was deep. . . . It was made by a sharp instrument, and as it appeared from the preliminary information, by the dagger which exactly corresponded in width with the size of the wound.

The interior examination revealed a wound in the right lung and the pleura, inflammation of the lung and haemorrhage in the cavity of the pleura.

As far as I can remember, the doctors arrived approximately at the following conclusion: (a) death was caused by anaemia consequent on a great loss of blood; the loss of blood was explained by the presence of a gaping wound on the right side of the breast. (b) the wound on the head must be considered a serious injury, and the wound in the breast was undoubtedly mortal; the latter must be reckoned as the immediate cause of death. (c) the wound on the head was given with a blunt instrument; the wound in the breast by a sharp and probably a double-edged one. (d) the deceased could not have inflicted all the above-mentioned injuries upon herself with her own hand; and (e) there probably had been no offence against feminine honour.

In order not to put it off till Doomsday and then repeat myself, I will give the reader at once the picture of the murder I sketched while under the impression of the first inspections, two or three examinations, and the perusal of the report of the post-mortem examination.

Olga, having left the rest of the party, walked about the wood. Lost in a reverie or plunged in her own sad thoughts – the reader will remember her mood on that ill-fated evening – she wandered deep into the forest. There she was met by the murderer. When she was standing under a tree, occupied with her own thoughts, the man came up and spoke to her. . . . This man did not awaken suspicions in her, otherwise she would have called for help, but that cry would not have been heart-rending. While talking to her the murderer seized hold of her left arm with such strength that he tore the sleeve of her bodice and her chemise and left a mark in the form of four spots. It was at that moment probably that she shrieked, and this was the shriek heard by the party. . . . She shrieked from pain and evidently because she read in the face and movements of the murderer what his intentions were. Either wishing that she should not shriek again, or perhaps acting under the influence of wrathful feelings, he seized the bodice of her dress near the collar, which is proved by the two upper buttons that were torn off and the red line the doctors found on her body. The murderer in clutching at her breast and shaking her, had tightened the gold watch-chain she wore round her neck. . . . The friction and the pressure of the chain produced the red line. Then the murderer dealt her a blow on the head with some blunt weapon, for example, a stick or even the scabbard of the dagger that hung from Olga's girdle. Then flying into a passion, or finding that one wound was insufficient, he drew the dagger and plunged it into her right side with force – I say with force, because the dagger was blunt.

This was the gloomy aspect of the picture that I had the right to draw on the strength of the above-mentioned data. The question who was the murderer was evidently not difficult to determine and seemed to resolve itself naturally. First the murderer was not guided by covetous motives but something else. . . . It was impossible therefore to suspect some wandering vagabond or ragamuffin, who might be fishing in the lake. The shriek of his victim could not have disarmed a robber: to take off the brooch and the watch was the work of a second.

Secondly, Olga had purposely not told me the name of the murderer, which she would have done if he had been a common thief. Evidently the murderer was dear to her, and she did not wish that he should suffer severe punishment on her account. . . . Such people could only have been her mad father; her husband, whom she did not love, but before whom she felt herself guilty; or the Count, to whom perhaps in her soul she felt under a certain obligation. . . . Her mad father was sitting at home in his little house in the forest on the evening of the murder, as his servant affirmed afterwards, composing a letter to the chief of the district police, requesting him to overcome the imaginary robbers who surrounded his house day and night. . . . The Count had never left his guests before and at the moment the murder was committed. Therefore, the whole weight of suspicion fell on the unfortunate Urbenin. His unexpected appearance, his mien, and all the rest could only serve as good evidence.

Thirdly, during the last months Olga's life had been one continuous romance. And this romance was of the sort that usually ends with crime and capital punishment. An old, doting husband, unfaithfulness, jealousy, blows, flight to the lover-Count two months after the marriage. . . . If the beautiful heroine of such a romance is killed, do not look for robbers or rascals, but search for the heroes of the romance. On this third count the most likely hero – or murderer – was again Urbenin.

XXVIII

I made the preliminary examinations in the mosaic room in which I had loved at one time to loll on the soft divan and pay court to gipsies.

The first person I examined was Urbenin. He was brought to me from Olga's room, where he continued to sit on a stool in a corner and never removed his eyes from the empty bed. . . . For a moment he stood before me in silence, looking at me with indifference, then probably thinking that I wanted to speak to him in my character of examining magistrate, he said in the tired voice of a man who was broken by grief and anguish:

'Sergey Petrovich, examine the other witnesses first, please, and me afterwards. . . . I can't . . .'

Urbenin considered himself a witness, or thought that he would be considered one.

'No, I must examine you at once,' I said. 'Be seated, please. . . .'

Urbenin sat down opposite me and bent his head. He was weary and ill, he answered reluctantly, and it was only with difficulty I was able to squeeze his deposition out of him.

He deposed that he was Pëtr Egorych Urbenin, nobleman, fifty years of age, belonging to the Orthodox Faith. That he owned an estate in the neighbouring K— district where he was on the electoral roll, and had served for the last three terms as honorary magistrate. Being ruined, he had mortgaged his estate and had considered it necessary to go into service. He had entered the Count's service as bailiff six years ago. Liking agriculture, he was not ashamed of being in the service of a private individual, and considered that it was only the foolish who were ashamed of work. He received his salary from the Count regularly, and he had nothing to complain of. He had a son and a daughter from his first marriage, etc., etc., etc.

He had married Olga because he was passionately in love with her. He had struggled long and painfully with his feelings, but neither common sense nor the logic of a practical elderly mind – in fact, nothing had effect: he was obliged to succumb to his feelings and he got married. He knew that Olga did not marry him for love, but considering her to be moral in the highest degree, he decided to content himself with her faithfulness and friendship, which he had hoped to merit.

When he came to describe his disenchantment and the wrongs done to his grey hairs, Urbenin asked permission not to speak of 'the past which God will forgive her' or at least to defer the conversation about that to a future time.

'I can't. . . . It's hard. . . . Besides, you yourself saw it.'

'Very well, let us leave it for another time. . . . Only tell me now, did you beat your wife? It is reported that one day, finding a note from the Count in her possession, you struck her. . . .'

'That is not true. . . . I only seized her by the arm, she began to cry, and that same evening she went to complain. . . .'

'Did you know of her connection with the Count?'

'I have begged that this subject should be deferred. . . . And what is the use of it?'

'Answer me only this one question, which is of great importance. . . . Was your wife's connection with the Count known to you?'

'Certainly. . . .'

'I shall write that down, and all the rest concerning your wife's unfaithfulness can be left for the next time. . . . Now we will revert to another question. Will you explain to me how it came that you were in the forest where Olga Nikolaevna was murdered? . . . You were, you say, in town . . . How did you come to be in the forest?'

'Yes, sir, I had been living in town with a cousin ever since I lost my place. . . . I passed my time in looking for a place and in drinking to forget my sorrows . . . I had been drinking specially hard this last month. For example, I can't remember what happened last week as I was always drunk. . . . The day before yesterday I got drunk too. . . . In a word I am lost. . . . Irremediably lost! . . .'

'You were going to tell me how it was that you came to be in the forest yesterday.'

'Yes, sir. . . . I awoke yesterday morning early, about four o'clock. . . . My head was aching from the previous day's drink, I had pains in all my limbs as if I had a fever. . . . I lay on my bed and saw through the window the sun rise, and I remembered . . . many things. . . . A weight was on my heart . . . Suddenly I wanted to see her . . . to see her once more, perhaps for the last time. I was seized by wrath and melancholy. . . . I drew from my pocket the hundred-rouble note the Count had sent me. I looked at it, and then trampled it underfoot. . . . I trampled on it till I decided to go and fling this charity into his face. However hungry and ragged I may be, I cannot sell my honour, and every attempt to buy it I consider a personal insult. So you see, sir, I wanted to have a look at Olga and fling the money into the ugly mug of that seducer. And this longing overpowered me to such an extent that I almost went out of my mind. I had no money to drive here; I could not spend *his* hundred roubles on myself. I started on foot. By good luck a muzhik I know overtook me, and drove me eighteen versts for ten kopecks, otherwise I might still have been trudging along. The muzhik set me down in Tenevo. From there I came here on foot and arrived about four o'clock.'

'Did anybody see you here at that time?'

'Yes, sir. The watchman, Nikolai, was sitting at the gate and told me the masters were not at home, they had all gone out shooting. I was almost worn out with fatigue, but the desire to see my wife was stronger than my weariness. I set off on foot without a moment's rest to the place where they were shooting. I did not go by the road, but started through the forest. I know every tree, and it would be as difficult for me to lose myself in the Count's forests as it would be in my own house.'

'But going through the forest and not by the road you might have missed the shooting party.'

'No, sir, I kept so close to the road all the time that I could not only hear the shots but the conversations too.'

'So you did not expect to meet your wife in the forest?'

Urbenin looked at me with astonishment, and, after thinking for a short time, he replied:

'Pardon me, but that is a strange question. One doesn't *expect* to meet a wolf, any more than one expects to meet a terrible misfortune. God sends them unexpectedly. For example, this dreadful occurrence . . . I was walking through the Ol'khovsky wood, not on the lookout for trouble because I have enough trouble as it is, when suddenly I heard a strange shriek. The shriek was so piercing that it seemed almost as if somebody had cut into my ear. . . . I ran towards the cry. . . .'

Urbenin's mouth was drawn to one side, his chin trembled, his eyes blinked, and he began to sob.

'I ran towards the cry, and suddenly I saw . . . Olga lying on the ground. Her hair and forehead were bloody, her face terrible. I began to shout, to call her by her name. . . . She did not move. . . . I kissed her, I raised her up. . . .'

Urbenin choked and covered his face with his hands. After a minute he continued:

'I did not see the scoundrel. . . . When I was running towards her I heard somebody's hasty footsteps. He was probably running away.'

'All this is an interesting story, Pëtr Egorych,' I said. 'But you must know that magistrates are little inclined to believe in such rare occurrences as the coincidence of the murder with your accidental walk, etc. It's not a bad fabrication, but it explains very little.'

'What do you mean?' Urbenin asked, opening his eyes wide. 'I have fabricated nothing, sir. . . .'

Suddenly Urbenin got very red and rose.

'It appears that you suspect me . . .' he mumbled. 'Of course, anybody can suspect, but you, Sergey Petrovich, have known me long. . . . It's a sin for you to brand me with such a suspicion. . . . You know me.'

'I know you, certainly . . . but my private opinion is here of no avail. . . . The law reserves the right of private opinion to the jurymen, the examining magistrate has only to deal with evidence. There is much evidence, Pëtr Egorych.'

Urbenin cast an alarmed look at me and shrugged his shoulders.

'Whatever the evidence may be,' he said, 'you must understand. . . . Now, could I kill? . . . Could I! And if so, whom? I might be able to kill a quail or a woodcock, but a human being . . . a woman who was dearer to me than life, my salvation . . . the very thought of whom illuminates my gloomy nature like the sun. . . . And suddenly you suspect me!'

Urbenin waved his hand resignedly and sat down again.

'As it is, I long for death, and now in addition you traduce me. If some official I didn't know had spoken thus, I'd say nothing, but you, Sergey Petrovich! . . . May I leave now, sir?'

'You may. . . . I shall examine you again tomorrow, and in the meantime, Pëtr Egorych, I must put you under arrest. . . . I hope that before tomorrow's examination you will have had time to appreciate the importance of all the evidence there is against you, and you will not waste time uselessly, but confess. I am convinced that Olga Nikolaevna was murdered by you. . . . I have nothing more to say to you today. . . . You may go.'

Having said this I bent over my papers. . . . Urbenin looked at me in perplexity, rose, and stretched out his arms in a strange way.

'Are you joking . . . or serious?' he asked.

'This is no time for joking,' I said. 'You may go.'

Urbenin remained standing before me. I looked up at him. He was pale and looked with perplexity at my papers.

'Why are your hands blood-stained, Pëtr Egorych?' I asked.

He looked down at his hands on which there still were marks of blood, and he moved his fingers.

'You ask why there is blood? . . . Hm . . . If this is part of the evidence, it is but poor evidence. . . . When I lifted up Olga after the murder I could not help my hands becoming bloody. I was not wearing gloves.'

'You just told me that when you found your wife all bloody, you called for help. . . . How is it that nobody heard your cries?'

'I don't know, I was so stunned by the sight of Olia, that I was unable to cry out. . . . Besides, I know nothing. . . . It is useless for me to try to exculpate myself, and it's against my principles to do so.'

'You would hardly have shouted. . . . Having killed your wife, you ran away, and were terribly astonished when you saw people on the clearing.'

'I never noticed the people. I paid no heed to people.'

With this my examination for that day was concluded. After that Urbenin was confined in one of the outhouses on the Count's estate and placed under guard.

XXIX

On the second or third day the Assistant Public Prosecutor, Polugradov, arrived post-haste from the town; he is a man I cannot think of without upsetting myself. Imagine a tall, lean man, of about thirty, clean shaven, smartly dressed, and with hair curled like a sheep's; his features were thin, but so dry and unexpressive that it was not difficult to guess the emptiness and foppishness of the individual to whom they belonged; his voice was low, sugary, and mawkishly polite.

He arrived early in the morning, with two portmanteaux in a hired calash. First of all he inquired with a very concerned face, complaining affectedly of fatigue, if a room had been prepared for him in the Count's house. On my orders a small but very cosy and light room had been assigned to him, where everything he might need, from a marble washstand right down to matches, had been arranged.

'I – I say, my good fellow! Bring me some hot water!' he began while settling down in his room, and fastidiously sniffing the air. 'Some hot water, please, I say, young man!'

Before beginning work he washed, dressed, and arranged his hair for a long time; he even brushed his teeth with some sort of red powder, and occupied about three minutes in trimming his sharp, pink nails.

'Well, sir,' he said at last, settling down to work, and turning over the leaves of our report. 'What's it all about?'

I told him what was the matter not leaving out a single detail. . . .

'Have you been to the scene of the crime?'

'No, not yet.'

The Assistant Public Prosecutor frowned, passed his white womanish hand over his freshly washed brow, and began walking about the room.

'I can't understand why you haven't been there,' he murmured.

'I should suppose that was the first thing that ought to have been done. Did you forget or did you think it unnecessary?'

'Neither the one nor the other: yesterday I waited for the police, and I intend to go today.'

'Now nothing will be left there: it has been raining for the last few days, and you have given the criminal time to obliterate his traces. Of course you placed a guard at the spot? No? I don't understand!'

He shrugged his shoulders.

'You'd better drink your tea, it's getting cold,' I said, in a tone of indifference.

'I like it cold.'

The Assistant Public Prosecutor bent over the papers, and with a loud sniff he began to read aloud in an undertone, occasionally jotting down his remarks and corrections. Two or three times his mouth was drawn to one side in a sarcastic smile: for some reason neither my official report nor the doctors' pleased this cunning rogue.* In this sleek, well-brushed, and cleanly-washed government official, stuffed full of conceit and a high opinion of his own worth, the pedant was clearly apparent.

By midday we were on the scene of the crime. It was raining hard. Of course we found no evidence or traces; all had been washed away by the rain. By some chance I found one of the buttons that were missing on Olga's riding habit, and the Assistant Prosecutor picked up a sort of reddish pulp, that subsequently proved to be a red wrapper from a packet of tobacco. At first we stumbled upon a bush which had two twigs broken at one side. The Assistant Prosecutor was delighted at finding these twigs. They might have been broken by the criminal and would therefore indicate the way he had gone after killing Olga. But the joy of the Prosecutor was unfounded: we soon found a number of bushes with broken twigs and nibbled leaves; it turned out that a herd of cattle had passed over the scene of the murder.

---

* Kamyshev abuses the Assistant Public Prosecutor quite without cause. The only thing for which this prosecutor can be blamed is that his face did not please M. Kamyshev. It would have been more honest to admit his own inexperience – or was this an intentional mistake?

After making a plan of the place, and questioning the coachmen we had taken with us as to the position in which they had found Olga, we returned to the house with long faces. An onlooker might have noticed a certain laziness and apathy in our movements while we were examining the scene of the crime. . . . Perhaps our movements were paralysed to a certain extent by the conviction that the criminal was already in our hands, and therefore it was unnecessary to enter on any Lecoq-like analysis.

On his return from the forest Polugradov again spent a long time washing and dressing, and he again called for hot water. Having finished his toilet he expressed a wish to examine Urbenin once more. Poor Pëtr Egorych had nothing new to tell us at this examination; as before he denied his guilt, and thought nothing of our evidence.

'I am astonished that I can be suspected,' he said, shrugging his shoulders. 'Strange!'

'My good fellow, don't be naive,' Polugradov said to him. 'Nobody is suspected without reason. Hence, if you are suspected, there must be a good reason for it!'

'Whatever the causes may be, however strong the evidence may be, one must reason in a humane manner! Don't you understand, I can't murder? I can't . . . What then is your evidence worth?'

'Well!' and the Assistant Prosecutor waved his hand: 'what a trouble these educated criminals are; one can make a muzhik understand, but try to talk to one of these! "I can't" . . . "in a humane manner" . . . they go harping on about psychology!'

'I am no criminal,' Urbenin said quite offended, 'I beg you to be more careful in your expressions. . . .'

'Hold your tongue, my good fellow! We have no time to apologize nor to listen to your dissatisfaction. . . . If you don't wish to confess, you need not confess, but allow us to consider you a liar. . . .'

'As you like,' Urbenin grumbled. 'You can do with me what you like now. . . . You have the power. . . .'

Urbenin made a gesture of indifference, and continued to look out of the window.

'Besides, it's all the same to me: my life is lost.'

'Listen to me, Pëtr Egorych,' I said, 'yesterday and the day before you were so overcome by grief that you were scarcely able to keep on your legs, and you were hardly able to give more than brief answers; today, on the contrary, you have a blooming – of course only comparatively blooming – and gay appearance, and even launch into idle chatter. Usually grieving people have no wish to talk, while you not only embark on long conversations, but even make all sorts of trivial complaints. How do you explain such a sudden change?'

'And how do you explain it?' Urbenin asked, screwing up his eyes at me in a derisive manner.

'I explain it in this way: that you have forgotten your part. It is difficult to act for any length of time; one either forgets one's part, or it bores one. . . .'

'So it was all a fabrication,' said Urbenin, smiling; 'and it does honour to your perspicacity. . . . Yes, you are right; a great change has taken place in me. . . .'

'Can you explain it to us?'

'Certainly, I see no cause for hiding it. Yesterday I was so entirely broken and oppressed by my grief, that I thought of taking my life . . . of going mad . . . but then I thought better of it . . . the thought entered my mind that death had saved Olia from a life of depravity, that it had torn her out of the dirty hands of that good-for-nothing who has ruined me. Death does not make me jealous; it is better for Olga to belong to death than to the Count. This thought cheered and strengthened me: now there is no longer the same weight on my soul.'

'A clever story,' Polugradov murmured under his breath, as he sat swinging his leg, 'he is never at a loss for an answer!'

'I know I am speaking the truth, and I can't understand that you cultivated men cannot see the difference between truth and false-hood! But I know there is prejudice against me. It is only too easy to get the wrong idea when I come up for trial. I can understand your position. . . . I can imagine how, taking into consideration my brutal physiognomy, my drunkenness . . . My physiognomy is not brutal, but prejudice will have its way. . . .'

'Very well, very well, enough,' Polugradov said, bending over his papers, 'Go! . . .'

After Urbenin had left, we proceeded to examine the Count.

His Excellency was pleased to come to the examination in his dressing-gown, with a vinegar bandage on his head; having been introduced to Polugradov he sank into an armchair, and began to give his evidence:

'I shall tell you everything from the very beginning. . . . Well, and how is your President Lionsky getting on? Has he still not divorced his wife? I made his acquaintance in Petersburg, quite by chance. . . . Gentlemen, why don't you order something to be brought? Somehow it's jollier to talk with a glass of cognac before you. . . . I have not the slightest doubt that Urbenin committed this murder.'

And the Count told us all that the reader already knows. At the request of the prosecutor he told us all the details of his life with Olga, and described the delights of living with a beautiful woman, and was so carried away by his subject that he smacked his lips, and winked several times. From his evidence I learned a very important detail that is unknown to the reader. I learned that Urbenin while living in the town had constantly bombarded the Count with letters; in some letters he cursed him, in others he implored him to return his wife to him, promising to forget all wrongs, and dishonour; the poor devil caught at these letters like a drowning man catches at straws.

The Assistant Prosecutor examined two or three of the coachmen and then, having had a very good dinner, he gave me a long list of instructions, and drove away. Before leaving he went into the adjoining house where Urbenin was confined, and told him that our suspicions of his guilt had become certainties. Urbenin only shrugged his shoulders, and asked permission to be present at his wife's funeral; this permission was granted him.

Polugradov did not lie to Urbenin: yes, our suspicions had become convictions, we were convinced that we knew who the criminal was, and that he was already in our hands; but this conviction did not abide with us for long! . . .

XXX

One fine morning, just as I was sealing up a parcel which I was about to send by the guard, who was to take Urbenin to be locked up in the castle-prison in town, I heard a terrible noise. Looking out of the window I saw an amusing sight: some dozen strong young fellows were dragging one-eyed Kuz'ma out of the servants' kitchen.

Kuz'ma pale and dishevelled had his feet firmly planted on the ground, and being deprived of the use of his arms, butted at his adversaries with his large head.

'Your Honour, please go and see him!' Il'ya said to me, in great alarm, 'he . . . does not want to come!'

'Who does not want to come?'

'The murderer.'

'What murderer?'

'Kuz'ma. . . . He committed the murder, your Honour . . . Pëtr Egorych is suffering unjustly. . . . As God is my witness, sir.'

I went into the yard and walked towards the servants' kitchen, where Kuz'ma, who had torn himself out of the strong arms of his opponents, was administering cuffs to right and left.

'What's the matter?' I asked, when I came up to the crowd.

Then I was told something very strange and unexpected.

'Your Honour, Kuz'ma killed her!'

'They lie!' Kuz'ma shouted. 'May God kill me if they don't lie!'

'But why did you, son of a devil, wash off the blood, if your conscience is clear? Stop a moment, his Honour will examine all this!'

One of the grooms, Trifon, riding past the river, had seen Kuz'ma washing something carefully in the water. At first Trifon thought he was washing linen, but looking more attentively he saw it was a poddevka★ and a waistcoat. He thought this strange: such clothes are not usually washed.

★ A sleeveless overcoat worn by coachmen and peasants.

'What are you doing?' Trifon called to him.

Kuz'ma became confused. Looking more attentively, Trifon noticed brown spots on the poddevka.

'I guessed at once that it must be blood . . . I went into the kitchen and told our people; they watched, and saw him at night hanging out the poddevka to dry. Of course they took fright. Why should he wash it, if he is not guilty? He must have something on his soul he is trying to hide. . . . We thought and thought, and decided to bring him to your Honour. . . . We were dragging him to you, but he keeps backing away and spitting in our eyes. Why should he back away if he is not guilty?'

From further examination it appeared that just before the murder, at the time when the Count and his guests were sitting in the clearing, drinking tea, Kuz'ma had gone into the forest. He had not helped in carrying Olga, and therefore could not have got blood on his clothes by this means.

When he was brought to my room Kuz'ma was so excited that at first he could not utter a word; turning up the white of his single eye he crossed himself and mumbled oaths.

'Be calm; tell me what you know and I will let you go,' I said to him.

Kuz'ma fell at my feet, stammering and calling on God.

'May I perish if I had anything to do with it. . . . May neither my father nor my mother . . . Your Honour! May God destroy my soul . . .'

'You went into the forest?'

'That's quite true, sir, I went. . . . I had served cognac to the guests and, forgive me, I had tippled a little; it went to my head, and I wanted to lie down; I went, lay down, and fell asleep. . . . But who killed her, or how I don't know, so help me God. . . . It's the truth I'm telling you!'

'But why did you wash off the blood?'

'I was afraid that people might imagine . . . that I might be taken as a witness. . . .'

'How did the blood get on your poddevka?'

'I don't know, your Honour.'

'Why don't you know? Isn't the poddevka yours?'

'Yes, certainly it's mine, but I don't know: I saw the blood when I woke up again.'

'So then, I suppose you dirtied the poddevka with blood in your sleep?'

'I suppose so. . . .'

'Well, my man, go and think it over. . . . You're talking nonsense; think well and tell me tomorrow. . . . Go!'

The following morning, when I awoke, I was informed that Kuz'ma wanted to speak to me. I ordered him to be brought in.

'Have you thought it over?' I asked him.

'Indeed, I have. . . .'

'How did the blood get on your poddevka?'

'Your Honour, I remember as if in a dream: I remember something, as in a fog, but if it is true or not I can't say.'

'What is it you remember?'

Kuz'ma turned up his eye, thought, and said:

'Extraordinary . . . it's like a dream or a fog. . . . I lay upon the grass drunk and dozing. I was not quite asleep. . . . Then I heard somebody passing, trampling heavily with his feet. . . . I opened my eyes and saw, as if I was unconscious, or in a dream; a gentleman came up to me, he bent over me and wiped his hands in my skirts. . . . He wiped them in my poddevka, and then rubbed his hands on my waistcoat . . . so.'

'What gentleman was it?'

'I don't know; I only remember it was not a muzhik, but a gentleman . . . in gentleman's clothes; but what gentleman it was, what sort of face he had I can't remember at all.'

'What was the colour of his clothes?'

'Who can say! Perhaps white, perhaps black. . . . I only remember it was a gentleman, and that's all I can remember. . . . Ach, yes, I can remember! When he bent down and wiped his hands he said: "Drunken swine!"'

'You dreamt this?'

'I don't know . . . perhaps I dreamt it. . . . But then where did the blood come from?'

'Was the gentleman you saw like Pëtr Egorych?'

'Not so far as I can tell . . . but perhaps it was. . . . But he would not swear and call people swine.'

'Try to remember. . . . Go, sit down and think. . . . Perhaps you may succeed in remembering.'

'I'll try.'

XXXI

The unexpected eruption of one-eyed Kuz'ma into this almost finished story confused things most dreadfully. I was quite bewildered, and did not know what to think about Kuz'ma's evidence. He denied any involvement, and the preliminary investigations were against his guilt. Olga had been murdered not from motives of greed; according to the doctors 'it was probable' that no attempt against her honour had been made; the only possible explanation if Kuz'ma had killed her was that he had done so for lust, or for money. He might have been drunk, or have strangled her in the course of an attack. But none of this tallied with the setting of the murder.

But if Kuz'ma was not guilty, why had he not explained the presence of blood on his poddevka, and why had he invented dreams and hallucinations? Why had he implicated this gentleman, whom he had seen and heard, but had forgotten so entirely that he could not even remember the colour of his clothes?

Polugradov hurried back post haste.

'Now you see, sir!' he said, 'if you had examined the scene of the crime at once, believe me all would have been plain now, as plain as a pikestaff! If you had examined all the servants at once, we could then have known who had carried Olga Nikolaevna and who had not. And now we can't even find out at what distance from the scene of the crime this drunkard was lying!'

He cross-questioned Kuz'ma for about two hours, but could get nothing new out of him; he only said that while half asleep he had seen a gentleman, that the gentleman had wiped his hands on the skirts of his poddevka and had cursed him for a 'drunken swine', but he could not say who this gentleman was, nor what his face and clothes were like.

'How much cognac did you drink?'

'I finished half a bottle.'

'Perhaps it was not cognac?'

'No, sir, it was real fine champagne.'

'So you even know the names of wines!' the Assistant Prosecutor said, laughing.

'How should I not know them? I've served my masters for more than thirty years, thank God! I've had time to learn. . . .'

For some reason the Assistant Prosecutor required that Kuz'ma should be confronted with Urbenin. . . . Kuz'ma looked for a long time at Urbenin, shook his head and said:

'No, I can't remember . . . perhaps it was Pëtr Egorych, perhaps not. . . . Who can say?'

Polugradov shrugged his shoulders and drove away, leaving me to choose which was the right one of the two murderers.

The investigations were protracted. . . . Urbenin and Kuz'ma were imprisoned in the guard-house of the village in which I lived. Poor Pëtr Egorych lost courage very much; he grew thin and grey and fell into a religious mood; two or three times he sent to me, begging to let him see the laws about punishments; it was evident he was interested in the extent of the punishment that awaited him.

'What will become of my children?' he asked me at one of the examinations. 'If I were alone your mistake would not grieve me very much; but I must live . . . live for the children! They will perish without me. Besides, I . . . I am not able to part from them! What are you doing with me?'

When the guards said 'thou' to him, and when he had to go a couple of times from my village to the town and back on foot under escort, in the sight of all the people who knew him, he became despondent and nervous.

'These are not lawyers,' he cried so that he was heard all over the guard-house. 'They are nothing but cruel, heartless boys, without mercy either for people or truth! I know why I am confined here, I know it! By casting the blame on me they want to hide the real culprit! The Count killed her; or if it was not the Count, it was his hireling!'

When he heard that Kuz'ma had been arrested, he was at first very pleased.

'Now the hireling has been found!' he said to me. 'Now he's been found!'

But soon, when he saw he was not released and when he was

informed of Kuz'ma's testimony, he again became depressed.

'Now I'm lost,' he said, 'definitely lost. In order to get out of prison this one-eyed devil will be sure sooner or later to name me and say it was I who wiped my hands in his skirts. But you yourself saw that my hands had not been wiped!'

Sooner or later our suspicions would have to be elucidated.

About the end of November of that year, when snow began to drift before my windows and the lake looked like an endless white desert, Kuz'ma asked to see me; he sent the guard to tell me he had 'thought things over'. I ordered him to be brought to me.

'I am very pleased that you have at last thought the matter over,' I greeted him. 'It is high time to finish with this dissembling and this leading us all by the nose like little children. Well, what do you have to say?'

Kuz'ma did not answer; he stood in the middle of my room in silence, staring at me without winking. . . . Fear shone in his eyes; his whole person showed signs of great trepidation; he was pale and trembling, and a cold perspiration poured down his face.

'Well, speak! What have you remembered?' I asked again.

'Something so extraordinary, that nothing can be more wonder-ful,' he said. 'Yesterday I remembered what sort of a tie that gentleman was wearing, and this night I was thinking and remembered his face.'

'Then who was it?'

'I'm afraid to say, your Honour; allow me not to speak: it's too strange and wonderful; I think I must have dreamt it or imagined it. . . .'

'Well, what have you imagined?'

'No, allow me not to speak. If I tell you, you'll condemn me. . . . Give me a little time to think, and I'll tell you tomorrow. I'm frightened!'

'Pshaw!' I began to get angry. 'Why did you trouble me if you can't speak? Why did you come here?'

'I thought I would tell you, but now I'm afraid. No, your Honour, please let me go. . . . I'd rather tell you tomorrow. . . . If I tell you, you'll get so angry that I'd sooner go to Siberia – you'll condemn me. . . .'

I got angry and ordered Kuz'ma* to be taken away. In the evening of that very day, in order not to lose time and to put an end to this tiresome murder case, I went to the guard-house and tested Urbenin by telling him that Kuz'ma had named him as the murderer.

'I expected it,' Urbenin said with a wave of his hand. 'It's all one to me. . . .'

Solitary confinement had greatly affected Urbenin's health; he had grown sallow and had shrunk to almost half his weight. I promised to order the guards to allow him to walk about the corridors during the daytime and even by night.

'I'm sure there's no fear of your trying to escape,' I said.

Urbenin thanked me, and after my departure he walked about the corridor; his door was no longer kept locked.

On leaving him I knocked at the door behind which Kuz'ma was seated.

'Well, have you thought it over yet?' I asked.

'No, sir,' a weak voice answered. 'Let the Prosecutor come; I will tell him, but I won't tell you.'

'As you like!'

The next morning it was all over.

The watchman Egor came running to me and informed me that one-eyed Kuz'ma had been found dead in his bed. I hastened to the guard-house to assure myself of the fact. The strong, big muzhik, who the day before was full of health and inventing all sorts of tales to get himself free, was stark and cold as a stone. . . . I will not try to describe the horror the guards and I felt; it will be understood by the reader. Kuz'ma was important to me both as accuser and as witness; to the warders he was a prisoner for whose death or flight they would be severely punished. . . . Our horror was only increased when at the post-mortem examination it was discovered that he had died a violent death. . . . Kuz'ma had died from suffocation. . . . Once convinced that he had been suffocated, I

---

* A fine examining magistrate! Instead of continuing the examination and extorting the necessary evidence, he gets angry – something quite out of place for such an official. Besides, I put little trust in all this. . . . Even if M. Kamyshev cared so little about his duties, simple human curiosity ought to have obliged him to continue the examination. – A. Ch.

began to search for the culprit, and I had not long to search. . . .
He was near. . . .

'You scoundrel! It was not enough for you to kill your wife,' I
said, 'but you must take the life of the man who convicted you!
And you continue to act out this filthy comedy.'

Urbenin grew deadly pale and began to shake. . . .

'You lie!' he cried, striking himself on the breast with his fist.

'I do not lie! You shed crocodile tears at our evidence and made
game of it. . . . There were moments when I was tempted to
believe you rather than the evidence. . . . Oh, you are a good
actor! . . . But now I won't believe you, even should blood flow
from your eyes instead of these play-actor's false tears! Admit that
you killed Kuz'ma!'

'You are either drunk or laughing at me! Sergey Petrovich,
patience and submissiveness has its limits; I can bear this no
longer!'

And Urbenin, with flashing eyes, struck the table with his
clenched fist.

'Yesterday I was imprudent enough to give you more liberty,' I
continued, 'by allowing you that which no other prisoner is
allowed, to walk about the corridors. And now it appears, out of
gratitude you went to the door of that unfortunate Kuz'ma and
suffocated a sleeping man! Do you know that you have not only
killed Kuz'ma; the warders will also be ruined on your account.'

'What have I done, good God?' Urbenin said, seizing hold of his
head.

'Do you want the proofs? I will give them. . . . By my orders
your door was left open. . . . The foolish warders opened the door
and forgot to hide the lock. . . . All the cells are opened with the
same key. . . . In the night you took your key and going into the
corridor, you opened your neighbour's door with it. . . . Having
smothered him, you locked the door and put the key into your
own lock.'

'Why should I smother him? Why?'

'Because he denounced you. . . . If yesterday I had not given
you this news, he would have been alive now. . . . It is sinful and
shameful, Pëtr Egorych!'

'Sergey Petrovich,' the murderer suddenly said in a soft, tender voice, seizing me by the hand, 'you are an honest and respectable man! Do not ruin and sully yourself with false suspicions and over-hasty accusations! You cannot understand how cruelly and painfully you have wounded me by casting upon my soul, which is wholly innocent, a new accusation. . . . I am a martyr, Sergey Petrovich! You should be afraid to wrong a martyr! The time will come when you will have to beg my pardon, and that time will be soon. . . . You can't really want to accuse me! But this pardon will not satisfy you. . . . Instead of assailing me so terribly with insults, it would have been better if you had questioned me in a humane – I will not say a friendly – way (you have already renounced all friendly relations). If we take this new accusation . . . I could tell you much. I did not sleep last night, and heard everything.'

'What did you hear?'

'Last night, at about two o'clock . . . all was dark. . . . I heard somebody walking about the corridor very softly, and constantly touching my door. . . . He walked up and down, and then opened my door and came in.'

'Who was it?'

'I don't know; it was dark – I did not see. . . . He stood for about a minute and went away again . . . exactly as you said. . . . He took the key out of my door and opened the next cell. Two minutes later I heard a guttural sound and then a commotion. I thought it was the warder rushing around, and the sounds I took for snores, otherwise I would have raised the alarm.'

'Fables,' I said. 'There was nobody here but you who could have killed Kuz'ma. The warders were all asleep. The wife of one of them, who could not sleep last night, has given evidence that all three warders slept like dead men and never left their beds for a minute; the poor fellows did not know that such brutes as you could be found in this miserable guard-house. They have been serving here for more than twenty years, and during all that time they have never had a single case of a prisoner having escaped, to say nothing of such an abomination as a murder. Now, thanks to you, their life has been turned upside down; I, too, will have to suffer on your account because I did not send you to the town prison, and even gave you the liberty of walking about the corridors. Thank you!'

This was my last conversation with Urbenin. I never spoke to him again, if I do not count the two or three answers I gave to the questions he put to me when he was seated in the dock.

XXXII

I have said that my novel is a story of crime, and now, when the case of the murder of Olga Urbenin has been complicated by another murder, in many ways mysterious and incomprehensible, the reader is entitled to expect that the novel will enter upon its most interesting and exciting phase. The discovery of the criminal, and the reasons for his crime, offer a wide field for the display of ingenuity and sharp-wittedness. Here evil will and cunning are at war with knowledge and skill, a war that is interesting in all its manifestations. . . .

I was the general leading the battle, and the reader has the right to expect me to describe the means that led to my victory. Doubtless he is expecting all sorts of detective finesses such as adorn the novels of Gaboriau and our Shklyarevsky; and I am ready to satisfy his expectations, but . . . one of the chief characters leaves the field of battle without waiting for the end of the combat – he is not made a participator in the victory; all that he has done so far is lost for him – he goes over into the crowd of spectators. That character in the drama is your humble servant. On the day following the above conversation with Urbenin I received an invitation, or, more correctly speaking, an order to hand in my resignation. The tittle-tattle and talk of our district gossips had done its work. . . . The murder in the guard-house, the evidence that the Assistant Prosecutor had collected, unknown to me, from the servants, and, if the reader still remembers it, the blow I had dealt a muzhik on the head with an oar on the occasion of one of our former revels, had all greatly contributed to my dismissal. The muzhik started the case. All sorts of charges were made. In the course of two days I had to hand over the investigation to the magistrate in charge of specially important cases.

Thanks to the talk and the newspaper reports, the Prosecutor became absorbed in the affair. He came in person to the Count's estate every other day and assisted at the examinations. The official reports of our doctors were sent to the medical board, and higher. There was even a question of exhuming the bodies and making a fresh post-mortem examination, which, by the way, would have led to nothing.

Urbenin was taken a couple of times to the chief town of the district to have his mental capacities tested, and both times was found quite normal. I was given the part of witness.* The new examining magistrates were so carried away by their zeal that even my Polycarp was called as a witness.

A year after my resignation, when I was living in Moscow, I received a summons to appear at Urbenin's trial. I was glad of the opportunity of seeing again the places to which I was drawn by habit, and I went. The Count, who was residing in Petersburg, did not attend, but sent a medical certificate instead.

The case was tried in our district town in a division of the Court of Justice. Polugradov – that same Polugradov who cleaned his teeth four times a day with red powder – conducted the prosecution; a certain Smirnyaev, a tall, lean, fair-haired man with a sentimental face and long straight hair, acted for the defence. The jury was exclusively composed of shopkeepers and peasants, of whom only four could read and write; the others, when they were given Urbenin's letters to his wife to read, sweated and got confused. The chief juryman was Ivan Dem'yanych, the shopkeeper from my village, after whom my late parrot had been named.

When I came into the court I did not recognize Urbenin; he had become quite grey, and looked twenty years older. I had expected to read on his face apathy, and indifference to his fate, but I was mistaken. Urbenin was deeply interested in the trial; he raised objections to three of the jurymen, gave long explanations, and questioned the witnesses; he absolutely denied any guilt, and questioned all the witnesses who did not give evidence in his favour, very minutely.

The witness Pshekhotsky deposed that I had had a connection with the late Olga.

* A part that was certainly better suited to M. Kamyshev than the part of examining magistrate: in the Urbenin case he could not be examining magistrate – A. Ch.

'That's a lie!' Urbenin shouted. 'He lies! I don't trust my wife, but I trust him!'

When I gave my evidence the counsel for the defence asked me in what relation I stood to Olga, and told me of the evidence Pshekhotsky, whose unwelcome applause I had once earned, had presented. To have spoken the truth would have been to give evidence in favour of the accused. The more depraved the wife, the more lenient the jury is towards the Othello-husband. I understood this. . . . On the other hand, if I spoke the truth I would have wounded Urbenin . . . in hearing it he would have felt an incurable pain. . . . I thought it better to lie.

'No,' I said.

In his speech the Public Prosecutor described Olga's murder in vivid colours and drew especial attention to the brutality of the murderer, to his malignancy. . . . 'An old, worn-out voluptuary saw a girl, young and pretty. Knowing the whole horror of her position in the house of her mad father, he enticed her to come to him by offering her board and lodging, and a few bright-coloured rags. . . . She agreed. An old, well-to-do husband is more easily endured than a mad father and poverty. But she was young, and youth, gentlemen of the jury, possesses its own inalienable rights. . . . A girl brought up on novels, in the midst of nature, sooner or later was bound to fall in love. . . .' And so on in the same style. It finished up with 'He who had not given her anything more than his age and a few bright-coloured rags, seeing his prize slipping away from him, becomes as furious as an animal newly branded. He had loved her like an animal and must hate like an animal,' etc., etc.

In charging Urbenin with Kuz'ma's murder, Polugradov drew special attention to the stealthy processes, well thought out and weighed, that accompanied the murder of a 'sleeping man who the day before had had the imprudence to give testimony against him'. 'I suppose you cannot doubt that Kuz'ma wanted to tell the Public Prosecutor something specially concerning him.'

The counsel for the defence, Smirnyaev, did not deny Urbenin's guilt; he only begged them to admit that Urbenin had acted under the influence of a state of temporary insanity, and to have indulgence for him. When describing how painful the feelings of jealousy are, he cited as an example Shakespeare's 'Othello'. He looked at that 'universal human figure' from every side, giving extracts from various critics, and became so confused that the presiding judge had to stop him with the remark that 'a knowledge of foreign literature was not obligatory for the jurymen'.

Taking advantage of having the last word, Urbenin called God to witness that he was not guilty either in deed or thought.

'It is all the same to me where I am – in this district where everything reminds me of my unmerited shame and of my wife, or in penal servitude; but it is the fate of my children that is troubling me.'

And, turning to the public, Urbenin began to cry, and begged that his children might be cared for.

'Take them. The Count will not lose the opportunity of vaunting his generosity, but I have already warned the children; they will not accept a crumb from him.'

Then, noticing me among the public, he looked at me with suppliant eyes and said:

'Defend my children from the Count's favours!'

He apparently had quite forgotten the impending verdict, and his thoughts were only centred on his children. He talked about them until he was stopped by the presiding judge.

The jury were not long in consultation. Urbenin was found guilty, without extenuating circumstances on any count.

He was condemned to the loss of all civil rights, transportation and hard labour for fifteen years.

So dearly had he to pay for his having met on a fine May morning the poetical girl in red.

More than eight years have passed since the events described above happened. Some of the actors in the drama are dead and buried, others are bearing the punishment of their sins, others still are wearily dragging on their lives, struggling with boredom and awaiting death from day to day.

Much is changed during these eight years. . . . Count Karnéev, who has never ceased to entertain the sincerest friendship for me, has sunk into utter drunkenness. His estate which was the scene of the drama has passed from him into the hands of his wife and

Pshekhotsky. He is now poor, and is supported by me. Sometimes of an evening, lying on the sofa in my room in the boarding-house, he likes to remember the good old times.

'It would be fine to listen to the gipsies now!' he murmurs. 'Serezha, send for some cognac!'

I am also changed. My strength is gradually deserting me, and I feel youth and health leaving my body. I no longer possess the same physical strength, I have not the same alertness, the same endurance which I was proud of displaying formerly, when I could carouse night after night and could drink quantities which now I could hardly lift.

Wrinkles are appearing on my face one after the other; my hair is getting thin, my voice is becoming coarse and less strong. . . . Life is finished.

I remember the past as if it were yesterday. I see places and people's faces as if in a mist. I have not the power to regard them impartially; I love and hate them with all my former intensity, and never a day passes that I, being filled with feelings of indignation or hatred, do not hold my head in my hands. As formerly, I consider the Count odious, Olga infamous, Kalinin ludicrous owing to his stupid presumption. Evil I hold to be evil, sin to be sin.

But not infrequently there are moments when, looking intently at a portrait that is standing on my writing-table, I feel an irresistible desire to walk with the girl in red through the forest, under the sounds of the tall pines, and to press her to my breast regardless of everything. In such moments I forgive the lies, the fall into the abyss, I am ready to forgive everything, if only a small part of the past could be repeated once more. . . . Wearied of the dullness of town, I want to hear once again the sound of the giant lake and gallop along its banks on my Zorka. . . . I would forgive and forget everything if I could once again go along the road to Tenevo and meet the gardener Franz with his vodka barrel and jockey-cap. . . . There are moments when I am even ready to press the blood-stained hand of good-natured Pëtr Egorych, and talk with him about religion, the harvest, and the enlightenment of the people. . . . I would like to meet 'Screw' and his Nadenka again. . . .

Life is mad, licentious, turbulent – like a lake on an August night. . . . Many victims have disappeared for ever beneath its dark waves. . . . They lie, like sediment in wine, at its bottom.

But why, at certain moments, do I love it? Why do I forgive it, and in my soul hurry towards it like an affectionate son, like a bird released from a cage?

At this moment the life I see from the window of my room in these chambers reminds me of a grey circle; it is grey in colour without any light or shade. . . .

But, if I close my eyes and remember the past, I see a rainbow formed by the sun's spectrum. . . . Yes, it is stormy there, but it is lighter too. . . .

S. ZINOV'EV.

THE END

POSTSCRIPT

At the bottom of the manuscript there is written:

<small>To the Editor</small>
Dear Sir, – I beg you to publish the novel (or story, if you prefer it) which I submit to you herewith, as far as possible, in its entirety, without abridgment, cuts or additions. However, changes can be made with the consent of the author. In case you find it unsuitable I beg you to keep the MSS. to be returned. My address (temporary) in Moscow is the Anglia Chambers, on the Tverskoy.
<small>Ivan Petrovich Kamyshev.</small>

P.S. – The fee is at the discretion of the Editor.
Year and date.

Now that the reader has become acquainted with Kamyshev's novel I will continue my interrupted talk with him. First of all, I must inform the reader that the promise I made to him at the start of this novel has not been kept: Kamyshev's novel has not been printed without omissions, not *in toto*, as I promised, but considerably shortened. The fact is, that 'The Shooting Party' could not be printed in the newspaper which was mentioned in the first chapter of this work, because the newspaper ceased to exist just when the manuscript was sent to press. The present editorial board, in accepting Kamyshev's novel, found it impossible to publish it without cuts. During the time it was appearing, every chapter that was sent to me in proof was accompanied by an editorial request to 'make changes'. However, not wishing to take on my soul the sin of changing another man's work, I found it better and more profitable to leave out whole passages rather than make possibly unsuitable changes. With my assent the editor left out many passages that shocked by their cynicism, or were too long, or were abominably careless in style. These omissions and cuts demanded both care and time, which is the cause that many chapters were late. Among other passages we left out two descriptions of nocturnal orgies. One of these orgies took place in the Count's house, the other on the lake. We also left out a description of Polycarp's library and of the original manner in which he read; this passage was found over-extended and exaggerated.

The chapter I was most anxious to retain and which the editor chiefly disliked, was one in which the desperate card gambling that was the rage among the Count's servants was minutely described. The most passionate gamblers were the gardener Franz and the old woman nicknamed the Scops-Owl. While Kamyshev was conducting the investigations he passed by one of the summer-houses, and looking in he saw mad play going on; the players were the Scops-Owl, Franz and – Pshekhotsky. They were playing 'Stukol-ka', at twenty kopeck points and with a fine that reached thirty roubles. Kamyshev joined the players and 'cleared them out' as if they had been partridges. Franz, who had lost everything but wished to continue, went to the island where he had hidden his money. Kamyshev followed him, marked where he had concealed his money, and afterwards robbed the gardener, not leaving a kopeck in his hoard. The money he had taken he gave to the fisherman Mikhey. Such strange charity admirably characterizes this hare-brained magistrate, but the chapter was written so carelessly and the conversation of the gamblers glittered with such pearls of obscenity that the editor would not consent to its inclusion even after alterations had been made.

The description of certain meetings of Olga and Kamyshev are omitted; an explanation between him and Nadenka Kalinin, etc., etc., are also left out. But I think what is printed is sufficient to characterize my hero. *Sapienti sat*. . . .

Exactly three months later the door-keeper Andrey announced the arrival of the gentleman 'with the cockade'.

'Ask him in!' I said.

Kamyshev entered, the same rosy-cheeked, handsome and

healthy man he had been three months before. His steps, as formerly, were noiseless. . . . He put down his hat on the window with so much care that one might have imagined that he had deposited something heavy. . . . Out of his eyes there shone, as before, something childlike and infinitely good-natured.

'I am troubling you again!' he began smiling, and he sat down carefully. 'I beg you, forgive me! Well, what? What sentence has been passed on my manuscript?'

'Guilty, but deserving of indulgence,' I replied.

Kamyshev laughed and blew his nose in a scented handkerchief.

'Consequently, banishment into the flames of the fireplace?' he asked.

'No, why be so savage? It does not merit punitive measures; we will employ a corrective treatment.'

'Must it be corrected?'

'Yes, certain things must be omitted. . . . By mutual consent. . . .'

We were silent for a quarter of a minute. I had terrible palpitations of the heart and my temples throbbed, but showed no outward sign of agitation.

'By mutual consent,' I repeated. 'Last time you told me that you had taken the subject of your novel from real life.'

'Yes, and I am ready to confirm it now. If you have read my novel, may I have the honour of introducing myself as Zinov'ev.'

'So it was you who were best man at Olga Nikolaevna's wedding.'

'Both best man and friend of the house. Do I not come out of this story well?' Kamyshev laughed, stroked his knees and got very red. 'A fine fellow, eh? I ought to have been flogged, but there was nobody to do it.'

'So, sir. . . . I liked your story: it is better and more interesting than most crime novels. Only you and I must agree together on certain radical changes to be made.'

'That's possible. What do you want to change?'

'The very *habitus* of the novel, its character. It has, as in all novels treating of crimes, everything: crime, evidence, an inquest, even fifteen years' penal servitude as a climax, but the most essential thing is lacking.'

'What is that?'

'The real culprit does not appear. . . .'

Kamyshev opened his eyes wide and rose.

'To be frank, I don't understand you,' he said after a short pause. 'If you do not consider the man who commits murder and strangles to be a real culprit, then I don't know who can be considered so. Criminals are, of course, the product of society, and society is guilty, but . . . if one is to devote oneself to the higher considerations one must cease writing novels and write reports.'

'Ach, what sort of higher considerations are there here! It was not Urbenin who committed the murder!'

'How so?' Kamyshev asked, approaching nearer to me.

'Not Urbenin!'

'Perhaps. *Errare humanum est* – and magistrates are not perfect: there are often errors of justice under the moon. You consider that we were mistaken?'

'No, you did not make a mistake; you wished to make a mistake.'

'Forgive me, I again do not understand,' and Kamyshev smiled. 'If you find that the inquest led to a mistake, and even, if I understand you right, to a premeditated mistake, it would be interesting to know your point of view. Who was the murderer in your opinion?'

'You!'

Kamyshev looked at me with astonishment, almost with terror, grew very red and stepped back. Then turning away, he went to the window and began to laugh.

'Here's a nice go!' he muttered, breathing on the glass and nervously drawing figures on it.

I watched his hand as he drew, and it appeared to me that I recognized in it the iron, muscular hand that, with a single effort, would have been able to strangle the sleeping Kuz'ma, or mangle Olga's frail body. The thought that I saw before me a murderer filled my soul with unwonted feelings of horror and fear . . . not for myself – no! – but for him, for this handsome and graceful giant . . . and for mankind in general. . . .

'You murdered them!' I repeated.

'If you are not joking, allow me to congratulate you on the discovery,' Kamyshev said laughing, but still not looking at me.

'However, judging by your trembling voice, and your pallor, it is difficult to suppose that you are joking. What a nervous man you are!'

Kamyshev turned his flushed face towards me and, forcing himself to smile, he continued:

'I should like to know how such an idea could have come into your head! Have I written something like that in my novel? By God, that's interesting. . . . Tell me, please! I should like, just once in a lifetime, to know what it feels like to be looked upon as a murderer.'

'You are a murderer,' I said, 'and you are not able to hide it. In the novel you lied, and now you are proving yourself a poor actor.'

'This is really quite interesting; upon my word, it would be curious to hear. . . .'

'If you are curious, then listen.'

I jumped up and began walking about the room in great agitation. Kamyshev looked out of the door and closed it tight. By this precaution he gave himself away.

'What are you afraid of?' I asked.

Kamyshev became confused, coughed and shrugged his shoulders.

'I'm not afraid of anything, I only . . . only looked – looked out of the door. Well, now tell me!'

'May I ask you some questions?'

'As many as you like.'

'I warn you that I am no magistrate, and no master in cross-examination; do not expect order or system, and so don't try to disconcert or puzzle me. First tell me where you disappeared after you had left the clearing in which the shooting party was feasting?'

'In the novel it is mentioned: I went home.'

'In the novel the description of the way you went is carefully effaced. Did you not go through the forest?'

'Yes.'

'Consequently, you could have met Olga?'

'Yes, I could,' Kamyshev said smiling.

'And you met her.'

'No, I did not meet her.'

'In your investigations you forgot to question one very important witness, and that was yourself. . . . Did you hear the shriek of the victim?'

'No. . . . Well, baten'ka,* you don't know how to cross-examine at all.'

This familiar 'baten'ka' jarred on me; it accorded ill with the apologies and the embarrassment Kamyshev had shown when conversation began. Soon I noticed that he looked upon me with condescension, and almost with admiration of the determination I showed in questioning him.

'Let us admit that you did not meet Olga in the forest,' I continued, 'though it was more difficult for Urbenin to meet her than for you, as Urbenin did not know she was in the forest, and therefore did not look for her, while you, being flushed with drink, would have been more likely to do so. You certainly did look for her, otherwise what would be your object in going home through the forest instead of by the road? . . . But let us admit that you did not meet her. . . . How is your gloomy, your almost mad frame of mind, in the evening of the fatal day, to be explained? What induced you to kill the parrot as it cried out about the husband who killed his wife? I think he reminded you of your own evil deed. That night you were summoned to the Count's house, and instead of beginning your investigations at once, you delayed until the police arrived almost twenty-four hours later. Perhaps you yourself did not notice this. . . . But only a magistrate who already knew the criminal's identity would have delayed. . . . Further, Olga did not mention the name of the murderer because he was dear to her. . . . If her husband had been the murderer she would have named him. Since she was capable of informing against him to her lover the Count, it would not have cost her anything to accuse him of murder: she did not love him, and he was not dear to her. . . . She loved you, and you were the only person dear to her . . . she wanted to spare you. . . . Allow me to ask, why did you delay asking her a straight question when she regained consciousness for a moment? Why did you ask her all sorts of questions that had nothing to do with the matter? I suggest that you did this only to mark time, in order to prevent her from

---

* The diminutive of otets – father, a very familiar form of address.

naming you. Then Olga dies. . . . In your novel you do not say a word about the impression that her death made on you. . . . In this I see caution: you do not forget to write about the number of glasses you emptied, but such an important event as the death of "the girl in red" is passed over in the novel without the slightest mention. . . . Why?'

'Go on, go on. . . .'

'You made all your investigations in a most slovenly way. . . . It is hard to believe that you, a clever and very cunning man, did not do so purposely. All your investigations remind one of a letter purposely written with grammatical errors. Why did you not examine the scene of the crime? Not because you forgot to do so, or considered it unimportant, but because you waited for the rain to wash away your traces. You write little about the examination of the servants. Thus Kuz'ma was not examined by you until he was caught washing his poddevka. . . . You evidently had no reason to involve him in the affair. Why did you not question any of the guests, who had been feasting with you in the clearing? They had seen the blood stains on Urbenin, and had heard Olga's shriek, – they ought to have been examined. But you did not do it, because one of them might have remembered at his examination that shortly before the murder you had suddenly gone into the forest and been lost. Afterwards they probably were questioned, but this circumstance had already been forgotten by them. . . .'

'Very clever!' Kamyshev said, rubbing his hands; 'go on, go on!'

'Is it possible that what has already been said is not enough for you? . . . To prove conclusively that Olga was murdered by you, and nobody else, I must remind you that you were her lover, whom she had jilted for a man you despised! A husband can kill from jealousy. I presume a lover can do so, too. . . . Now let us return to Kuz'ma. . . . To judge by his last interrogation, that took place on the eve of his death, he had you in mind; you had wiped your hands on his poddevka, and you had called him a swine. . . . If it had not been you, why did you interrupt your examination at the most interesting point? Why did you not ask about the colour of the murderer's necktie, when Kuz'ma had informed you he had remembered what the colour was? Why did you relax the guard on Urbenin just when Kuz'ma remembered the name of the murderer? Why not before or after? It was evident you required a man who might walk about the corridors at night. . . . And so you killed Kuz'ma, fearing that he would denounce you.'

'Well, enough!' Kamyshev said laughing. 'That will do! You are in such a passion, and have grown so pale that it seems as if at any moment you might faint. Do not continue. You are right. I really did kill them.'

This was followed by a silence. I paced the room from corner to corner. Kamyshev did the same.

'I killed them!' Kamyshev continued. 'You've found out – good luck to you. Not many will have that success. Most of your readers will accuse Urbenin, and be amazed at my magisterial cleverness and acumen.'

At that moment my assistant came into the office and interrupted our conversation. Noticing that I was occupied and excited he hovered for a moment around my writing-table, looked at Kamyshev, and left the room. When he had gone Kamyshev went to the window and began to breathe on the glass.

'Eight years have already passed since then,' he began again, after a short silence, 'and for eight years I have borne this secret within me. But it is impossible for a human being to keep such a secret; it is impossible to know without torment what the rest of mankind does not know. For all these eight years I have felt myself a martyr. It was not my conscience that tormented me, no! Conscience is a thing apart . . . and I don't pay much attention to it. It can easily be stifled by rationalizing about its flexibility. When reason does not work, I smother it with wine and women. With women I have my former success – this I only mention by the way. But I was tormented by something else. The whole time I thought it strange that people should look upon me as an ordinary man. During all these eight years not a single living soul has looked at me searchingly; it seemed strange to me that there was no need for me to hide. A terrible secret is concealed in me, and still I walk about the streets. I go to dinner-parties. I flirt with women! For a man who is a criminal such a position is unnatural and painful. I would not be tormented if I had to hide and dissemble. Psychosis, baten'ka! At last I was seized by a kind of passion. . . . I suddenly wanted to pour out my feelings in some way on everybody, to shout my secret aloud, though I care nothing for what people think . . . to do something extraordinary. And so I wrote this novel – an indictment, which only the witless will have any difficulty in recognizing me as a man with a secret. . . . There is not a page that does not give the key to the puzzle. Is that not true? You doubtless understood it at once. When I wrote it I took into consideration the intelligence of the average reader. . . .'

We were again disturbed. Andrey entered the room bringing two glasses of tea on a tray. . . . I hastened to send him away.

'Now it is easier for me,' Kamyshev said smiling, 'now you look upon me not as an ordinary man, but as a man with a secret. . . . But . . . It is already three o'clock, and somebody is waiting for me in the cab. . . .'

'Stay, put down your hat. . . . You have told me what made you take up authorship, now tell me how you murdered.'

'Do you want to know that in addition to what you have read? Very well. I killed in a state of momentary aberration. Nowadays people even smoke and drink tea under the influence of aberration. In your excitement you have taken up my glass instead of your own, and you are smoking more than usual. . . . Life is all aberration . . . so it appears to me. . . . When I went into the wood my thoughts were far away from murder; I went there with only one object: to find Olga and continue to torment and scold her. . . . When I am drunk I always feel the necessity to quarrel. . . . I met her about two hundred paces from the clearing. . . . She was standing under a tree and looking pensively at the sky. . . . I called to her. . . . When she saw me she smiled and stretched out her arms to me. . . .

' "Don't scold me, I'm so unhappy!" she said.

'That night she looked so beautiful, that I, drunk as I was, forgot everything in the world and pressed her in my arms. . . . She swore to me that she had never loved anybody but me . . . and that was true . . . she really loved me . . . and in the very midst of her assurances she suddenly took it into her head to say something terrible: "How unhappy I am! If I had not got married to Urbenin, I might now have married the Count!" All that was boiling in my breast bubbled over. I seized the vile little creature by the shoulder and threw her to the ground as you throw a ball. My rage reached

its peak. . . . Well . . . I finished her. . . . I just finished her. . . .
You understand about Kuz'ma. . . .'

I glanced at Kamyshev. On his face I could neither read
repentance nor regret. 'I just finished her' was said as easily as 'I
just had a smoke.' In my turn I also experienced a feeling of wrath
and loathing. . . . I turned away.

'And Urbenin is in penal servitude?' I asked quietly.

'Yes. . . . I heard he had died on the way, but that is not
certain. . . . What then?'

'What then? An innocent man is suffering and you ask "What
then?"'

'But what am I to do? Go and confess?'

'I should think so.'

'Well, let us suppose it! . . . . I have nothing against taking
Urbenin's place, but I won't do it voluntarily. . . . Let them take
me if they want, but I won't give myself up. Why did they not take
me when I was in their hands? At Olga's funeral I wept so long,
and had such hysterics that even a blind man should have known
the truth. . . . It's not my fault that they are stupid.'

'You are odious to me.'

'That is natural. . . . I am odious to myself. . . .'

There was silence again. . . . I opened the cash-book and began
mechanically to count the figures. . . . Kamyshev took up his hat.

'I see you feel stifled by my presence,' he said. 'By-the-by, don't
you want to see Count Karnéev. There he is sitting in the cab!'

I went up to the window and glanced at him. . . . Sitting in the
cab with his back towards us sat a small stooping figure, in a
shabby hat and a faded collar. It was difficult to recognize in him
one of the actors of the drama!

'I heard that Urbenin's son is living here in Moscow in the
Andréev Chambers,' Kamyshev said. 'Do you know what I want,
what I am going to do? I'll ruin the Count, I'll bring him to such a
pass that he'll be asking Urbenin's son for money. That will be his
punishment. But I must say good-bye. . . .'

Kamyshev nodded and left the room. I sat down at the table and
gave myself up to bitter thoughts.

I felt stifled.